PENGUIN BOOKS

THE PENGUIN BOOK OF
SCOTTISH SHORT STORIES

J. F. Hendry was born in Glasgow in 1912. He was best known as the pioneering editor, with Henry Treece, of the anthologies *The New Apocalypse*, *White Horsemen* and *Crown and Sickle*, and as the author of two volumes of verse, *The Bombed Happiness* and *Orchestral Mountain*, and of the epic poem *Marimarusa*. He was for many years Director of the School of Translators and Interpreters at Laurentian University, Ontario, Canada. He died in Toronto in 1986.

The Penguin Book
of Scottish Short Stories

COMPILED WITH AN INTRODUCTION
BY J. F. HENDRY

PENGUIN BOOKS

PENGUIN BOOKS

Published by the Penguin Group

Penguin Books Ltd, 80 Strand, London WC2R 0RL, England

Penguin Group (USA) Inc., 375 Hudson Street, New York, New York 10014, USA

Penguin Group (Canada), 90 Eglinton Avenue East, Suite 700, Toronto, Ontario, Canada M4P 2Y3
(a division of Pearson Penguin Canada Inc.)

Penguin Ireland, 25 St Stephen's Green, Dublin 2, Ireland (a division of Penguin Books Ltd)

Penguin Group (Australia), 250 Camberwell Road, Camberwell, Victoria 3124, Australia
(a division of Pearson Australia Group Pty Ltd)

Penguin Books India Pvt Ltd, 11 Community Centre, Panchsheel Park, New Delhi – 110 017, India

Penguin Group (NZ), 67 Apollo Drive, Rosedale, Auckland 0632, New Zealand
(a division of Pearson New Zealand Ltd)

Penguin Books (South Africa) (Pty) Ltd, 24 Sturdee Avenue, Rosebank,
Johannesburg 2196, South Africa

Penguin Books Ltd, Registered Offices: 80 Strand, London WC2R 0RL, England

www.penguin.com

First published in Penguin Books 1970
Reissued in this edition 2011

1

This edition produced for The Book People Ltd,
Hall Wood Avenue, Haydock, St Helens WA11 9UL

Printed in Great Britain by Clays Ltd, St Ives plc

ISBN: 978-0-241-95547-5

www.greenpenguin.co.uk

Penguin Books is committed to a sustainable
future for our business, our readers and our
planet. This book is made from paper certified
by the Forest Stewardship Council.

CONTENTS

CONTENTS

INTRODUCTION

THERE has been too much talk of 'roots', 'tradition' and even 'nation' in the past. The writer in Scotland has in fact been bedevilled and in a way censored, as he is on the other side of the Iron Curtain, to see if what he writes may be given the stamp of official approval. His enemy has been within as well as without.

In this collection the heretical principle has been adopted that if a writer *is* Scots, something of the Scottish spirit must inevitably emerge from his work.

Attempt has nevertheless been made to strike some sort of balance between older and younger writers, as also between stories with a purely Scottish background and others, which are just as traditional. Absence of the habitual macabre may be due to the fact that it is suffering from anaemia, and in any case was probably something of a gimmick. Since television, 'the gift' is played out. Like Harry Lauder's crook, the eerie, the ghostly, the psychic, the morbid come into the category of entertainment, not literature or art. Perhaps to the Scot they always were in that category, and it was his misfortune that others took him seriously when he indulged, as they did, in extravaganza. The best Scottish writing is clear, objective, 'realistic', in the sense of facing up to all aspects of reality, as opposed to hiding in one.

Of the authors included, George Mackay Brown has achieved prominence in a new genre with his recent collection of tales of the Orkneys. Ian H. Finlay is well-known for his work in concrete poetry and art. Neil Paterson's story, once filmed as *The Kidnappers*, has been extremely appreciated and is well worth reprinting for its associations with Scottish emigration, as well as its literary merit.

The contribution by Naomi Mitchison, which is unpublished, throws a useful light on the Roman occupation of Britain, as well as on the historical nature of our religious preoccupations.

Of Lewis Grassic Gibbon, the author of the classic 'A Scots Quhair', or of Neil Gunn, that admirable stylist, there is little need to speak. They are already part of our history and their work will live among us.

Among younger writers, the story by Muriel Spark is in a way a foil to one of my own, included at the insistence of several of the contributors, dealing as it does with a rather neglected subject, the Home Front in London during the war.

Fred Urquhart's *Collected Stories* appeared recently and were universally acclaimed by reviewers for their highly individual character. It is to be hoped that we shall have a novel from him before long, as we have had in the past. He is a gusty writer, who brings an authentic reality.

Edward Gaitens's death was a great loss to Scottish literature. He too brought an authentic reality with him and promised mature Scottish work, though what he has left deserves to be much better known in the English-speaking world.

Neil McCallum and James Allan Ford have given us novels and short stories since the war, the latter being no less a figure than the Registrar-General for Scotland, whose book *Season of Escape* won the Frederick Niven Award for 1965.

Neil McCallum's book *My Enemies Have Sweet Voices* was a finely observed collection of stories dealing with the last war.

One of the justifications for this volume, then, besides those already cited, is that writers such as these have been brought together to provide a composite picture of the various facets of Scottish writing today.

It is my sincere hope that a reading of the collection will convey as much pleasure to others as the compilation has done to me.

Selection of these stories has been made on a broad basis, abjuring any requirements that the story deal with the 'Scottish Scene', a restriction as limiting to creative writers as requirements that Scottish poets write in 'Scots', 'Lallans', or Gaelic, rather than English, as though the writing of *poetry* were incidental.

We have tried to allow real freedom of expression throughout.

J. F. HENDRY

George Mackay Brown

THE STORY OF JORKEL HAYFORKS

THE week before midsummer Jorkel and six others took ship at Bergen in Norway and sailed west two days with a good wind behind them. They made land at Whalsay in Shetland and were well entertained at a farm there by a man called Veig. After they had had supper one of Jorkel's men played the harp and recited some verses. The name of this poet was Finn.

As soon as Finn had sat down, Brenda, the daughter of Veig the Shetlander, came to her father and said, 'Offer Finn a horse and a piece of land, so that he will be pleased to stay here.'

Veig made the offer to Finn, but Finn said, 'We are sailing to Orkney on a certain urgent matter in the morning. I can't stay.'

Veig repeated Finn's remark to Brenda.

At midnight when the men were drinking round the fire, Brenda rose out of bed and said to her father Veig, 'I can't get to sleep. Offer Finn a gold arm-band and a silver ring to stay here in Shetland.'

Veig called Finn aside and made this offer. Finn said, 'I am a poor man and a happy man, and gold and women would distract me from the making of verses. Besides, we have an appointment to keep in Orkney on midsummer day.'

Veig told Brenda what Finn had said.

At dawn, though the ale keg was empty, the men were still sitting at the fire. Some of them were lying under the benches drunk, but Finn was discussing metres with the Shetlanders. 'I would argue better,' said Finn, 'if I was not so dry.'

Soon after that Brenda came in and offered Finn a cup of ale.

With the froth still wet on his beard, Finn turned to Brenda and said, 'Did you brew this ale, woman?' Brenda said that she alone had made it. Then Finn said, 'On account of this ale I will stay for a while with you here in Shetland.'

I

Then the sun got up and the Norwegians stirred themselves and went on board their ship. But Finn was nowhere to be found, and the door of Brenda's room was barred. Jorkel was very angry about that.

They say that Finn made no more poems after that day. Brenda bore him twelve children. He died there in Shetland before there was a grey hair in his beard. He was drunk most days till his death, and he would drink from no cup but Brenda's. He was totally dependent on her always. It was thought rather a pity that such a promising poet should make such an ordinary end.

'She bewitched him, that bitch,' said Jorkel.

In the afternoon of the same day, Jorkel's ship reached Fair Isle. They saw some sheep on a hillside there. Flan, who was a blacksmith back in Norway, said they were fine sheep. 'And my wife,' said he, 'will be looking for a present from the west. I will bring her a fleece from Fair Isle.'

Before they could stop Flan he leapt overboard and swam ashore. The sheep were grazing at the edge of a high cliff. Flan climbed up this face, disturbing the sea birds that were there, and laid hands on the first sheep he saw. He was raising his axe to dispatch the ewe when another sheep ran terrified between his legs and toppled him over the edge of the crag, so that the sea birds were wildly agitated for the second time that day.

'Flan's descent is much quicker than his going up,' said Jorkel. 'What does a blacksmith know about shepherding?'

They anchored that night under the cliffs of Fair Isle.

They left Fair Isle at dawn and had a rough crossing to the Orkneys. There was a strong wind from the east and the sea fell into the ship in cold grey lumps, so that they were kept busy with the bailing pans.

Then Mund who had a farm east in Sweden laid down his bailing pan.

He said, 'I have made deep furrows in the land with my plough but I did not believe there could be furrows in the world like this.'

The men went on bailing.

Later Mund said, 'When Grettir lay dying in his bed at Gothenburg last summer his face was like milk. Is my face that colour?'

Jorkel said his face was more of a green colour, and urged the men to bail all the harder, since now Mund was taking no part in the game.

At noon Mund said, 'I was always a gay man at midsummer, but I do not expect to be dancing round a Johnsmas fire this year.'

The men went on bailing, until presently the wind shifted into the north and moderated, so that they were able to cook a meal of stewed rabbit and to open a keg of ale.

But when they brought the meat and ale to Mund, they found him lying very still and cold against a thwart.

'Mund will not be needing dinner any more,' said Jorkel.

They reached Papa Westray soon after that. There were some decent farms in the island, and an ale-house near the shore, and a small monastery with a dozen bald-headed brothers beside a loch.

The people of the island gave them a hospitable welcome, and sold them fish and mutton, and showed them where the best wells were.

The twelve brothers trooped into the church for vespers.

After the necessary business of victualling had been transacted, the Norwegians went into the ale-house to drink.

They played draughts and sang choruses so long as there was ale in the barrel. Then, when the keeper of the ale-house was opening a new barrel, Jorkel noticed that Thord was missing.

'He will have gone after the women of Papa Westray,' said Sweyn. Thord was known to be a great lecher back home in Norway.

3

The church bell rang for compline.

There was some fighting in the ale-house when they were midway through the second barrel, but by that time they were too drunk to hurt each other much. When things had quietened down, Jorkel remarked that Thord was still absent.

'No doubt he is stealing eggs and cheese, so that we can vary our diet on the ship,' said Valt. Thord was a famous thief on the hills of southern Norway, when it was night and everyone was sitting round the fires inside and there was no moon.

They went on drinking till the lights of yesterday and to-morrow met in a brief twilight and their senses were reeling with ale and fatigue.

'This is a strange voyage,' said Jorkel. 'It seems we are to lose a man at every station of the way.'

They heard the bell of the church ringing. Jorkel went to the door of the ale-house. Thirteen hooded figures passed under the arch to sing matins.

Jorkel returned to the ale-barrel and said, 'It seems that Thord has repented of his drinking and whoring and thieving. Yesterday there were twelve holy men in Papa Westray. This morning I counted thirteen.'

He lay down beside his companions, and they slept late into the morning.

Now there were only three men on the ship, Jorkel and Sweyn and Valt.

'We will not stop until we reach Hoy,' said Jorkel. 'Every time we stop there is one kind of trouble or another.'

They were among the northern Orkneys now, sailing through a wide firth with islands all around.

It turned out that none of the three knew where exactly Hoy was.

Sweyn said, 'There is a man in that low island over there. He has a mask on and he is taking honey from his hives. I will go ashore and ask him where Hoy is.'

'Be careful,' said Jorkel. 'We will have difficulty in getting to Hoy if there are only two of us left to work the ship.'

4

Sweyn waded ashore and said to the bee-keeper, 'Be good enough to tell us how we can recognize the Island of Hoy.'

The man took off his mask and replied courteously that they would have to sail west between the islands until they reached the open ocean, and then keeping the coast of Hrossey on the port side and sailing south they would see in the distance two blue hills rising out of the sea. These blue hills were Hoy.

Sweyn thanked him and asked if he was getting plenty of honey.

The man replied that it was a bad year for honey. The bees had been as dull as the weather.

'Still,' the bee-keeper said, 'the next comb I take from the hive will be a gift for you.'

Sweyn was deeply touched by the courtesy and kindness of the bee-keeper.

It happened that as the man was bending over the hive, a bee came on the wind and settled on his neck and stung him.

The bee-keeper gave a cry of annoyance and shook off the bee.

Sweyn grew angry at the way the insects repaid with ingratitude the gentleness of the Orkney bee-keeper. He suddenly brought his axe down on the hive and clove it in two.

Jorkel and Valt were watching from the ship, and they saw Sweyn run screaming round the island with a cloud of bees after him. It was as if he was being pelted with hot sharp sonorous hail stones.

Sweyn ran down into the ebb and covered himself with seaweed.

When Jorkel and Valt reached him, he told them where Hoy was. Then his face turned blind and blue and swollen and he died.

Jorkel and Valt got horses at a farm called the Bu in Hoy and rode between the two hills till they came to a place called Rackwick. There was a farm there and five men were working in the hayfield. It was a warm bright day, and the faces of the labourers shone with sweat.

Jorkel asked them if a man called Arkol lived nearby.

'Arkol is the grieve at this farm,' said one of the labourers, 'but he often sleeps late.'

'We work in the daytime,' said another, 'but Arkol does most of his labouring at night.'

'Arkol is a great man for the women,' said a third, and winked.

Jorkel said he thought that would be the man they were looking for.

Presently the labourers stopped to rest and they invited Jorkel and Valt to share their bread and ale. They sat under a wall where there was shadow and Valt told all that had happened to them from the time they left Bergen. But Jorkel sat quietly and seemed preoccupied. They noticed too that he did not eat or drink much.

'Who is the owner of this farm?' said Valt when he had finished his story of the voyage.

The labourers said the farmer in Rackwick was a man called John. They spoke highly of him. He was a good master to them.

Just then a man with a dark beard crossed the field. He ordered the labourers to resume their work, and then looked suspiciously at Jorkel and Valt. They were rather scruffy and dirty after their voyage.

Jorkel asked him if his name was Arkol Dagson.

The man yawned once or twice and said that it was.

'In that case,' said Jorkel, 'I must tell you that my sister Ingirid in Bergen bore you a son at the beginning of June.'

Arkol made no answer but yawned again. Then he laughed.

'And I want to know,' said Jorkel, 'if you will pay for the fostering of the child.'

Arkol said he would not discuss so intimate a matter with two tramps. So far he had not been in the habit of paying for the fostering of any child that he had fathered, and he doubted whether it was wise to begin now, especially as Norway was so far away. Furthermore, he could hardly be expected to believe the unsupported testimony of two tramps, one of whom claimed to be Ingirid's brother. Ingirid had been a most lovely and

6

gently-reared girl, and Arkol did not think the scarecrow standing before him could really be the brother of such a delightful
bedmate. Besides, he had been busy all night in another sweet
bed, and now he was very tired, and he begged the two gentlemen of the roads to excuse him.

Jorkel said, 'Will you pay now for the fostering of your son?'

Arkol turned away and yawned.

Jorkel drove his dagger into Arkol's throat, so that he fell
dead at once on the field.

The labourers jumped down from the haystack and ran at
Jorkel and Valt with their forks.

'I wish the others were here now,' said Jorkel as he turned
to face them. 'Now I would be glad to have Finn and Flan and
Mund and Thord and Sweyn at my side.'

Valt was quickly pronged to death there, and though Jorkel
defended himself well and was still on his feet when John of
Rackwick appeared on the scene, he was so severely lacerated
that he lay between life and death in the farm for more than a
week.

The three farm girls looked after him well till he recovered.
They hovered around him day and night with oil and sweet
water and beeswax.

On the day they took the last bandages from Jorkel's arm,
John of Rackwick came to him and said mildly, 'Arkol, my
grieve, was in many ways an evil lecherous man, and for that
he must answer to a higher lord than the Earl of Orkney or the
King of Norway. But also he was a loyal servant of mine, and
because of that you must pay me as compensation your ship
that is anchored off Selwick. You are welcome to stay here in
Hoy, Jorkel, for as long as you like. There is a small vacant
croft on the side of the hill that will support a cow and an
ox and a few sheep. It will be a tame life for a young man,
but now you are disabled because of the hay forks, and if
you till your field carefully nothing could be more pleasing
to God.'

Jorkel accepted that offer. He lived there at Upland for the
rest of his life. In Orkney he was nicknamed 'Hayforks'. He

put by a little money each harvest so that one day he would be able to return to Norway, but the years passed and he could never get a passage.

The summer before his death Jorkel went to Papa Westray in a fishing boat. At the church there he inquired for Thord, and presently Thord came out to meet him. They were two old men now, bald and toothless. They embraced each other under the arch. They were like two boys laughing to each other over an immense distance, thin affectionate lost voices.

Jorkel took a purse from his belt and counted five pieces of silver into Thord's hand. 'I have been saving this money for forty years,' he said, 'so that some day I could go home to Norway. But it is too late. Who would know me in Bergen now? I should prepare, instead, for the last, longest journey. Will you arrange for masses to be said in your church for Finn and Flan and Mund and Sweyn and Valt?'

Thord said that masses would certainly be offered for those dead men and for Jorkel himself too. Then he embraced Jorkel and blessed him. Jorkel turned round. He was at peace. The long silver scars of the hayforks troubled his body no longer.

Half-way to the boat he turned back. He gave Thord another silver coin. 'Say a mass for Arkol Dagson also,' he said.

They smiled at each other, crinkling their old eyes.

Elspeth Davie

OUT OF HAND

THESE nightly wrestlings with newspaper began quietly. A faint rustling of pages – giving no more warning of turmoil than the first, surreptitious scrapes of leaves in the night. After all, they were less than the familiar cracklings with which, throughout years and yards of newsprint, the old man had displayed his massive discontent with the world. Hadn't he all his life ravaged and worried the pages the better to get to grips with the clots of black headline which hid in the folds before he'd got the paper properly opened up? With one brisk shake and a bounce-up of his boney knee, he would free the poisonous black cockroach of print from its crack, revealing it in all its rustling insect slyness. It was a poisonous world but he'd kept up with it, following it step by step on its downward path. Yes, it was going down. No, it had not been better in his young days nor in his father's either ! He did not fall into that particular trap laid for him by his clever middle-aged children and his clever teenage grandchildren, nor even by the clever, impudent newsboy who hurled the paper in at the open window in summertime or used it as a brush to whiffle off balls of snow from the hedge in winter. No, and no better in his grandfather's either ! There was no first or last place on a downward slope, no one part worse than another on the sheer curve that had started as soon as human beings had anything to do with it. All this – explosive cracklings, exclaimings and paper-jabbings – had been a natural part of every day. But this year his verbal protests had grown less. During one week he made only two remarks as he sat with his paper on his lap. When words stopped the rustlings increased prodigiously. And they were of an unfamiliar kind.

He would lift the paper high in the air and lay it down again slowly and with infinite care on his knee, softly smoothing

9

out the flaws with the backs of his hands, would stare at it
for a while, pick it up, fold it back from the centre, lay it down
again and begin painstakingly creasing down a long thin edge
with his thumb, lift it up, open it out and fold it back, lay it
down again and softly pleat its edge, take it up, shake it out
and stare at it for a long time. Sometimes he would give the
whole thing an almighty shake-up, pages would drop out and
he would lift them from the floor, contemptuous, on the toe
of his shoe and fit them together again with a flailing of his
angry arms around his head. He sat now in a continual whirl-
wind of moving paper.

'He hasn't read a word for weeks. You know that, of course,'
said his granddaughter one night after he had gone to bed. It
was a windy autumn night and the gusts blew everything towards the window. They heard the leaves, dust, the hard pellets
of rain – and other less familiar sounds – twigs, or the dry
snappings of insects jet-propelled against glass, siftings. and
slidings and the brush of the bending tree on the wall. No one
spoke. After a few minutes the girl looked round again at her
father, her mother and her brother, and answered herself
briskly: 'That's right. I've been watching him. He's folding up.'
Her mother, daughter of the old man, looked taken aback not
so much at this phrase as at the briskness with which it was
uttered. Though she was a quick and opinionated woman
herself, she became very slow, very vague, when the word 'death'
came up. She thought a lot about it though, and from time to
time she moved about the idea of her own death as though
padding softly in bedroom slippers round an invalid's bed. The
man's approach was different. On most things his opinions
were cautious, but on the subject of death he could be boisterous.
If ever the word was thrown out in company, he made a grab
at it, bounced it about like a hard ball from hand to hand,
giving it a kick now and then to send it up. He could be kinder
than his wife, but about people's deaths – the sudden over-
forties anyway – he was sorry, cheerful and rather ruthless,
his view being that there was not much you could say about
death and about a possible after life – nothing at all. He talked

a lot all the same. And it was he who now answered his daughter:

'Folding up, is he? Why, isn't he well? I'd even say he was better a lot, physically, than last year.' She insisted. 'Folding himself up is nearer it. I've watched him all this week and that's exactly how it looks.' There was some discussion about colour and appetite and the doctor's opinion. The girl was stubborn and after a time they all fell silent and went on with what they'd been doing. The woman was knitting something for herself in bright orange wool on huge needles. It was going to take days not months, and she was using an up-to-the-minute pattern. All the same she now knitted very rapidly indeed as though to dispel some distant or not so distant image of herself. Her husband went back to his own paper. He turned the pages, when he had to, briskly and neatly, taking care to make as little noise and fuss about it as possible.

Much later the girl went to make coffee for herself and her brother followed, catching up the old man's newspaper from the rug on the way out. 'What exactly are you trying to say about him?' he asked when they were on their own in the kitchen.

'Every time I open my mouth you ask what I'm trying to say. It's become a habit. And a bad one.'

'No, I'm interested.'

'I'm not trying. This is what I mean. I do think he's wrapping it up. Would it be strange at that age?'

'Not at all. But what interests me is what goes on behind it all. Who or what is he wrapping?'

'Sometimes he's tucking himself in. Sometimes smoothing himself out. Once in a while he flings it all up and kicks himself free again.'

'A do-it-yourself dying?'

'Well, if ever a thing's to be done alone, this is it.'

'To my mind, it's a tidying up. The nearest thing to it is that park attendant across there, coming in after the weekend. No sooner in the gate but he's tying up and wrapping and jabbing and sometimes kicking. I wouldn't get in his way for worlds. A mixture of fury and forbearance. Do you mind talking about the old man?'

'No, I mind for him though. I hope he manages to his satisfaction. He's had some grudges in his day.'

'So it's the world he's tidying up.'

'If it is, he's got his work cut out. He's been a regular angry old man for years.'

They were silent. The boy lifted up a corner of the paper and held it, ducking his head sideways to look. It had been a rough week — so bad it had been difficult to fit the dark stuff into the columns apportioned for it. Natural catastrophe and human violence jostled for precedence. Chunks of distant stuff had to be cut drastically for injuries nearer home. Famine had made shift for riot and yesterday's American hurricane was already howled down by angry mobs in Europe. The boy glanced over all this, but he also examined closely the actual stuff of the paper. For there were two kinds of reading here. As well as the print there were the pleats that his grandfather had made, the crumples he had attempted to smooth. To the boy this also seemed important.

'All the same, he's going to take his time about it,' he said at last, putting down the paper as though having made a careful diagnosis of its skin creases. 'I hope to God we'll manage it.'

'How *we'll* manage?'

'Certainly. Look how the evening's folded up already. Everyone stuck in his own thoughts. Silent.'

'But how about us? Don't we talk?'

'A bit. There's still chunks of stuff, though, we don't even touch. I don't feel I'm saying the half.'

As a family they got on well. Outside, in their official family roles of parent, grandparent, son and daughter, they had all of them thrown themselves dutifully into the divided generations debate, the endless age-group wrangle. But with forced gusto. The heart wasn't exactly in it. The grandfather and the equality of his glassy plunge could have had something to do with it. Also they liked one another. Yet at the same time it was true that this idea of death — even an old man's death — had divided them a bit. In the end – and barring the catastrophe which hung over everyone – it could be boiled down to a practical matter of year-counting. And the family counts came out different. The old man was beyond it, his grandchildren hadn't begun, and the father and mother, consciously or not, were counting all the time – counting out the years of their life as though, at some unspecified mid-term, a time-watch had been placed at their elbow, silent, but working industriously away. At any moment the alarm could buzz. How many of their friends had lately been staggered by such alarms – struck down by heart attacks or suicidal depressions, slowly or shatteringly waking up to cancer, to coronaries, finding the harmless stiffness in the finger dangerously related to the stiffness in the toe, the familiar headache turned menacing, the cough which had kept them company for years turned killing? Even pleasures could now be counted with a sense of loss. The once-a-year friends, the once-in-two-year travels. Sometimes the question burst with appalling force. How many more times would they actually see this person, visit that country? Twenty for some things, ten for others. Five, three or less. None perhaps if you happened to be too ambitious. Was the Far East finally out then? Greenland's mountains still in the question mark bracket? The old desire for South America came back in force, stripped of all sophisticated explanations about culture. Now it was raw, black longing. It was nothing more nor less than the need to put an oar down into the thick mud of the Amazon river, to part the great glittering leaf-fronds overhead. You could say they actually hungered for crocodile. But not for the same crocodile. The idea that anyone should think them a contented couple with identical tastes seemed to drive them wild.

The fact that the old man had reached his eighty-second year was neither here nor there. It merely reminded them of their restlessness. There was nothing calm about him either, nothing resigned. He still struggled to get on top of the wilful paper, while rejecting utterly the soothing note that had crept into visitors' voices. But didn't people need comfort when they came to the end of their lives? What exactly did they need?

Did this old unbeliever want reassurance of some other existence?

'You never know what's going on in people's heads when they fall silent,' said the woman. 'They can change. They can change absolutely.' She was thinking about herself too. Her claim on a completely different kind of life. Here and now. When she said this her husband removed himself, but her son showed interest.

'You may want it,' he said. 'But does that make it any more likely?'

'Well at least I know the places are there. There are maps and photos. I could make the effort.'

'Which is different from a possible other existence. It can't be comprehended. So what efforts can you make towards it? Far less help anyone else. My guess is as good as yours – yours or an Archbishop's or Himalayan hermit's.'

'People like us are always rushing in to shout that they're as well up, any day, as Archbishop, Pope or hermit.'

'And so they should. They've got to go on and on insisting that on certain things we're absolute ignoramuses, one and all. You can't let up for an instant!' But other, uncalled-for questions on time cropped up in the midst of it all, and once in a while the woman could meditate by herself on the problem of when exactly a stole became a shawl with much the same solemnity as theologians discuss at what instant the body can be said to possess a soul.

Weeks later the independent old man entered a new stage in relation to his newspaper. Sometimes he would hand it over, open and scarcely crumpled, to whoever happened to be near with the brusque command: 'Here!' He waited, and as he waited he would fix that person with his eyes. It happened more often with neighbours who had looked in, and they responded in various ways. Some took the paper and let it lie on their knees while they ran over it quickly to see if they could find the particular paragraph which demanded comment. And they would find some bit which they read out hesitatingly or pounced on, with an exclamation. No, they'd failed to hit the mark. The paper was at once withdrawn. Worst of all when a woman neighbour with an unflinching rectitude, more stubborn than ill-will, insisted on reading aloud to him, working haphazardly down through robberies and recipes, crashes, rockets, round-table conferences and farmhouse murders – enunciating all benignly as a bedtime story – one with a sick twist here and there, but a bedtime story all the same. For a time the old man sat paralysed. Then in mid-sentence he left the room. They saw him pass the window outside, gesticulating, cautioning the disordered clouds overhead and kicking up some dark, imagined dust from the paving-stones of the path. There were some who took the paper he offered, folded it and put it aside. Or used it to swat wasps. Or as a baton to conduct a conversation, as a fire-screen, as a lap-tray for a cup of tea. He watched angrily, incredulously or with desperate intensity as though at any moment they might hit on the one thing which would satisfy him. No one knew what he wanted. Did he know himself?

'We wants to be finished,' said the granddaughter. 'And it all goes on. He goes on. The papers go on, the talk, the laughing, the coughing, the silence, plates coming and going, the forks and knives, dressing and undressing – day in day out, it all goes on. He's kept up with the world. Now there's the moon. The planets are coming into view. But the clouds are in the way, crumbs, dust – and paper, scraps of crumpled paper and falling pages. It's all got out of hand!'

Late one night, out of his hand, he let the paper slide to the floor. They heard the slow, rustling breath of the pages and above it the quick, rustling breath of the old man. It was a racer's breath, changing quickly from rustling to raucous as he put on the spurt towards his goal. The rims of his nostrils were hard and white as he sucked in the air. While the woman went to the phone his grandson crouched beside him and for a moment or two suffocated with him. But as suddenly the boy withdrew and his breath calmed. The gap between living and dying widened slowly, minute by minute. And soon the boy was no more than a sympathetic onlooker – glad to live and cool again like someone who had been ordered to step back and get on with his own business. He waited. There was now some division in his grandfather. While the upper part of his body still laboured for air, one hand felt along the ground at his side. He found the paper, handed it to the boy, at the same time turning his eyes to give him a look.

'All right. All right!' the boy said briskly. For a moment he knelt above the open pages wondering what he would do. The look had not been angry, not appealing. It was wildly expectant. He began to fold the newspaper rapidly, turning it first one way then the other, creasing with his thumb and pressing down with his fist as he went. His own antics gave him the notion that this was a parcel he was making up. But it was a parcelling done at speed as though a violent turmoil had to be smoothed and sealed, smoothed and sealed again and again until the frenzy of paper turned to a firm square and the square to a tight packet, hard as a little spade. Then the boy got up and started to fit it into the big loose pocket of his grandfather's dressing-gown. It was a tough job but he managed to push the whole thing tightly down until the woollen flap covered it.

If only for this instant – chaos was contained. He stood back, silently congratulating himself and the old man on this prodigious feat. And immediately he saw the old man's hand come up and give the pocket a light, sharp tap. The strained head turned his way to signal its ironic, still undeceived, but unmistakable relief.

THE MONEY

AT one period in my life, as a result of the poverty I was suffering, it became impossible for me to tell a lie. Consequently, I
became the recipient of National Assistance money. But it all
began when I applied for Unemployment Benefit money at the
little Labour Exchange in the nearest town.

As I entered the building, the typist turned to the clerk
and I heard her whisper, 'The artist is here again.' No, she gave
me a capital – 'Artist.' The clerk rose, and, making no attempt
to attend to me, crossed to the door marked 'Welfare Officer'
and gave it a knock.

The clerk was seated. Presently the Welfare Officer appeared.
He is, or I should say, was then, a rather stout, unhappy looking person in his early forties. This afternoon, as if he had
known I was coming to see him, he wore a fashionable sports
jacket and a large, arty and gaudy tie. My heart went out to
him as he advanced towards the counter saying: 'I've told you
before. We have no jobs for you. You are simply wasting our
time.'

Somehow, I had got myself into a ridiculous *lolling* position,
with my elbows on the counter and my hand supporting my
chin. I gazed up at the Welfare Officer and replied timidly,
'I haven't come about a job. I have *been* in a job. Now I have
come to ask you for Unemployment Benefit money.'

As I spoke, I could not help glancing at the large, locked safe
that stood in the far corner of the room. Out of it, distinctly, a
curious silence trickled, rather as smoke trickles out of the stove
in my cottage. I had no doubt it was the silence of The Money
I had just referred to.

'What!' exclaimed the Welfare Officer, raising his black,
bushy eyebrows. 'You have been in a job!'

I nodded. 'I was editing a magazine.'

'And may I ask what salary you received?' he said, his tone disguising the question as an official one.

'One pound, three and sixpence,' I answered, for, as I explained, I could not tell a lie.

'Per month?' he suggested.

'Per week,' I replied with dignity. 'And it was only a part-time job.'

'Hum! In that case, assuming that you have been in part-time employment and did not leave it of your own accord you will be entitled to claim part-time Unemployment Benefit money from this Labour Exchange,' he informed me, all in one breath.

'What? But that isn't fair!' I retorted. My cheeks crimsoned; I took my elbows off the counter and waved my hands. 'That isn't just! I paid *full-time* National Insurance money. So I should draw *full-time* Unemployment Benefit money from this Labour Exchange!'

My impassioned outburst brought a nervous titter from the typist and an astonished rustle from the young clerk. The Welfare Officer, however, only glanced at me for an instant, turned his back on me, strode into his office and shut the door.

I waited a few moments. Then, 'Do you think I have offended him?' I asked the clerk. 'Am I supposed to go away now? Do you know?'

But before I had received an answer to my unhappy question, the Welfare Officer appeared once more, bearing two large volumes – no, *tomes*, in his arms. CRASH! He dropped the tomes on the counter, right under my nose.

Then he opened one of the tomes; and slowly, silently, with brows sternly knitted, he began to thumb his way through the thick and closely printed sheets. Page 100 ... Page 250. ... And he still had the second of the tomes in reserve.

I moistened my lips, and said weakly, 'Very well, I give in. I am only entitled to draw part-time Unemployment money from this Labour Exchange.'

'That is correct,' observed the Welfare Officer. Closing the tome, and flexing his muscles, he bent to push it aside. Then he took a step or two towards the safe. That, at least, was my impression. Looking back on the incident, I see that he was really going to the cupboard to fetch forms.

But the sight of his too-broad figure retreating to fetch me The Money touched my heart. True, he had won a hollow victory, but I did not mind, and I wanted him to know I did not mind.

'Thank you,' I said, in low, sincere tones.

The Welfare Officer stopped at once. He turned to face me again. 'Thank you? Why are you saying thank you? You haven't got the money yet, you know,' he warned me.

'I know that,' I said, and I apologized to him. He appeared to accept my apology, and, turning, took another step or two towards the cupboard – or, as I thought, the safe.

Again I was touched. It was the combination of my poverty, his pathetic appearance in his rich clothes, and the thought of The Money he was about to give me. It was as if he was generously giving it to me out of his own pocket, I felt.

'But honestly,' I sighed, 'I'm awfully grateful to you. You see, if you give me The Money, I'll be able to work ... I'll be free to work – at last!'

'Work? What work?' exclaimed the Welfare Officer. He halted, flew into a rage, and once more turned to face me. 'If you are going to be working you cannot claim Unemployment Benefit money! Don't you understand that!' he shouted.

At this moment, the typist intervened, saying, 'He doesn't mean work. What he means is, taking pictures. Like that one – I forget his name – who cut off his ear.'

I, too, flew into a rage, and not only at this mention of *ears*.

'*Taking* pictures? T A K I N G pictures? P A I N T I N G pictures if you don't mind!' I fixed the typist with my eye, and as a sort of reflex action, she bent forward and typed several letters on her machine. Then, looking at the Welfare Officer, I asked: 'Just tell me, yes, do tell me, how is a person to work when they are in a job? I can only work when I am N O T in a job? When I am in a job I C A N N O T work, do you understand?'

'Are you working or are you not working?' shouted the

exasperated Welfare Officer at the very top of his voice. 'Think it over will you, and let me know!'

So I thought it over, and that very night, by the light of my oil lamp, I wrote a polite letter to the authorities in the Labour Exchange. In effect, what I said was: 'I resign.' And the following morning, I handed the letter to the postman when he delivered the bills at my mountain-cottage.

But in the afternoon, when I was painting in my kitchen, I happened to look through the window, and I saw a neat little man. Clothed in a pin-striped office-suit and clasping a briefcase, he was clinging rather breathlessly to the fence. Several sheep had ceased to crop the hillside and were gazing at him with evident surprise.

As he did not look like a shepherd, I at once concluded that he must be – could only be – an art-dealer. Overjoyed, I thrust my hairless brushes back in their jam-pot, threw the door open, and ran out into the warm summer sunshine to make him welcome.

My collie dog, swinging the shaggy pendulum of his tail, and barking furiously, preceded me. 'Don't be afraid!' I shouted to the art-dealer. However, he had already scrambled back over the fence, and was standing, at bay, in the shade of the wood.

Calling the dog off, I opened the gate, and, smiling, advanced to meet him with outstretched hand. 'Good afternoon. I'm very glad to see you,' I said. The art-dealer took my hand, shook it warmly, and replied, 'I am from the National Assistance Board. Good afternoon.'

It was then I noticed he had been holding *forms*. The collie still bounded about us, leaping up on the stranger so as to sniff his interesting office-y smells. 'Fin McCuil,' I ordered, 'you mustn't touch *those*. Bad. Go away, now. Chew your bone instead!'

Then I turned to the National Assistance man, and I explained to him, with many apologies, that I had resigned.

He listened sympathetically, but when I had finished speaking, he came a step nearer to me, placed his arm around my shoulder, and said softly, 'Son, there is no need to feel like that, you are perfectly entitled to take this money.'

He tapped his brief-case. He meant, of course, the National Assistance money.

'But I don't feel *like that*,' I assured him. 'Believe me, I feel grateful ... I mean, ungrateful ... bringing you all this way ... But I have resigned ... I don't think I fit in very well, you see ...'

'Son,' said the National Assistance man, speaking as no art-dealer ever did, 'I understand your position. No, don't look surprised. I do understand it. For you see, my own brother is a violinist ...' And breaking off for a moment, he gazed thoughtfully down the steep and rickety, old path up to my house. Here was a green, ferny landing; there a hole in the bannisters of bracken where a sheep had crashed through. 'He lives in a garret,' he continued. 'He is in the same ... er ... position ... you see, as you are. He sits up there all day playing his violin.'

So there had been a mistake. It was just as I thought, and almost as bad as if I had told a lie. 'But I don't play the violin,' I pointed out. 'I don't play anything. You see, there's been a mistake.'

'No, no, I understand. You don't play the violin. You paint pictures,' said the National Assistance man soothingly. 'By the way,' he added, 'what do you do with them?'

'Do with them?' I repeated, at a loss. 'Ah, do with them: I see. Well, the big ones I put upstairs, in the attic. The little ones I put downstairs, in the cupboard.'

'You don't ever think of selling them?' he asked gently.

'Selling them! HA, HA! No, I don't,' I said, deighted by the fantasy of the question.

There was a pause. Suddenly he looked me straight in the eye, and he asked me, point-blank, 'Son, do you want this money?'

I could not tell a lie. 'I do,' I said.

So he thrust his hand into his brief-case. He offered me the Money, and, without looking at It, I put It in my pocket as fast as I could. Money is a great embarrassment when you are poor.

'Just fill those in,' he explained.

So, I thought to myself, they are not pound notes; they are postal-orders. But when we had shaken hands and said good-bye to each other, I found they were not postal-orders, either; they were forms ...

And I filled them in. And thereafter, till my truthfulness got me into fresh trouble (for, of course, I had been brought up to look on charity as trouble) they sent me a regular weekly cheque. For my part, I was requested to fill in a form stating what Employment I had undertaken during the week and how much money I had earned by it. As painting was not Employment, though it was Work, I very carefully wrote the words 'None' and 'Nil' in the appropriate columns. After five or six weeks they gave me a seven-shilling rise.

Then I sold a picture. And I was inspected at the same time by an unfamiliar National Assistance man.

It was a breezy, blue and golden day in early autumn when he arrived at the door of my cottage. No sooner had I answered his knock than he cheerfully apologized. 'Sorry, old chap. Can't wait long today. Two ladies down in the car ...'

'I expect you are going out for a picnic,' I observed, wondering if I ought or ought not to return his wink.

'Ha, ha, old boy, you are quite right there !' he answered.

'Well, do come in for just a moment,' I said. 'I shan't keep you, I promise.'

Lifting my easel out of the way, and hastily removing my wet palette from a chair, I invited him into my kitchen, and he sat down. On my palette, as it happened. He had sat on the chair on to which I had removed it; I at once ran for the turpentine and the cloth.

When we had cleaned him up, I put in tentatively: 'There is something I wanted to ask you. It's er ... it's about those ... er ... form ...'

'Forms?' His bright face clouded over. I was spoiling his picnic with my Prussian Blue paint and my silly questions.

'Those ... er ... weekly forms that you send me ...'

'Oh, those. You mean that you complete those, do you?' He seemed astonished that I did.

But I could not tell a lie. 'I'm afraid I do,' I confessed. 'Do you think it matters very much?'

'Ah, well, no harm done, I suppose.'

'Then there is a difficulty,' I announced. And quickly, so as not to keep the ladies waiting, I mentioned the awful problem I was now faced with. Painting, I explained, was not Employment, though it was *Work*. And even if I stretched a point and called it Employment, still it was not employment undertaken *this week*. The picture I had sold had been painted a whole year ago ... How was I to inform them of the money I had received for it?

'I want to be quite truthful, you see,' I added. 'The form applies only to the present week ... So, you see, it is difficult to be truthful.'

'If you want my advice, old boy, *be* truthful,' he answered. 'Yes, be truthful, that is always best. Or nearly always best, eh? HA, HA! Ah, hmm ...' He rose, and moved to the door. 'I say,' he whispered to me, 'do I smell of turpentine?'

I sniffed at him, and assured him that he did not. 'The very best of luck then, old chap.' We shook hands. Halting to wave to me at frequent intervals, he hurried down the path, and I returned to the house.

There and then, determined to be truthful at all costs, I set about filling in my weekly form. 'Employment Undertaken – None.' And under 'Money Earned.' I carefully wrote – '£5. 5. 0.' It had, I reflected, that slight suggestion of paradox one expects with the truth.

I posted the form, and, by return of post, I was sternly summoned to the central office of the National Assistance Board.

When I entered the building, and gave my name at the desk, I was at once led, like a very special sort of person, down several long passages and into a room. There, I was awaited. Several men, all of whom, it was plain, were awaiting me, were seated rather grimly around a table. On the table lay my form. Strange to say, it looked completely different there; *absurd*.

On my arriving in the room, one of the men – their spokesman or perhaps the head one – pointed to my form, and said, 'What is *that*?'

'That? Why, it's my weekly form,' I replied.

'Can you explain it to us?' another asked me.

'Yes, easily,' I answered. And I proceeded to explain it to them. Time. Money. Work. Truth. When I had completed my explanation, one of them got up from his chair and fetched a tome. It was a signal, for, at this, they all left their chairs and fetched back tomes. They threw them open on the table.

I grew nervous. After a while, I looked at the one who had first addressed me, and, pointing to his tome, I said, 'You are wasting your time. *I am not in it.*' He looked at me, but he did not smile or reply.

'Gentlemen – ,' I began, interrupting them. 'Gentlemen, I think it would be best if I gave up The Money. I don't quite fit in, I quite see that. I sympathize with you. So I resign.'

At this, there was a sudden and very noticeable change in the atmosphere. They were obviously relieved at my decision. They smiled at me. But one of them said: 'There is no need to be hasty.' And another added: 'We wish you well.'

'Then I am to go on taking The Money, am I?' I asked.

But once more there was a change in the atmosphere. The men became grim again, and put on frowns.

'I see,' I said. 'Then I have no alternative but to resign.'

Smiles. Relief. Opening of silver cigarette-cases. 'There is no need to be hasty.' 'We wish you well.'

'I believe you,' I assured them. 'Will you send on the forms or shall I just fill them in now?'

'Now!' said the men, speaking all at once.

So I completed the forms of resignation, and I left the building a free man.

Ian Hamilton Finlay

THE POTATO PLANTERS AND
THE OLD JOINER'S FUNERAL

THE potato planters had only just started work again after having their dinner. They were spread out in almost a straight line across their first drills in the middle of the field.

There were seven planters, two men, two women, and three young tinker girls. The old tinker who was carrying the potatoes to them had filled their sack-aprons, and was opening more sacks with his clasp-knife farther down the drills.

The old tinker grimaced when he discovered that all the sacks he opened were filled with big potatoes. That was bad for whoever was carrying to the planters. Before he had got three sacks opened, the seven planters had emptied their aprons and he had to walk back up the drills and fill them all over again. He staggered across the drills, between the planters and the sacks, with the heavy wire basket held at arm's length against his belly.

As soon as they had got their potatoes, the three young tinker girls started to plant them out. They held up their rough heavy sack-aprons as if they were pinafores filled to the brim with pretty flowers. The two men went on planting methodically while the other two women began to move away out in front as if there was a race down to the fence at the bottom of the field.

It was a hot spring day. The seven planters were sweating already. As the old tinker said, it was far too hot a day for working; they ought to have been fast asleep under some trees where it was shady and cool. A white heat-haze hung on the hills. The sun was like a huge marigold in the blue sky right above their heads. Away on the far side of the field one of the tractors was droning. The potatoes fell with little thuds into the hot, dry earth where spiders scurried among the grains of the potato manure like cooking-salt.

The planters moved slowly down the field, repeating their mechanical movements below the fiery sun that stung their necks. The old tinker filled their sack-aprons with the big potatoes as quickly as he could.

Before the planters had reached the bottom of their first drills they all stopped work for a time and stared down the field to the main road. They all stared at the motor hearse going up the road to collect the body of an old joiner who had died that week. They all stared till the black, shiny vehicle went out of sight behind the blue pine trees. The old joiner, they remembered, was to be buried that afternoon at 2.30 in the cemetery on the far side of the village, three miles away. When they had thought about this for several seconds, they all called to have their sack-aprons filled – all seven of them at once.

The tinker ripped open a fresh sack with his clasp-knife. His face was thickly coated with pale dust; it was almost the colour of candle-grease. He leaned his weight on the heavy sack to spill a basket-load of potatoes into the basket at his feet. Before he could get the heavy sack righted again the potatoes had over-flowed the basket and spilled on the ground. He had a sudden desire to beat his breast.

Suddenly, while they waited for the old tinker to come with potatoes, the seven planters noticed that the other old man, who had been carrying potatoes in the morning, was not there. They thought about him not being there and each one, secretly, arrived at the conclusion that he was away at the funeral of the old joiner who was being buried that afternoon at 2.30 in the cemetery on the other side of the village, three miles away. They went on noticing that the old man was not there each time they ran short of potatoes and had to wait for the old tinker to hurry along to them, with his heavy basket.

The seven planters reached the bottom of their first drills. They moved into seven new drills and started back up the field. Now they had their backs to the main road and they had an awful feeling that the funeral would sneak by silently without them seeing it. But they had reached the top of the field and turned around again before the funeral went by.

There were more cars than anyone had expected there would be. There were seven cars, not even counting the hearse with the old joiner laid in it, on his way to be buried in the cemetery on the far side of the village, three miles away. The minister's small, streamlined car was in the middle of the line. Because of its shape – like a pullet's egg – it was easy to pick out, and with its bright blue colour it looked very gay among all the other cars that were mostly black. The seven cars kept the same distance apart, and it looked at first as if the hearse was towing them along slowly on one long rope. Then the minister's car started to catch up on the car in front, and the cars in behind it had to hurry to catch up too.

The seven planters stared fixedly at the funeral. Being Protestants they did not cross themselves, or say or do anything whatever. They just stared. The two men did think of raising their caps but it seemed to them that the habit of doing that must have died out. The two women thought of saying something but they were each afraid to speak in case they said the wrong thing. The one in the green apron had a growing feeling that the funeral would have to hurry if it was to be down at the cemetery on the far side of the village by 2.30, as it ought to be.

There was silence for several moments after the funeral had gone out of sight behind the trees. Then there were seven small thuds because all the seven planters dropped the potatoes they had been holding when they stopped to watch. They started to move on again in a crooked line, under the hot sun like a huge marigold in the sky.

Suddenly the old tinker stopped, and laid his wire basket down on the earth. He bent his knees slightly, and raised his right arm, pointing upwards. The seven planters looked questioningly at him.

'Death !' said the old tinker, waving his left arm about. ''Tis terrible what Death will do to a man . . .'

The seven planters stared at the tinker with vacant expressions on their sweaty faces.

'Take that man there,' said the tinker, lowering his arm to

27

point after the funeral. 'I was speaking to that man, there, only on Saturday ...'

'No,' said the woman in the green apron, breaking in on the tinker. 'Not that man. Another man. It was a different man you were speaking to.'

The old tinker let his arm drop down to his side. He turned his face towards the woman in the green apron. Trickles of sweat had drawn tragic lines down his grey cheeks.

'A different man!' he said. 'And is *he* dead as well?'

'They are both dead,' said the woman in green, lowering her sack-apron a little.

'They are both dead. But the man you were speaking to was a different man. I know he was a different man because I saw you speaking to him. I happened to see you speaking to him last Saturday morning, about 10 o'clock, and it was not the same man.'

'A different man!' exclaimed the old tinker, shaking his head sadly. He lifted his basket and staggered towards the planters with it held against his belly.

The half-past bus came out from behind the pine trees with a sudden flash of windows. The planters all stopped planting and looked at the bus going along the main road.

'I thought that,' said the woman in green. 'I knew that all along. It will take that funeral all its time to be down at the cemetery by half-past two.'

One of the two men planters took out his watch slowly, looked at it intently, then put it away. The seven planters moved down the field in the intense heat. They reached down to the bottom of the drills and turned up again.

A few minutes later there was a further interruption as a tractor came racing into the potato field through the far gate. The trailer was loaded high with more potato-sacks and on top of the load stood the gay young tinker, the old tinker's son. He stood with his legs wide apart, lashing the tractor with a long, imaginary whip. Plainly he was imagining himself to be a cossack or something.

'Tallyho! Crack! Crack! Yipee!' he kept on shouting at the top of his voice.

The old tinker scowled when he discovered that the new sacks, too, were filled with big potatoes. He seemed to see two old men stretched out under shady trees, and though one of them, he knew, was different he could not think why that was the case.

The hot sun, like a huge marigold, beat down on the field.

The other old man, who was away at the funeral, did not get back to the potato field till almost four o'clock. The old tinker asked him where he had been.

J. A. Ford

THE DEVIL AND THE DEEP BLUE SEA

MONTGOMERY Jones stood with his back to the window and
led the case for Art. Behind him, the leaf and stone of Edinburgh in the autumn, when the black trees weaken and become
light-headed with colour and the grey stone walls are warmed by
the long light from the south. In front of him, his gathering of
fellow-advocates and influential solicitors and their wives and
some English acquaintances who had come north for the Festival. He held his lapels – he knew that his friends expected him
to pose – and spoke splendidly of Art.

As in court he could always see over his argument the re-
actions of judge and jury, so now he could, while pleading
special privileges for the artist, watch every movement of his
wife and his devil who were distributing the drinks and the
savouries. His wife had a thrifty way of chatting as she threaded
her way slowly and gracefully among the guests and offered
refreshment, but the dullwitted young devil spoke in abrupt
monosyllables and splashed drinks around with reckless generosity. It had been a mistake to ask him to help.

The devil was not the only source of irritation. There was
an old solicitor who presumed upon the bulk and glitter of
court practice to play Philistine in an effort to confound
counsel.

'The artist, like the rest of us, sells his talents,' he said roughly.
'If he can't find a purchaser, the plain assumption is that he has
nothing of worth to sell.'

This was an expression of the apathy that Montgomery Jones
had for years been trying to convert into passion. Not that there
was anything patently passionate about Montgomery Jones himself. Gently, his thumbs caressing his lapels, he said, 'Money
may stimulate artistic effort, but the withholding of money

cannot alter the fact of art. The artist confers a right upon us. There is an aesthetic obligation on us to enjoy that right, and a moral and sometimes legal obligation towards the artist. The artist gives us the chance to lead a fuller life, and we must give him the like chance. He finds a place for us among the universals and the abstractions, and we must find a place for him in society.'

But the younger ladies were becoming restive and he abandoned his judicial pose and slipped his hands into his pockets, Montgomery Jones, host and patron, the man who during last year's Festival had entertained a Spanish Dancer, a French novelist, and two German trombonists. He continued, 'Whatever you think of artists I hope you'll all be able to stay till my last guest arrives. I'd like you to meet him, P. S. Foley.'

There was a gratifying stir of expectancy among the younger guests and an infuriating lapse by the devil. He dropped an opened bottle on the Wilton and hesitated for a few expensive moments before he righted the bottle and mopped the carpet with his handkerchief. 'Foley?' he asked abruptly, still on his hands and knees. The man had no social presence. 'Is Foley coming here?'

Montgomery Jones turned from the offensive incredulity and spoke to an advocate's wife who was asking whether Mr Foley would recite one of his poems. 'You can never tell what may happen here. We had Spanish dancing last year.' The novelist had been rather quiet, but French. The trombonists had both vomited in the bathroom. 'But we mustn't press old P.S. We must make him feel at home.' He glanced at the old solicitor. 'P.S. is established now, with an international reputation, but where would he have been if someone hadn't taken him up in his early years?'

'What d'you mean "taken up"?' asked the solicitor.

'Why, brought him out, encouraged him.'

The solicitor drained his glass. 'D'you mean giving him money?'

'If necessary.'

'Is there anything of Foley's on your shelves?' The old Philistine grasped the back of his chair as if he threatened to rise and explore for himself.

'Alison,' Montgomery Jones was saying, 'now you can ask P.S. what he meant by "Sweet from their Adam's eve paint their cheeks apple."'

Alison Temple smiled too lazily, veiled her too innocent eyes.

'Sorry,' Montgomery Jones turned to the solicitor again, 'Anything of Foley's? I hope there is something left ... Same again, old man?' Adroitly he made for the sideboard.

He had never bought any of Foley's works, had never read any more of them than had appeared in the reviews. But he had discussed Foley at greater length and to better purpose than had, say, his devil, who could quote Foley as fluently as the old solicitor could quote Burns. There is little merit in reading except in so far as it leads to understanding, and Montgomery Jones could understand without a pedantic scrutiny of texts. He had discredited expert witnesses out of their own mouths, confounded a mariner without going to sea, and undermined a veterinary surgeon's confidence without ever taking a close look at a cow. And in the same way he could explain Foley, Sartre and Kafka out of the mouths of the labourers in the Parnassian vineyards.

The door-bell tinkled. Everyone fell silent. 'That'll be old P.S. now,' said Montgomery Jones.

The devil, who had been acting as usher as well as waiter, was already on his way to the door. Montgomery Jones urbanely tried to keep the conversation going, but the responses were formal, the guests were poising themselves for introduction. The devil was taking an infernally long time. Montgomery Jones murmured an apology, put a cigarette in his mouth, and went to the door.

Foley had brought a woman with him. She stood neglected while the devil addressed Foley in a state of feverish excitement. Montgomery Jones bit angrily on his cigarette and walked forward. 'So glad you managed to come, old man.'

Foley glanced up. 'Oh, hello,' he said. 'I'll have a word with you later,' he promised to the devil. He was jerking about uneasily. 'Oh, you're Mr Jones?'

Montgomery Jones clenched his jaws. Foley had been a little tight when they were introduced the previous night, but if he could not remember a face and a name for less than twenty-four hours he might at least dissemble his forgetfulness.

'I brought my wife along.'

The woman nodded. 'How do you do, Mr Jones.' She was dressed like a countrywoman and stood with her legs apart as if she were waiting for a horse.

With an effort Montgomery Jones found his pose again, host and patron, ready to trample conventions to beat out a social path for the artist. 'Nice to see you again, P.S.'

In the few moments that it took to lead them into the lounge, he contrived to put his hand on Foley's shoulder and burst into laughter at the little poet's comment on the sharpness of the air outside. It was a splendid entrance, the radiant host, the bewildered poet, the countrywoman with a cavalry stride, and – damn him! – the devil hovering awkwardly in the background.

But, even while he was making the introductions, Montgomery Jones overheard the murmur of one of his colleagues: 'Most of M. J.'s lions turn out to be mice.' He was furious. Foley did look extraordinarily unlike an artist of genius. He was small and pale, carefully dressed in blue serge and gently clumsy as if he had recently been fitted out with new hands and feet. This was not the bright-eyed visionary of the previous night.

Deliberately, Montgomery Jones made for the sideboard. Mrs Foley wanted a sherry, a dark sherry. 'And you, P.S.?'

'Oh, Lor',' exclaimed the countrywoman, 'don't give him anything stronger than lime juice. He has a tummy.'

'Ulcer?' inquired the old solicitor feelingly.

Foley nodded, coloured slightly, and tried to edge into a less conspicuous position.

'All the Foleys have ulcers,' said the countrywoman complacently. 'Nothing like that on my side.'

Montgomery Jones found himself wishing that her horse would arrive and carry her away. He looked at the lime juice and his head swam with a sudden nostalgia for the sun and the deep blue sea. Edinburgh was too cold for the passion that engendered art, for the enthusiasm that inspired culture. It was too far north for the full life, north of normal. In his mind there circled hazy images that had haunted him from school-days – men and their monuments beside the deep blue sea, all under the broad light of the sun that shone from the pages of Homer and Virgil.

With a little support, a little encouragement in his early years he might have been a considerable artist himself. Now all that was left of those years was the memory of crumbling statuary beside the sea ... and the desire to give some other artist hospitality and encouragement. Every artist looks for encouragement, for art is the loneliest of ventures.

He turned to Foley with fresh interest. 'Well, have you told Alison all about Adam's eves?'

The poet was startled. He looked for his hands, laid them away behind his back, and smiled. 'You musn't look too closely at the things I did in the genesis of my career.'

Montgomery Jones and two other advocates laughed.

'But Mr Foley,' said Alison, 'you never write love poetry.' Her blue gaze suggested that she herself was ready to burst into the song of the Shulamite.

'All my poetry,' said Foley with desperate humour, 'is about love.'

The old solicitor cleared his throat. 'Have you read Burns?'

'Oh, yes.'

'Nothing obscure about Burns, Mr Foley. Why are modern poets obscure?'

Foley looked quickly around again, as if he were keeping in mind the route to the door. 'I don't know. Really. We may be surveying new territory in inadequate symbols, or straining language to describe old territory in fresh terms. Both, maybe?'

'You sound like an explorer,' said Alison softly. Perhaps it had been a mistake to invite her. She was becoming obvious.

'But Burns –'

The devil interrupted the old solicitor. He would learn manners in his unaccompanied pacings of Parliament House. 'Times change,' he said. 'You don't practise eighteenth-century law, so why should you expect poetry to stand still?'

'I don't. But I expect it to remain intelligible.'

'New things are always more difficult to understand than old things. Take statutory instruments, for example.' He was speaking angrily, as if honour or income were at stake, and Montgomery Jones intervened.

'If there is any estrangement between poet and public just now, there may be faults on both sides.' He had taken hold of his lapels again. 'Perhaps personal contact like this will help to bridge the gap.'

The old solicitor turned to Foley. 'Do *you* think there's any danger of a real artist being lost to the world through lack of support and encouragement?'

'I don't know. Really. But artists are men. Encouragement helps.' Foley looked suddenly reckless.

'Without encouragement,' said Montgomery Jones deliberately, 'many young artists go to the wall.'

Foley nodded. 'It's the young who need the help. We should listen to them even although they're just tuning up.' He stared at the devil. 'Why don't you read one of your poems now?'

The devil turned red as fire.

'Tumblers and poets,' said Foley, and there was for the first time a note of authority in his voice. 'Poets and tumblers, we must take our chances when they come.'

And to Montgomery Jones's horror, the devil stood back against the sideboard and began to recite. His redness gave way to pallor. His voice came tight from his throat. Until at last he felt himself less than his words. Then there was no nervous devil, but only his words in the silence and the failing light, around the dark figures of men and women and against the leaf and the stone. Only his words and the passion that suddenly flowered out of his loneliness.

When he finished he trembled slightly as if he were cold. The guests stirred and coughed uneasily and murmured approval. Foley, his eyes and mouth tired, said, 'What can I say? You have put a few lines between yourself and despair. They – I enjoyed them.'

There was a silence. Then, mercifully, Alison crossed to speak to the devil, and Mrs Foley, staring out of the window, said, 'Takes a long time for night to fall in the North.' Everyone was glad to agree.

Montgomery Jones stood with his hands by his sides. He too was cold, and he knew that it was beyond him to revive the party, to create a memorable occasion. The devil had seen to that, clouding the air with embarrassment. An awkward, ungrateful, and egotistical young man. It had been a mistake to invite him.

Edward Gaitens

A WEE NIP

A MACDONNEL party was nearly always an informal affair. Guests were never invited by card or telephone. They just 'got to know' and drifted in, irresistibly drawn by the prospect of free drink and uproarious song. John Macdonnel always insisted that there were people in the Gorbals who possessed second-sight in the matter of parties. Fellows like Squinty Traynor, Baldy, Flynn and bowlegged Rab Macpherson and ladies like wee Mrs Rombach, Tittering Tessie and wee Minnie Milligan – though why she always showed up at parties when she was a Rechabite and never touched a drop, he couldn't understand – could smell a wake or a wedding a mile off and always crept in at the exact moment when there was still plenty of drink going and everybody was too drunk to ask or care if they had been invited.

Sometimes the nucleus of a Macdonnel party was formed in the Ladies' Parlour of a local pub from which Mrs Macdonnel would emerge with some shawled cronies and confer on the pavement, deciding whether they should continue their tippling in another Ladies' Parlour or in one of their own kitchens. Owing to this erratic behaviour on the part of his wife, Mr Macdonnel occasionally returned from his day's work to find her absent – when he went round her friends' kitchens in search of her – or at home with several lady friends all jolly and mildly drunk. If he was hungry and in sober mood his icy glare sent all his wife's friends flying like snow in a wintry blast, but if he yearned for spirits he thawed and deferred his displeasure till the following morning when the mere thought of work was a nightmare to his aching head.

Every time Jimmy Macdonnel came home from sea there was a party and a few more after it till his pay of several months was burned right up. Even if Mrs Macdonnel had been six

months teetotal, she couldn't resist taking one wee nip to celebrate her son's return and that wee nip somehow multiplied,
had bairns, as she would laughingly tell you herself.

Returning from his last voyage before World War I, Jimmy
Macdonnel, after a year's absence as cook on a tramp steam-
ship, was the originator of a famous Macdonnel party. It was
a bright July Saturday afternoon when Jimmy unexpectedly
arrived. A delicious smell of Irish stew was still hanging around
the Macdonnel kitchen. Mrs Macdonnel was a rare cook and
Mr Macdonnel who loved her cooking had dropped into a
smiling drowse, dazed by his enormous meal. At the open
window Eddy Macdonnel was seated on the dishboard of the
sink muttering to himself the Rules of Syntax out of an English Grammar, asking himself how it was that Donald Hamilton
could repeat from memory whole pages of the Grammar and
yet couldn't write a grammatical sentence, while he, who could
hardly memorize a couple of Rules, could write perfect English
with the greatest of ease. But he drove himself to the unpleasant
exercise of memorizing, resisting the temptation to bask in the
powerful sunshine and listen to the children playing at an old
singing-game, The Bonny Hoose O' Airlie O. The children
were gathered near the backcourt wash-house, round the robber
and his wife. First the little girl sang:

> 'Ah'll no' be a robber's wife,
> Ah'll no' die wi' your penknife
> Ah'll no' be a robber's wife
> Doon b' the bonny hoose o' Airlie, O.'

then the boy answered, taking her hand,

> 'Oh you sall be a robber's wife,
> An' ye'll die wi' my penknife
> You sall be a robber's wife
> Doon b' the bonny hoose o' Airlie, O.'

The old ballad tune seemed to come out of the heart of young
Scotland, out of the childhood of his country's life. Eddy wanted
to dream into that bygone poetry. Ach! He drove his mind

again to memorizing the lesson for his night-school class. Mr Henderson, the English teacher, had a biting tongue for lazy students. He turned back the page, started again, and his muttered Rules mingled with the snores of his father and his mother's whispers as she sat at the table scribbling a shopping-list on a scrap of paper and continually pausing to count the silver in her purse.

Just then there was a knock at the stairhead door and Mrs Macdonnel, touching back her greying, reddish hair, rose in a fluster to open, exclaimed, 'My Goad, it's Jimmy!' and returned followed by a slim, dapper young man of twenty-nine, with bronzed features, in the uniform of a petty-officer of the Merchant Service and carrying a sailor's kitbag which he dumped on the floor.

'Did ye no' ken Ah was comin' hame the day?' he asked resentfully; 'Ah sent ye a postcard fae Marsels.'

'Och, no son!' said his mother, blaming in her heart those "forrin' postcairds" which always bewildered her. 'Shure yer da would hiv come tae meet the boat. Ye said the twenty-seeventh,' and she began searching in a midget bureau on the dresser to prove her words, then she gazed mystified at the 'Carte Postale' with the view of Marseilles Harbour. 'Och, Ah'm haverin'!' she cried, 'it says here the seeventeenth!'

'Ach away! Ye're daft!' said Jimmy. 'How could ye mistake a "one" for a "two"?'

Mr Macdonnel woke up, rubbing his eyes, Eddy got down from the dishboard, closing his Grammar; and they all stared at Jimmy in silent wonder. He certainly looked trim as a yacht in his blue reefer suit, white shirt, collar and black tie, but they weren't amazed at his spruceness nor by his unexpected arrival but by the fact that he stood there as sober as a priest. For ten years Jimmy had been coming home from sea at varying intervals and had never been able to get up the stairs unassisted; and here he was, after a six months voyage, not even giving off a smell of spirits. Mr Macdonnel put on his glasses to have a better look at him. What was wrong with Jimmy? They wondered if he was ill, then the agonizing thought that he had been robbed occurred simultaneously to the old folk, and Jimmy was about to ask them what they were all looking at when his mother collected herself and embraced him and his father shook his hand, patting his shoulder.

Jimmy flushed with annoyance at his mother's sentiment as he produced from his kitbag a large plug of ship's tobacco for his da, a Spanish shawl of green silk, with big crimson roses on it for his mother, and a coloured plaster-of-paris plaque of Cologne Cathedral for his Aunt Kate, then, blushing slightly, he took his seaman's book from his pocket and showed them the photograph of a young woman. 'That's Meg,' he said, 'Meg Macgregor. She's a fisher-girl. I met her at the herring-boats when ma ship called in at Peterhead.'

His mother was delighted with his taste and knew immediately why he had arrived sober. She passed the photograph to her husband, who beamed at it and said heartily, 'My, she's a stunner, Jimmy boy! A proper stunner! She'll create a sensation roun' here!' Mr Macdonnel usually awoke ill-tempered from his after-dinner naps, but his indigestion vanished like magic as he imagined the glorious spree they were going to have on Jimmy's six months' pay; and he swore he had never seen such a beautiful young woman as Meg Macgregor. Then Jimmy startled them all by announcing, as if he was forcing it out of himself: 'Meg's awfu' good-livin', mother, an' she's asked me tae stoap drinkin' for the rest o' ma life. Ah've promised her Ah will.'

Mr Macdonnel glared wildly at his son, then gave a sour look at the portrait and, handing it back without a word, rolled down his sleeves and pulled up his braces. He was dumbfounded. What had come over his son Jimmy? Teetotal for the rest of his life! Was he going to lose his head over that silly-faced girl? Mrs Macdonnel studied Jimmy with plaintive anxiety while he described Meg's beauty and goodness. 'Ach, she was made tae be adored b' everybody!' he said, and warned his mother to steer clear of the drink and keep her house in order to receive his beloved, whom he had invited to come and stay with the family.

His mother promised to love Meg as a daughter and silently hoped that the girl would stay at home. She was too old now to be bothered by a healthy young woman with managing ways. Jimmy swore he hadn't touched a drop since he had sailed from Peterhead and described the tortures of his two-days' self-denial so vividly that his father shivered and hurried into the parlour to get his coat and vest. Jimmy said he was finished with the sea and booze; sick of squandering money. He was determined to settle on shore, get married, and spend all his money on Meg's happiness.

A miserly gleam beamed in his mother's eye when he said that and she wondered how much his new devotion would limit his contribution to her purse. Jimmy took a bundle of notes from his inside breast-pocket and handed her thirty pounds, reminding her that she had already drawn advance-sums from his shipping office. Mrs Macdonnel said he was too kind and offered to return five notes with a drawing-back movement, but Jimmy refused them with a bluff, insincere gesture, for there was a flash of regret in his eye as she tucked the wad in her purse, but, with genuine feeling he invited her and his da out to drink him welcome home. 'Ah'll have a lemonade,' he said, gazing piously at the ceiling as though at the Holy Grail. His mother thought he was being too harsh with himself. 'Shure ye'll hiv a wee nip wi' me an' yer da, son. A wee nip won't kill ye!' she laughed slyly, and Jimmy promised to drink a shandy-gaff just to please her, sighing with relief when he thought of the dash of beer in the lemonade. He called his father who came in from the parlour wrestling with a white dickey which he was trying to dispose evenly on his chest. 'Ah won't keep ye a jiffy, laddie!' he said, facing the mirror and fervently praying that the smell of the pub would restore poor Jimmy to his senses.

As she put on her old brown shawl Mrs Macdonnel was disappointed at Jimmy's insistence that they should go to an out-of-the-way pub. She wanted to show off her bonny son; he was so braw; so like a captain! She imagined the greetings they would get going down the long street.

'Ay, ye've won hame, Jimmy, boay? My, ye're lookin' fine,

mun! Goash, ye oaght tae be a prood wumman the day, Mrs
Macdonnel! Jimmy's a credit tae ye!' and she foretasted the
old sweet thrill of envy and flattery. But Jimmy said he would
never drink again with the corner-boys. Love had made a new
man of him!

When they had all gone out Eddy Macdonnel hurried into
the small side bedroom to read the book on PSYCHOLOGY AND
MORALS he had borrowed from the Corporation Library. Inspired by Jimmy's miraculous conversion he crouched over the
volume, concentrating fiercely on the chapters headed WILL
POWER AND SIN, and his heart swelled with a reformer's zeal
as he saw himself one day applying all these marvellous laws
to the human race, hypnotizing countless millions of people
into sobriety.

Three hours later he heard a loud clamour in the street below.
Throwing his book on the bed he raised the window and looked
over and his uplifted heart sank down, for he saw Jimmy
stumbling happily up the street with his Aunt Kate's hat on
his head and his arm round his father's neck. They were lustily
singing 'The Bonny Lass O' Ballochmyle'. Mr Macdonnel's
dickey was sticking out like the wings of a moulted swan and
large bottles of whisky waggled from the pockets of the two
men. Behind them, laughing like witches, came Mrs Macdonnel
and Aunt Kate with the sailor's cap on, followed by six of
Jimmy's pals who were carrying between them three large
crates of bottled beer.

Eddy closed the window quickly and stared sadly at the
wall. Jimmy, the idol of his dream, himself had shattered it!
As he turned into the lobby, Jimmy opened the stairhead door
and thrust his pals into the kitchen, which already seemed
crowded with only two members of the family. John Macdonnel,
now a fair young man of twenty-five, just home from overtime
at the shipyards, leant in his oil-stained working clothes against
the gas stove, reading about the Celtic and Rangers match in
the Glasgow *Evening Times* and regretting that he had missed
a hard-fought game which his team had won. With a wild
'whoopee' Jimmy embraced his brothers, who smiled with

embarrassment. John was proud of Jimmy's prestige with the corner-boys, though he knew it was the worthless esteem for a fool and his money; Eddy saw Jimmy as a grand romantic figure, a great chef who had cooked for a millionaire on his yacht and had seen all the capital cities of the world, and Jimmy's kitbag, lying against a home-made stool by the dresser, stuffed with cooks' caps and jackets, radiated the fascination of travel.

Aunt Kate, a tiny, dark woman of remarkable vitality, went kissing all her nephews in turn and the party got into full swing. Liquor was soon winking from tumblers, teacups, egg-cups – anything that could hold drink – and Aunt Kate, while directing the young men to bring chairs from the parlour, sang 'A Guid New Year Tae Ane an' A',' disregarding the fact that it was only summer-time, and Jimmy, thinking a nautical song was expected from him, sang 'A Life on the Ocean Wave!' in a voice as flat as stale beer that drowned his aunt's pleasant treble. But somebody shouted that he sang as well as John McCormack and he sat down with a large tumbler of whisky, looking as if he thought so himself.

Then Aunt Kate told everybody about her marvellous meeting with Jimmy whose voice she had heard through the partition as she sat in the Ladies' Parlour in The Rob Roy Arms and Eddy learned how his brother had fallen. Jimmy, it appeared, felt he must toast Meg Macgregor in just one glass of something strong; that dash of beer in lemonade had infuriated his thirst and in a few minutes he had downed several glasses of the right stuff to his sweetheart, proving to his aunt's delight that he was still the same old jovial Jimmy.

John Macdonnel, all this while, was going to and fro, stumbling over out-thrust feet between the small bedroom and kitchen sprucing himself up to go out and meet his girl. From feet to waist he was ready for love. His best brown trousers with shoes to match adorned his lower half, while his torso was still robed in a shirt blackened with shipyard oil and rust. He washed himself at the sink, laughing at his Aunt's story, then turned, drying himself, to argue with his mother about his 'clean change'. Mrs Macdonnel waved her cup helplessly, saying she couldn't help the indifference of laundrymen and John implored Eddy to shoot downstairs and find if the family washing had arrived at the receiving-office of the Bonnyburn Laundries.

Visitors kept dropping in for a word with the sailor and delayed their departure while the drinks went round. Rumour had spread the report that Jimmy Macdonnel was home flush with money and a Macdonnel party was always a powerful attraction. The gathering was livening up. Two quart bottles of whisky had been absorbed and beer was frothing against every lip when Eddy returned triumphantly waving a big brown paper parcel in John's direction.

It was at the right psychological moment, when a slight lull in the merriment was threatening, that Rab Macpherson romped from his hiding-place in the doorway into the middle of the kitchen and suddenly burst out singing at the top of his voice:

> 'Le – et Kings and courteers rise an' fa'
> This wurrld has minny turns,
> But brighter beams abune them a'
> The star o' Rabbie Burns!'

Rab's legs were very bow and wee Tommy Mohan, who was talking to his pal John Macdonnel at the sink, sunk down on his hunkers and gazed under his palm, like a sailor. Looking straight at her husband standing in the kitchen doorway and returning her stare with a malignant leer, Aunt Kate filled a large cup with whisky from a bottle on the dresser and, still singing, handed it to him with a mock bow. On similar occasions Mr Hewes had been known to dash the cup from her hand and walk out and desert her for six months, but this time he seized it, swallowed the drink in one gulp, hitched up his belt and joined the party.

Eddy crushed a way through to his seat on the sink and watched his uncle, who, seated beside Mr Macdonnel, eyed with hostility every move of his popular wife. There was an excess of spite in Mr Hewes and he loved to hate people. Time, accident and ill-nature had ruined his face. A livid scar streamed from his thin hair down his right temple to his lip; his broken nose had reset all to one side, his few teeth were black and his little moustache as harsh as barbed wire; and with a blackened sweatrag round his neck he looked like a being from some underworld come to spy on human revels. He was called upon for a song when the applause for his wife had ended, and he stood up and roared, glaring at her:

> 'Am Oi a man, or am Oi a mouse
> Or am I a common artful dodger?
> Oi want to know who is master of my house!
> Is ut me or Micky Flanagan the lodger?'

Shouts of 'ongcore!' egged him on to sing the verse several times, his glare at his smiling wife intensifying with each repetition. He was suspected of having composed the song himself and the neighbours always knew he was going to desert his wife when he came up the stairs singing it. His whole body was humming like a dynamo after two large cups of Heather Dew and as his wife began chanting an old Irish jig he started to dance. Throwing off his jacket he roared 'B' Jasus!' tightened his belt and rolled up his sleeves, revealing thick leather straps round his wrists, and his hob-nailed boots beat a rapid deafening tattoo on the spot of floor inside the surrounding feet. His wife's chant became shriller and the whole company began clapping hands, stamping and yelling wild 'hoochs!' that drove the little gasworker to frenzy. John Macdonnel, all dressed to go out with a new bowler hat perched on his head, lifted a poker from the grate and thrust it into the dancer's hand. Mr Hewes tried to twirl it round his head between finger and thumb like a drum-major, then smashed it on the floor in passionate chagrin at his failure. 'B' Jasus Oi could dance ye'se all under the table!' he yelled, and with head and torso held stiff and arms working like pistons across his middle, he pranced like an enraged cockerel.

Faster he hopped from heel to heel, still packed with energy after a hard day shovelling in a hot atmosphere; sweat glistened on his grey hair and beaded his blackened cheeks; he twisted his feet in and out in awkward attempts at fancy steps and looked as if he would fly asunder in his efforts to beat the pace of his accompanists; then, with a despairing yell of 'B' Jasus!' he stopped suddenly, gasped, 'Och, Oi'm bate!' and hurled dizzily behind foremost into his chair.

It was a hefty piece of furniture but it couldn't stand up to his violence; with a loud crack its four legs splayed out and the gasworker crashed like a slung sack into the hearth, smashing the polished plate-shelf sticking out beneath the oven; his head struck heavily the shining bevel of the range; the snapped chair-back lay over his head, and there was a roar of laughter which stopped when he was seen to lie still among the wreckage.

His wife and Mr Macdonnel bent over him, but he pushed them away, staggered erect and, shaking himself like a dog after a fight, snatched and swallowed the cup of whisky which Mrs Macdonnel had poured quickly for him while looking ruefully at her shattered chair and plate-shelf. The blow had hardly affected him and, as Mrs Hewes anxiously examined his head he pushed her rudely aside, shouting, 'B' Jasus! Oi'll give ye'se "The Enniskillen's Farewell!" and he roared boastfully the Boer War song of an Irish regiment's departure. Suddenly he realized that attention was diverted over the sea, away through Rab's legs all the time he was singing. Everybody was convulsed with laughter and Mrs Macdonnel was so pleased with Rab, that she got up, still laughing, and with her arm around his neck, gave him a good measure of whisky in a small cream jug.

Suddenly everybody fell silent to listen to Jimmy Macdonnel, who had been up since three that morning and half-asleep was trolling away to himself 'The Lass that Made the Bed For Me', and Mrs Steedman, a big-bosomed Orangewoman, startled the company by shouting, 'Good aul' Rabbie Burns! He ken't whit a wumman likes the maist!' There was a roar of laughter at this reminder of the poet's lechery, then Aunt Kate insisted that Mr Macdonnel should sing 'I Dreamt I Dwelt in Marble Halls', while her sister, Mrs Macdonnel, asked him for 'The Meeting of the Waters' because it reminded her of their honeymoon in Ireland. Mr Macdonnel, assisted by the table, swayed to his feet as pompously as Signor Caruso, twirled his moustache, stuck his thumbs behind his lapels, like the buskers of Glasgow backcourts, and 'hemmed' very loudly to silence the arguing sisters. He always sang with his eyes closed and when the gaslight shone on his glasses he looked like a man with four eyes, one pair shut, the other brilliantly open. He honestly believed he had a fine tenor voice and with swelled chest he bellowed:

> 'Yes! Let me like a soldier fall, upon some open plain!
> Me breast boldly bared to meet the ball
> That blots out every stain!'

The china shivered on the shelves above the dresser and Eddy Macdonnel, lost in some vision of bravery, stared with pride at his father. Halfway through the ballad, Mr Macdonnel forgot the words but sang on, 'tra-laing' here, pushing in his own words there, and sat down well satisfied to a din of hand-claps and stamping feet.

Jimmy was blasted into wakefulness by his father's song and he washed himself sober and led out all the young men to help him buy more drink. When they returned, well-stocked, half an hour later, Mr Macdonnel had the whole crowd singing.

> 'I'll knock a hole in McCann for knocking a hole in me can!
> McCann knew me can was new
> I'd only had it a day or two,
> I gave McCann me can to fetch me a pint of stout
> An' McCann came running in an' said
> That me can was running out!'

This was Mr Macdonnel's winning number at every spree and the refrain had echoed several times through the open windows to the street and backcourt before the young men returned. In the comparative silence of clinking bottles and glasses, Jimmy told his laughing guests of the night when he had served up beer in chamber-pots to a party of corner-boys. A dozen chamber-pots were arrayed round the table and twelve youths sat gravely before them while Jimmy muttered a Turkish grace over the beer and told them that was the way the Turks drank their drink and they believed him because he had been six times round the world.

When Aunt Kate had recovered from her delight in this story she asked Eddy to run up and see if her 'bonny wee man' was home from the gasworks. Eddy raced up to the top storey, knocked on a door, and started back as his uncle's gargoyle face thrust out at him and barked, 'Where's Katey? Am Oi a man or a mouse? B' the Holy Saint Pathrick Oi'll murther the lazy cow!' Eddy said faintly, 'Jimmy's home an' we're having a party. Will ye come down?' and Mr Hewes followed him downstairs muttering threats of vengeance on his wife for neglecting his tea.

The gathering had overflowed into the parlour when Eddy returned with the gasworker behind him; the lobby was crowded with newly-arrived guests listening to Aunt Kate singing 'The Irish Emigrant's Farewell'; the eyes of all the women were wet with film-star tears and the singer herself seemed to be seeing a handsome Irish youth as she looked from him; someone in the packed lobby was crying, 'Here's Big Mary! Make way for Blind Mary!' and Mr Hewes, grasping his jacket from Mr Macdonnel's hand, slung it across his shoulder, stared malignantly at everyone and pushed uncivilly out of the house.

The Widow Loughran, who was being guided in by Jerry Delaney and his wife, was a magnificent Irishwoman, well over six feet, round about forty, and round about considerably more at waist and bosom. The habit of raising the head in the manner of the blind made her appear taller and gave her a haughty look, but she was a jolly, kind woman in robust health, and her rosy face and glossy, jet hair, her good-humoured laughter, caused one to forget her blindness. Blind Mary was the wonder of the Gorbals. She drank hard and regularly and stood it better than the toughest men. 'Mary's never up nor doon,' they said, and she boasted that she had never known a 'bad moarnin' in her life. She also wore a tartan shoulder-shawl of the Gordon clan, a widow's bonnet, and a bright print apron over her skirt. Mrs Macdonnel led her to a seat and she stood up, her hands searching around for Jerry Delaney when she heard there wasn't a chair for him. He was pushed into her arms and she pulled him into a tight embrace on her ample knees. Mr Delaney, popularly known as 'One-Eyed Jerry' since a flying splinter, at his work as a ship's carpenter, had deprived him of his right eye, was no light weight, but Mary handled him like a baby, and Mrs Macdonnel shrieked with laughter: 'Blind Mary's stole yer man, Bridget!' and Mrs Delaney, a dark beauty of five-and-thirty, laughed back, 'Ach away! She's welcome tae him! Shure they're weel matched wi' yin eye atween them!' This so tickled Mary and Jerry that they almost rolled on the floor with helpless laughter, and Mrs Macdonnel looked very worried, expecting every minute to see another of her chairs smashed to smithereens.

Aunt Kate had vanished in pursuit of her man and returned at this moment, pale with anger, to announce publicly that he had skedaddled, but that she would set the police at his heels and make him support her; then she sang in her sweetest voice, 'O My Love is Like a Red, Red Rose!' followed by a delicate rendering of 'Ae Fond Kiss'. But no one was surprised by her instant change from wrath to tenderness, except young Eddy, who felt that this was his most profitable 'psychological' evening as he watched Blind Mary with her hands boldly grasping Mr Delaney's thighs and began excitedly composing an essay on 'Psychology And The Blind' for his night-school class.

Someone called for a song from Blind Mary, and One-Eyed Jerry courteously handed her to her feet. She stood dominating the whole room, protesting that she couldn't sing a note, but everyone cried: 'Strike up, Mary! Ye sing like a lark!' and she began singing 'Bonny Mary O' Argyle' to the unfailing amazement of young Eddy, who could never understand why her voice that was so melodious in speech was so hideous when she sang. In his boyhood Eddy had always loved to see her in the house, finding a strange sense of comfort in her strength and cheerful vitality. Coming in from school his heart had always rippled with delight to see her gossiping and drinking with his mother and some neighbours. Her rich brogue always welcomed him, 'Ach, it's me wee Edward. Come here ye darlin'!' and there was always a penny or sixpenny bit for him, hot from her fat hand, or a bag of sweets, warm from her placket-pocket, their colours blushing through the paper. He enjoyed the strong smell of snuff from her soft fingers when they fondled his hair or read his face and the smell of her kiss, scented with whisky or beer, had never repelled him.

Mary had only sung two lines, when she was sensationally interrupted by Bridget Delaney, who suddenly leapt from her feet and shrieked indignantly: 'Ach, don't talk tae me aboot legs! Is there a wumman in this house has a better leg than meself? Tae hell wi' Bonny Mary O' Argyle! I'll show ye'se the finest leg on the South Side this night!' and she bent and pulled her stocking down her left leg to the ankle, whipped up her blue satinette skirt and pulled up a blue leg of bloomer so fiercely that she revealed a handsome piece of behind. 'There ye are!' cried Bridget, holding forth her leg. 'Ah defy a wumman among ye'se tae shake as good a wan!'

Blind Mary stood silent and trembling in a strange listening attitude, thinking a fight had begun, and everyone was astounded. Jerry Delaney, blushing with shame, plucked nervously at his bedfellow's skirt, but Bridget pulled it up more tightly and shouted: 'Awa'! Ye've seen it oaften enough! Are ye ashamed o' it?' while Jerry told her he had always said she had the finest leg in Glasgow and acted as if he had never beheld such a distressing sight. Beside them a very dozy youth gazed dully at Bridget's fat, white thigh, and from the rose-wreathed wallpaper Pope Pius X, in a cheap print, looked sternly at the sinful limb.

Mrs Macdonnel hurried her hysterical sister-in-law into the small bedroom, and the only comment on the incident was, 'Blimey! Wot a lark!' from Mrs Bills. Blind Mary asked excitedly what had happened. Some of the ladies, while affecting shocked modesty, trembled with desire to take up Bridget's challenge; but no one could have explained her hysteria, except, perhaps, Mr Delaney. His one eye always glowed with admiration for a fine woman and he had gazed warmly all evening at Blind Mary. But Bridget's astonishing behaviour was superseded for the moment by the arrival of Wee Danny Quinn 'wi' his melodyin',' whom Jimmy Macdonnel himself introduced as the guest of honour.

The street-musician, a pug-nosed, dwarfish Glaswegian, bow-legged and very muscular, drank two large glasses of whisky, wiped his lips and began playing. The mother-o'-pearl keys of his big Lombardi piano-accordion flashed in the gaslight as his fingers danced skilfully among them, and while he leant his ear to the instrument, his little dark eyes looked up with a set smile, like a leprechaun listening to the earth. He played jigs and reels and waltzes; all the furniture in the kitchen was pushed to the wall and all who could find room to crush around were soon dancing through the lobby and back again.

It was late in the night, when the dancers had paused for refreshment, that Willie McBride the bookmaker, a six-foot red-headed Highlandman, suddenly reappeared arm-in-arm with his wife, he dressed in her clothes and she in his. They had disappeared for fifteen minutes and effected the change with the connivance of Aunt Kate, who slipped them the key of her house. Mr McBride had somehow managed to crush his enormous chest into the blouse of his slim wife; between it and the skirt, his shirt looked out, and from the edge of the skirt, which reached his knees, his thick, pink woollen drawers were visible; Mrs McBride, drowned in his suit, floundered, bowing to the delighted company.

This wild whim of the McBrides heated everyone like an aphrodisiac, and very soon Aunt Kate's but-an'-ben became the dressing-room for the transformation of several ladies and gentlemen. The two Delaneys exchanged clothes and Bridget showed to advantage her splendid legs swelling out her husband's trousers; Aunt Kate retired with a slight youth and reappeared in his fifty-shilling suit as the neatest little man of the evening; then Mrs Macdonnel walked in disguised as her husband, even to his glasses and cap, and was followed by him gallantly wearing the Spanish shawl, in which, after filling out his wife's blouse with two towels, he danced what he imagined was a Spanish dance and sang a hashed-up version of the 'Toreador Song' from *Carmen*.

Danny Quinn's playing became inspired and his volume majestic as he laughed at the dressed-up couples dancing around. The house was throbbing like a battered drum when heavy thumps shook the stairhead door. 'It's the polis,' cried everyone with amused alarm. Mrs Macdonnel rushed to open and a soft Irish voice echoed along the lobby: 'Ye'se'll have to make less noise. The nayburs is complainin'!'

'Ach, come awa in, Tarry, an' have a wee deoch-an'-doris!' cried Mrs Macdonnel, holding the door wide for the portly constable who stood amazed at her masculine garb, while Willie McBride was roaring, 'Do Ah hear me aul' freend Boab Finnegan? Come ben an' have a drink, man! Shure you an' me's had many a dram when yer inspector wisnae lookin'!' and Mrs Macdonnel conducted into the parlour Police-Officer Finnegan followed by a tall, young Highland officer, a novice in the Force, with finger at chinstrap and a frown of disapproval. The two policemen were welcomed with full glasses, and Mr Finnegan, known all over the Gorbals as 'Tarry Bob' because his hair and big moustache were black as tar and his heavy jowls became more saturnine with every shave he had, surveyed the strange gathering with a clownish smile, while Mr McBride, the street bookie, told the company how often he had dodged the Law by giving Tarry Bob a friendly drink.

In five minutes both policemen sat down and laid their helmets on the sideboard among the numerous bottles and fifteen minutes later they had loosened their tunics and were dancing with the ladies, their heavy boots creating a louder rumpus than they had come to stop.

Eddy Macdonnel stood in the crowded lobby craning his head over to watch the lively scene. After a long while he heard

his mother say to Tarry Bob, who was protesting he must go:
'Och, hiv another wee nip! Shure a wee nip won't kill ye!'
then he saw the good-natured policeman drench himself in beer
as he put on his helmet into which some playful guest had
emptied a pint bottle.

Eddy's wits were staggering. 'Human behaviour' had mud-
dled his understanding, and he mooned bewildered into the
kitchen where Jimmy sat half-asleep with a glass of whisky
trembling in his bronzed hand, while opposite him sat a youth
gazing in agony at the glass, expecting to see the darlin' drink
spilled on the floor.

Eddy took Jimmy's glass and placed it on the mantelshelf,
then picked up a postcard that lay face downward on the
floor. It was the picture of Meg Macgregor. He had fallen in
love with the picture himself and he looked at it again through
sentimental eyes that saw her average prettiness as dazzling
beauty. He had been nerving himself to ask Jimmy if he had a
photo of her to spare and was awaiting with adolescent im-
patience her sensational arrival. 'Ye've dropped Meg's photo,'
he said, holding it up to Jimmy's wavering stare. The sailor
thrust it aside. 'Take it away!' he said. 'Her face scunners me!'

'But it's Meg!' Eddy said. 'Meg Macgregor. The girl ye're
bringing home to marry!'

'"Take her away!" I said,' cried Jimmy with a royal wave
of the hand. 'There's nae wumman 'll run ma life for me!'
The youth sitting by the table nodded his approval, then stood
up and quickly drank off Jimmy's whisky.

Eddy studied his brother for a moment, desperately failing to
remember some part of his book on psychology that would
explain Jimmy's sudden jaundiced dismissal of Meg Macgregor.
Then he drifted solemnly into the lobby, opened the stairhead
door and wandered slowly down to the close-mouth. His confused head was ringing with a medley of folk-songs and music-
hall choruses and his heart held the streams and hills and the
women of the poetry of Robert Burns. He was thinking of
Jeannie Lindsay and wishing he might find her standing at
her close in South Wellington Street. But it was very late. He

hurried round the corner in a queer, emotional tangle of sexual shame and desire, his romantic thoughts of Jeannie mingled with the shameful memory of his mother and the women dressing up in men's clothes and Bridget Delaney pulling up her skirts to her hips to show her bare legs to the men.

SMEDDUM*

SHE'D had nine of a family in her time, Mistress Menzies, and brought the nine of them up, forby – some near by the scruff of the neck, you would say. They were sniftering and weakly, two-three of the bairns, sniftering in their cradles to get into their coffins; but she'd shake them to life, and dose them with salts and feed them up till they couldn't but live. And she'd plonk one down – finishing the wiping of the creature's neb or the unco dosing of an ill bit stomach or the binding of a broken head – with a look on her face as much as to say *Die on me now and see what you'll get!*

Big-boned she was by her fortieth year, like a big roan mare, and *If ever she was bonny 'twas in Noah's time*, Jock Menzies, her eldest son, would say. She'd reddish hair and a high, skeugh nose, and a hand that skelped her way through life; and if ever a soul had seen her at rest when the dark was done and the day was come he'd died of the shock and never let on.

For from morn till night she was at it, work, work, on that ill bit croft that sloped to the sea. When there wasn't a mist on the cold, stone parks there was more than likely the wheep of the rain, wheeling and dripping in from the sea that soughed and splashed by the land's stiff edge. Kinneff lay north, and at night in the south, if the sky was clear on the gloaming's edge, you'd see in that sky the Bervie lights come suddenly lit, far and away, with the quiet about you as you stood and looked, nothing to hear but a sea-bird's cry.

But feint the much time to look or to listen had Margaret Menzies of Tocherty toun. Day blinked and Meg did the same, and was out, up out of her bed, and about the house, making the porridge and rousting the bairns, and out to the byre to

* *Smeddum* is defined by the Scots dictionaries as meaning 'mettle, spirit, liveliness', but the best synonym is the colloquial 'guts'.

milk the three kye, the morning growing out in the east and a wind like a hail of knives from the hills. Syne back to the kitchen again she would be, and catch Jock, her eldest, a clout in the lug that he hadn't roused up his sisters and brothers; and rouse them herself, and feed them and scold, pull up their breeks and straighten their frocks, and polish their shoes and set their caps straight. *Off you get and see you're not late*, she would cry, *and see you behave yourselves at the school. And tell the Dominie I'll be down the night to ask him what the mischief he meant by leathering Jeannie and her not well ...*

They'd cry *Ay, Mother*, and go trotting away, a fair 'flock of the creatures, their faces red-scoured. Her own as red, like a meikle roan mare's, Meg'd turn at the door and go prancing in; and then at last, by the closet-bed, lean over and shake her man half-awake. *Come on then, Willie, it's time you were up.*

And he'd groan and say *Is't?* and crawl out at last, a little bit thing like a weasel, Will Menzies, though some said that weasels were decent beside him. He was drinking himself into the grave, folk said, as coarse a little brute as you'd meet, bone-lazy forby, and as sly as sin. Rampageous and ill with her tongue though she was, you couldn't but pity a woman like Meg tied up for life to a thing like *that*. But she'd more than a soft side still to the creature, she'd half-skelp the backside from any of the bairns she found in the telling of a small bit lie; but when Menzies would come paiching in of a noon and groan that he fair was tashed with his work, he'd mended all the ley fence that day and he doubted he'd need to be off to his bed – when he'd told her that and had ta'en to the blankets, and maybe in less than the space of an hour she'd hold out for the kye and see that he'd lied, the fence neither mended nor letten a-be, she'd just purse up her meikle wide mouth and say nothing, her eyes with a glint as though she half-laughed. And when he came drunken home from a mart she'd shoo the children out of the room, and take off his clothes and put him to bed, with an extra nip to keep off a chill.

She did half his work in the Tocherty parks, she'd yoke up

the horse and the sholtie together, and kilt up her skirts till you'd see her great legs, and cry *Wissh!* like a man and turn a fair drill, the sea-gulls cawing in a cloud behind, the wind in her hair and the sea beyond. And Menzies with his sly-like eyes would be off on some drunken ploy to Kinneff or Stonehive. Man, you couldn't but think as you saw that steer it was well that there was a thing like marriage, folk held together and couldn't get apart; else a black look-out it well would be for the fusionless creature of Tocherty toun.

Well, he drank himself to his grave at last, less smell on the earth if maybe more in it. But she broke down and wept, it was awful to see, Meg Menzies weeping like a stricken horse, her eyes on the dead, quiet face of her man. And she ran from the house, she was gone all that night, though the bairns cried and cried her name up and down the parks in the sound of the sea. But next morning they found her back in their midst, brisk as ever, like a great-boned mare, ordering here and directing there, and a fine feed set the next day for the folk that came to the funeral of her orra man.

She'd four of the bairns at home when he died, the rest were in kitchen-service or fee'd, she'd seen to the settling of the queans herself; and twice when two of them had come home, complaining-like of their mistresses' ways, she'd thrashen the queans and taken them back – near scared the life from the doctor's wife, her that was mistress to young Jean Menzies. *I've skelped the lassie and brought you her back. But don't you ill-use her, or I'll skelp you as well.*

There was a fair speak about that at the time, Meg Menzies and the vulgar words she had used, folk told that she'd even said what was the place where she'd skelp the bit doctor's wife. And faith! that fair must have been a sore shock to the doctor's wife that was that genteel she'd never believed she'd a place like that.

Be that as it might, her man new dead, Meg wouldn't hear of leaving the toun. It was harvest then and she drove the reaper up and down the long, clanging clay rigs by the sea, she'd jump down smart at the head of a bout and go gathering and binding swift as the wind, syne wheel in the horse to the cutting again. She led the stooks with her bairns to help, you'd see them at night a drowsing cluster under the moon on the harvesting cart.

And through that year and into the next and so till the speak died down in the Howe Meg Menzies worked the Tocherty toun; and faith, her crops came none so ill. She rode to the mart at Stonehive when she must, on the old box-cart, the old horse in the shafts, the cart behind with a sheep for sale or a birn of old hens that had finished with laying. And a butcher once tried to make a bit joke. *That's a sheep like yourself, fell long in the tooth.* And Meg answered up, neighing like a horse, and all heard: *Faith, then, if you've got a spite against teeth I've a clucking hen in the cart outbye. It's as toothless and senseless as you are, near.*

Then word got about of her eldest son, Jock Menzies, that was fee'd up Allardyce way. The creature of a loon had had fair a conceit since he'd won a prize at a ploughing match – not for his ploughing, but for good looks; and the queans about were as daft as himself, he'd only to nod and they came to his heel; and the stories told they came further than that. Well, Meg'd heard the stories and paid no heed, till the last one came, she was fell quick then.

Soon's she heard it she hove out the old bit bike that her daughter Kathie had bought for herself, and got on the thing and went cycling away down through the Bervie braes in that spring, the sun was out and the land lay green with a blink of mist that was blue on the hills, as she came to the toun where Jock was fee'd she saw him out in a park by the road, ploughing, the black loam smooth like a ribbon turning and wheeling at the tail of the plough. Another billy came ploughing behind, Meg Menzies watched till they reached the rigend, her great chest heaving like a meikle roan's, her eyes on the shape of the furrows they made. And they drew to the end and drew the horse out, and Jock cried *Ay*, and she answered back *Ay*, and looked at the drill, and gave a bit snort, *If your looks win prizes, your ploughing never will.*

Jock laughed, *Fegs, then, I'll not greet for that*, and chirked
to his horses and turned them about. But she cried him *Just
bide a minute, my lad. What's this I hear about you and Ag
Grant?*

He drew up short then, and turned right red, the other
childe as well, and they both gave a laugh, as plough-childes
do when you mention a quean they've known over-well in more
ways than one. And Meg snapped *It's an answer I want, not a
cockerel's cackle: I can hear that at home on my own dunghill.
What are you to do about Ag and her pleiter?*

And Jock said *Nothing*, impudent as you like, and next
minute Meg was in over the dyke and had hold of his lug and
shook him and it till the other childe ran and caught at her
nieve. *Faith, mistress, you'll have his lug off!* he cried. But Meg
Menzies turned like a mare on new grass. *Keep off or I'll have
yours off as well!*

So he kept off and watched, fair a story he'd to tell when he
rode out that night to go courting his quean. For Meg held
to the lug till it near came off and Jock swore that he'd put
things right with Ag Grant. She let go the lug then and looked
at him grim: *See that you do and get married right quick,
you're the like that needs loaded with a birn of bairns – to keep
you out of the jail, I jaloose. It needs smeddum to be either
right coarse or right kind.*

They were wed before the month was well out, Meg found
them a cottar house to settle and gave them a bed and a press
she had, and two-three more sticks from Tocherty toun. And
she herself led the wedding dance, the minister in her arms,
a small bit childe; and 'twas then as she whirled him about the
room, he looked like a rat in the teeth of a tyke, that he thanked
her for seeing Ag out of her soss, *There's nothing like a marriage for redding things up.* And Meg Menzies said *EH?* and
then she said *Ay*, but queer-like, he supposed she'd no thought
of the thing. Syne she slipped off to sprinkle thorns in the bed
and to hang below it the great handbell that the bothy-billies
took with them to every bit marriage.

Well, that was Jock married and at last off her hands. But

she'd plenty left still, Dod, Kathleen and Jim that were still at school. Kathie a limner that alone tongued her mother, Jeannie that next led trouble to her door. She'd been found at her place, the doctor's it was, stealing some money and they sent her home. Syne news of the thing got into Stonehive, the police came out and tormented her sore, she swore she never had stolen a meck, and Meg swore with her, she was black with rage. And folk laughed right hearty, fegs! that was a clout for meikle Meg Menzies, her daughter a thief!

But it didn't last long, it was only three days when folk saw the doctor drive up in his car. And out he jumped and went striding through the close and met face to face with Meg at the door. And he cried *Well, mistress, I've come over for Jeannie.* And she glared at him over her high, skeugh nose, *Ay, have you so then? And why, may I speir?*

So he told her why, the money they'd missed had been found at last in a press by the door; somebody or other had left it there, when paying a grocer or such at the door. And Jeannie – he'd come over to take Jean back.

But Meg glared. *Ay, well, you've made another mistake. Out of this, you and your thieving suspicions together!* The doctor turned red, *You're making a miserable error* – and Meg said *I'll make you mince-meat in a minute.*

So he didn't wait that, she didn't watch him go, but went ben to the kitchen, where Jeannie was sitting, her face chalk-white as she'd heard them speak. And what happened then a story went round, Jim carried it to school, and it soon spread out, Meg sank in a chair, they thought she was greeting; syne she raised up her head and they saw she was laughing, near as fearsome the one as the other, they thought. *Have you any cigarettes?* she snapped sudden at Jean, and Jean quavered *No,* and Meg glowered at her cold. *Don't sit there and lie. Gang bring them to me.* And Jean brought them, her mother took the pack in her hand. *Give's hold of a match till I light up the thing. Maybe smoke'll do good for the crow that I got in the throat last night by the doctor's house.*

Well, in less than a month she'd got rid of Jean – packed off to Brechin the quean was, and soon got married to a creature there – some clerk that would have left her sore in the lurch but that Meg went down to the place on her bike, and there, so the story went, kicked the childe so that he couldn't sit down for a fortnight, near. No doubt that was just a bit lie that they told, but faith! Meg Menzies had herself to blame, the reputation she'd gotten in the Howe, folk said, *She'll meet with a sore heart yet.* But devil a sore was there to be seen. Jeannie was married and was fair genteel.

Kathleen was next to leave home at the term. She was tall, like Meg, and with red hair as well, but a thin fine face, long eyes blue-grey like the hills on a hot day, and a mouth with lips you thought over thick. And she cried *Ah well, I'm off then, mother.* And Meg cried *See you behave yourself.* And Kathleen cried *Maybe; I'm not at school now.*

Meg stood and stared after the slip of a quean, you'd have thought her half-angry, half near to laughing, as she watched that figure, so slender and trig, with its shoulders square-set, slide down the hill on the wheeling bike, swallows were dipping and flying by Kinneff, she looked light and free as a swallow herself, the quean, as she biked away from her home, she turned at the bend and waved and whistled, she whistled like a loon and as loud, did Kath.

Jim was the next to leave from the school, he bided at home and he took no fee, a quiet-like loon, and he worked the toun, and, wonder of wonders, Meg took a rest. Folk said that age was telling a bit on even Meg Menzies at last. The grocer made hints at that one night, and Meg answered up smart as ever of old: *Damn the age! But I've finished the trauchle of the bairns at last, the most of them married or still over young. I'm as swack as ever I was, my lad. But I've just got the notion to be a bit sweir.*

Well, she'd hardly begun on that notion when faith! ill the news that came up to the place from Segget. Kathleen her quean that was fee'd down there, she'd ta'en up with some coarse old childe in a bank, he'd left his wife, they were off together, and she but a bare sixteen years old.

And that proved the truth of what folk were saying, Meg Menzies she hardly paid heed to the news, just gave a bit laugh like a neighing horse and went on with the work of park and byre, cool as you please – ay, getting fell old.

No more was heard of the quean or the man till a two years or more had passed and then word came up to the Tocherty someone had seen her – and where do you think? Out on a boat that was coming from Australia. She was working as stewardess on that bit boat, and the childe that saw her was young John Robb, an emigrant back from his uncle's farm, near starved to death he had been down there. She hadn't met in with him near till the end, the boat close to Southampton the evening they met. And she'd known him at once, though he not her, she'd cried *John Robb?* and he'd answered back *Ay?* and looked at her canny in case it might be the creature was looking for a tip from him. Syne she'd laughed *Don't you know me, then, you gowk? I'm Kathie Menzies you knew long syne – it was me ran off with the banker from Segget!*

He was clean dumbfounded, young Robb, and he gaped, and then they shook hands and she spoke some more, though she hadn't much time, they were serving up dinner for the first-class folk, aye dirt that are ready to eat and to drink. *If ever you get near to Tocherty toun tell Meg I'll get home and see her some time. Ta-ta!* And then she was off with a smile, young Robb he stood and he stared where she'd been, he thought her the bonniest thing that he'd seen all the weary weeks that he'd been from home.

And this was the tale that he brought to Tocherty, Meg sat and listened and smoked like a tink, forby herself there was young Jim there, and Jock and his wife and their three bit bairns, he'd fair changed with marriage, had young Jock Menzies. For no sooner had he taken Ag Grant to his bed than he'd started to save, grown mean as dirt, in a three-four years he'd finished with feeing, now he rented a fell big farm himself, well stocked it was, and he fee'd two men. Jock himself had grown thin in a way, like his father, but worse his bothy childes said, old Menzies at least could take a bit dram and get lost to the world but the son was that mean he might drink rat-poison and take no harm, 'twould feel at home in a stomach like his.

Well, that was Jock, and he sat and heard the story of Kath and her say on the boat. *Ay, still a coarse bitch, I have not a doubt. Well if she never comes back to the Mearns, in Segget you cannot but redden with shame when a body will ask 'Was Kath Menzies your sister?'*

And Ag, she'd grown a great sumph of a woman, she nodded to that, it was only too true, a sore thing it was on decent bit folks that they should have any relations like Kath.

But Meg just sat there and smoked and said never a word, as though she thought nothing worth a yea or a nay. Young Robb had fair ta'en a fancy to Kath and he near boiled up when he heard Jock speak, him and the wife that he'd married from her shame. So he left them short and went raging home and wished for one that Kath would come back, a summer noon as he cycled home, snipe were calling in the Auchindreich moor where the cattle stood with their tails a-switch, the Grampians rising far and behind, Kinraddie spread like a map for show, its ledges veiled in a mist from the sun. You felt on that day a wild, daft unease, man, beast and bird: as though something were missing and lost from the world, and Kath was the thing that John Robb missed, she'd something in her that minded a man of a house that was builded upon a hill.

Folk thought that maybe the last they would hear of young Kath Menzies and her ill-gettèd ways. So fair stammy-gastered they were with the news she'd come back to the Mearns, she was down in Stonehive, in a grocer's shop, as calm as could be, selling out tea and cheese and such-like with no blush of shame on her face at all, to decent women that were properly wed and had never looked on men but their own, and only on them with their braces buttoned.

It just showed you the way that the world was going to allow an ill quean like that in a shop, some folk protested to the creature that owned it, but he just shook his head, *Ah well, she works fine; and what else she does is no business of mine.*

So you well might guess there was more than business between the man and Kath Menzies, like.

And Meg heard the news and went into Stonehive, driving her sholtie, and stopped at the shop. And some in the shop knew who she was and minded the things she had done long syne to other bit bairns of hers that went wrong; and they waited with their breaths held up with delight. But all that Meg did was to nod to Kath *Ay, well, then, it's you – Ay, mother, just that – Two pounds of syrup and see that it's good*.

And not another word passed between them, Meg Menzies that once would have ta'en such a quean and skelped her to rights before you could wink. Going home from Stonehive she stopped by the farm where young Robb was fee'd, he was out in the hayfield coling the hay, and she nodded to him grim, with her high horse face. *What's this that I hear about you and Kath Menzies?*

He turned right red, but he wasn't ashamed. *I've no idea – though I hope it's the worse – It fell near is – Then I wish it was true, she might marry me, then, as I've prigged her to do.*

Oh, have you so, then? said Meg, and drove home, as though the whole matter was a nothing to her.

But next Tuesday the postman brought a bit note, from Kathie it was to her mother at Tocherty. *Dear mother, John Robb's going out to Canada and wants me to marry him and go with him. I've told him instead I'll go with him and see what he's like as a man – and then marry him at leisure, if I feel in the mood. But he's hardly any money, and we want to borrow some, so he and I are coming over on Sunday. I hope that you'll have dumpling for tea. Your own daughter, Kath.*

Well, Meg passed that letter over to Jim, he glowered at it dour, *I know – near all the Howe's heard. What are you going to do, now, mother?*

But Meg just lighted a cigarette and said nothing, she'd smoked like a tink since that steer with Jean. There was promise of strange on-goings at Tocherty by the time that the Sabbath day was come. For Jock came there on a visit as well, him and his wife, and besides him was Jeannie, her that had married the clerk down in Brechin, and she brought the bit creature, he fair was a toff; and he stepped like a cat through the sharn in the close; and when he had heard the story of Kath, her and her plan and John Robb and all, he was shocked near to death, and so was his wife. And Jock Menzies gaped and gave a mean laugh. *Ay, coarse to the bone, ill-gettèd I'd say if it wasn't that we came of the same bit stock. Ah well, she'll fair have to tramp to Canada, eh mother? – if she's looking for money from you.*

And Meg answered quiet *No, I wouldn't say that. I've the money all ready for them when they come.*

You could hear the sea splashing down soft on the rocks, there was such a dead silence in Tocherty house. And then Jock habbered like a cock with fits *What, give silver to one who does as she likes, and won't marry as you made the rest of us marry? Give silver to one who's no more than a –*

And he called his sister an ill name enough, and Meg sat and smoked looking over the parks. *Ay, just that. You see, she takes after myself.*

And Jeannie squeaked *How?* and Meg answered her quiet: *She's fit to be free and to make her own choice the same as myself and the same kind of choice. There was none of the rest of you fit to do that, you'd to marry or burn, so I married you quick. But Kath and me could afford to find out. It all depends if you've smeddum or not.*

She stood up then and put her cigarette out, and looked at the gaping gowks she had mothered. *I never married your father, you see. I could never make up my mind about Will. But maybe our Kath will find something surer. . . . Here's her and her man coming up the road.*

R. B. Cunninghame-Graham

MIRAHUANO

WHY Silvio Sanchez got the name of Mirahuano was difficult to say. Perhaps for the same reason that the Arabs call lead 'the light', for certainly he was the blackest of his race, a tall, lopsided negro, with elephantine ears, thick lips, teeth like a narwhal's tusks, and Mirahuano is a cottony, white stuff used to fill cushions, and light as thistledown. Although he was so black and so uncouth, he had the sweetest smile imaginable, and through his eyes, which at first sight looked hideous, with their saffron-coloured whites, there shone a light, as if a spirit chained in the dungeon of his flesh was struggling to be free. A citizen of a republic in which by theory all men were free and equal by the law, the stronger canon enacted by humanity, confirmed by prejudice, and enforced by centuries of use, had set a bar between him and his white brethren in the Lord which nothing, neither his talents, lovable nature, nor the esteem of everyone who knew him, could ever draw aside. Fate having doubly cursed him with a black skin and an aspiring intellect, he passed his life just as a fish might live in an aquarium, or a caged bird, if they had been brought up to think intelligently on their lost liberty.

The kindly customs of the republic, either derived from democratic Spain or taken unawares from the gentler races of the New World, admitted him, partly by virtue of his talents, for he was born a poet, in a land where all write verses, on almost equal terms to the society of men. Still there were little differences that they observed as if by instinct, almost involuntarily, due partly to the lack of human dignity conspicuous in his race; a lack which in his case, as if the very powers of nature were in league against him, seemed intensified, and made him, as it were, on one hand an archetype, so negroid that he almost seemed an ape, and yet in intellect superior to the majority of those who laughed at him. No one was ever heard to call him Don, and yet the roughest muleteer from Antióquia claimed and received the title as a right, as soon as he had made sufficient money to purchase a black coat.

In the interminable sessions in the cafés, where men sat talking politics by hours, or broached their theories at great length, on poetry, on international law, on government, on literature and art, with much gesticulation, and with their voices raised to their highest pitch – for arguments are twice as cogent when delivered shrilly and with much banging on the table – the uncouth negro did not suffer in his pride, for there he shouted with the rest, and plunged into a world of dialectics with the best of them. His Calvary came later, for when at last the apologetic Genoese who kept the café politely told his customers that it was time to close, and all strolled out together through the arcaded, silent streets built by the Conquerors, and stood about for a last wrangle in the plaza, under the China trees, as sometimes happened, one or two would go away together to finish off their talk at home. Then Mirahuano silently would walk away, watching the fireflies flash about the bushes, and with a friendly shout of 'Buenas noches, Mirahuano' ringing in his ears from the last of his companions as they stood on the threshold of their houses, holding the door wide open by the huge iron knocker, screwed high up, so that a man upon his mule could lift it easily.

Beyond that threshold he was never asked except on business, for there dwelt the white women, who were at once his adoration and despair. With them no talents, no kindliness or generosity of character, had any weight. They treated him, upon the rare occasions when he recited verses of his own composition at some function, with grave courtesy, for it was due to their own self-respect to do so, but as a being of another generation to themselves, who had, for so their priests informed them, an immortal soul, which after death might be as worthy of salvation as their own, in its Creator's eyes.

He, though he knew exactly his position, midway between that of the higher animals and man, was yet unable to resist the peculiar fascination that a white woman seems to have for those of coloured blood. Those of his friends who had his interests at heart, and were admirers of his talents, argued in vain, and pointed out that he was certain to bring trouble on his head if he attempted to presume upon his education and tried to be accepted as a man.

His means permitted him to live a relatively idle life, and as he read all kinds of books in French and Spanish, his intellect always expanded, and it was natural enough that he should think himself the equal of the best, unless he happened to take up a looking-glass and saw the injustice which from his birth both God and man had wrought upon him. As now and then he published poems, which, in a country where all write, were still above the average of those his brethren in the Muses penned (for all the whiteness of their skins), his name was noised abroad, and he was styled in newspapers the Black Alcaeus, the Lute of Africa, and a variety of other epithets, according to the lack of taste of those who make all things ridiculous which their fell pens approach.

The Floral Games were due. On such occasions poets write on themes such as 'To the Immortal Memory of the Liberator', or dedicate their lyrics to the 'Souls of those who fell at Mancavélica', or simply head their stuff 'Dolores', 'Una Flor Marchita', or something of the sort. Poets of all dimensions leave their counting-houses, banks, regiments, and public offices, and with their brows all 'wreathed in roses', as the local papers say, flock to the 'flowery strife'. All are attired in black, all wear tall hats, and all bear white kid gloves, sticky with heat, and generally a size or two too large for those who carry them.

Each poet in the breast-pocket of his long frock-coat has a large roll of paper in which in a clear hand are written out the verses that are to make his name immortal and crown his brow with flowers.

Now and again their hands steal furtively to touch the precious scrolls, just as a man riding at night in dangerous country now and then feels at the butt of his revolver to assure himself that it is there, when his horse pricks his ears or any of the inexplicable, mysterious noises of the night perplex and startle him. On this occasion, after the other sports, the running at the ring, the feats of horsemanship, in which men stopped their horses short before a wall, making them rear and place their feet upon the top, the tailing of the bulls, and all the other feats which Spanish Americans love to train their horses to perform, were over, the poets all advanced. In the fierce sun they marched, looking a little like a band of undertaker's mutes at an old-fashioned funeral, and stood in line before the jury, and each man in his turn read out his verses, swelling his voice, and rolling all the adjectives, like a delicious morsel, on his tongue. The audience now and then burst out into applause, when some well-worn and well-remembered tag treating of liberty, calling upon the Muses for their help, or speaking of the crimson glow, like blood of the oppressor, which tinged the Andean snows, making them blush incarnadine, or when a stanza dwelling on alabaster bosoms, teeth white as pearls, and eyes as black as those the Houris flash in Paradise, struck their delighted ears. All read and stood aside to wait, looking a little sourly on their fellow-competitors, or with their eyes fixed on a girl, the daughter of a Senator, who, dressed in white, sat in a box beside her father, ready to crown the successful poet with a limp wreath of flowers. The last to read was Mirahuano, and the Master of the Ceremonies, after due clearing of his throat, read out his title, 'Movements of the Soul.' Holding his hat in his left hand, and with the perspiration, which in a negro looks white and revolting to our eyes, standing in beads upon his face, and in the thick and guttural tones of all his race, the poet nervously began.

At first the audience maintained that hostile air which every audience puts on to those it does not know. This gradually gave place to one of interest, as it appeared the verses all ran smoothly; and this again altered to interest as the figure of the uncouth negro grew familiar to them. As he read on, tracing the movements of the soul, confined and fettered in the flesh, lacking advancement in its due development owing to circumstances affecting not itself, but the mere prison of the body, a prison that it must endure perforce, so that it may be born, and which it leaves unwillingly at last, so strong is habit, even to the soul, the listeners recognized that they were listening to a poet, and gazed upon him in astonishment, just as the men of Athens may have gazed on the mean-looking little Jew, who, beckoning with his head, after the manner of the natural orator, compelled their silence in the Agora. The poet finished in a blaze of rhetoric after the fashion that the Latin race in the republics of America demands, depicting a free soul, freed from the bonds that race, sex, or conditions have imposed on it, free to enjoy, to dare, to plan, free to work out its own salvation, free to soar upwards and to love.

He ceased, and a loud 'Viva!' rent the air, and though some of the men of property were evidently shocked at the implied intrusion of a mere negro soul into an Empyrean where their own would soon have atrophied, the poor and all the younger generation — for in America, whatever men become in after life, in youth they are all red republicans — broke out into applause.

Long did the jury talk the poems over, weighing judiciously the pros and cons, but from the first it was quite clear that Mirahuano's composition would receive most votes.

Again the Master of the Ceremonies stood up, and in dead silence proclaimed the prize had been adjudged to Señor Sanchez, and that he was requested to step forward and be crowned.

Shoving his papers hastily into his pocket, and clinging to his hat, just as a drowning sailor clutches fast a plank, the poet shuffled up towards the box in which the jury sat, and stood half proudly, half shamefacedly, to listen to the set oration which the President of the Floral Games stood ready to pronounce. Clearing his throat, he welcomed to Parnassus' heights another poet. He was proud that one of their town had won the prize. The Muses all rejoiced; Apollo had restrung his lyre and now stretched out his hand to welcome in the son of Africa. The eternal verities stood once more justified; liberty, poetry, and peace had their true home in the Republic. Europe might boast its Dantes and Shakkispers, its Lopes, Ariostos, and the rest, but Costaguano need not fear their rivalry whilst poets such as Mira – he should say as Silvio Sanchez – still raised their paeans to the great and indivisible.

He could say more, much more, but words, what were they in the face of genius? – so he would bring his discourse to a close by welcoming again the youngest brother of the lyre into the Muses' court. Now he would call upon the fairest of the fair, the Señorita Nieves Figueroa, to place the laurel on the poet's brow.

Applause broke out rather constrainedly, and chiefly amongst those who by the virtue of their station were able to express their feelings easily, really liked Mirahuano, and possibly admired the poem they had heard, that is as much of it as they had understood.

Dressed all in white, with a mantilla of white lace upon her head, fastened high on her hair to a tall comb, shy and yet self-possessed, the Señorita Nieves Figueroa advanced, holding a crown of laurel leaves, with a large silver ornament, shaped like a lyre, in front of it, and with long ribbons of the national colours hanging down behind. Her jet-black hair was glossy as a raven's wing. Her olive skin and almond eyes were thrown into relief by her white clothes, and gave her somewhat of the air of a fly dropped in milk, or a blackbird in snow. Clearly she was embarrassed by the appearance of the man she had to crown, who, on his side, stood quivering with excitement at his victory and the approach of the young girl.

Raising the crown, she placed it on the negro's head, where it hung awkwardly, half covering his eyes, and giving him the look as of a bull when a skilled bull-fighter has placed a pair of banderillas in his neck. Murmuring something about the Muses, poetry, and a lyre, she gracefully stepped back, and Mirahuano shuffled off, having received, as he himself observed, 'besides the wreath, an arrow in his heart'.

From that day forth he was her slave, that is, in theory, for naturally he never had the chance to speak to her, although no doubt she heard about his passion, and perhaps laughed with her friends about the ungainly figure she had crowned. Debarred from all chance of speech with her he called the 'objective of his soul', dressed in his best, he called each Thursday morning at Señor Figueroa's house to deliver personally a copy of his verses tied with blue ribbons at the door. The door was duly opened and the verses handed in for months, and all the town knew and talked of the infatuation of the negro poet, who for his part could have had no illusions on the subject, for from the moment of the Floral Games he had never spoken to the girl except, as he said, 'by the road of Parnassus', which after all is a path circuitous enough in matters of the heart.

His life was passed between the little house, buried in orange and banana trees, where his old mother, with her head wrapped in a coloured pocket-handkerchief, sat all the day, balanced against the wall in an old, high-backed chair, watching his sisters pounding maize in a high, hardwood mortar, with their chemises slipping off their shoulders, and the Café del Siglo, where all the poets used to spend their time.

Poets and verse-makers were as much jumbled up in people's minds in the republic as they are here, and anyone who had a rhyming dictionary and the sufficient strength of wrist to wield a pen, wrote reams of stuff about the pangs of love, the moon, water, and flashing eyes, with much of liberty and dying for their native land. When once they fell into the habit, it was as hard of cure as drinking, especially as most of them had comfortable homes, though they all talked of what they underwent in the Bohemia to which they were condemned. For hours they used to sit and talk, reading their verses out to one another or with their hats drawn down upon their brows to signify their state.

To these reunions of the soul, for so they styled them, Mirahuano came, sitting a little diffidently upon his chair, and now and then reciting his own verse, which, to speak truth, was far above the rest of the weak, wordy trash produced so lavishly. As it cost nothing to be kind to him, for he would never take even a cup of coffee, unless he paid for it himself, they used him kindly, letting him sit and read when they were tired, help them to consonants, and generally behave as a light porter to

72

the Muses, as he defined it in his half-melancholy, half-philosophizing vein.

One night as they sat late compassionating one another on their past luck, and all declaiming against envy and the indifference of a commercial world, whilst the tired waiters dozed, seated before the tables with their heads resting on the marble tops, and as the flies, mosquitoes, and the 'vinchucas' made life miserable, their talk drew round towards the hypothetical Bohemia in which they dreamed they lived. Poor Mirahuano, who had sat silently wiping his face at intervals with a red pocket-handkerchief – for in common with the highest and the lowest of his kind he loved bright colours – drew near, and sitting down among the poets, listened to their talk. The heavy air outside was filled with the rank perfume of the tropic vegetation. The fireflies flashed among the thickets of bamboos, and now and then a night-jar uttered its harsh note.

In the bright moonlight men slept on the stucco benches in the plaza, with their faces downwards, and the whole town was silent except where now and then some traveller upon his mule passed by, the tick-tack of the footfalls of his beast clattering rhythmically in its artificial pace, and sending up a trail of sparks as it paced through the silent streets. Nature appeared perturbed, as she does sometimes in the tropics, and as if just about to be convulsed in the throes of a catastrophe. Inside the café men felt the strain, and it seemed natural to them, when Mirahuano, rising to his feet, his lips blue, and his face livid with emotion, exclaimed, 'Talk of Bohemia, what is yours to mine! Mine is threefold. A poet, poor, and black. The last eats up the rest, includes them, stultifies you and your lives.' He paused, and, no one answering, unconscious that the waiters, awakened by his tones, were looking at him, half in alarm, half in amazement, broke out again. 'Bohemia! Think of my life; my very God is white, made in your image, imposed upon my race by yours. His menacing pale face has haunted me from childhood, hard and unsympathetic, and looking just as if He scorned us whom you call His children, although we know it is untrue. Your laws are all a lie. His too, unless it is that you have falsified them in your own interests and to keep us slaves.'

Seizing his hat, he walked out of the café without a salutation, leaving the company dumb with amazement, looking upon each other as the inhabitants of some village built on the slopes of a volcano long quiescent may look, when from the bowels of the sleeping mountain a stream of lava shoots into the sky. His brothers in the Muses missed him from his accustomed haunts for two or three days, and then a countryman reported he had seen in the backwater of a stream an object which he had thought was a dead bullock or a cow. Wishing to secure the hide, he had lassoed it, and to his great astonishment he found it was the body of a negro, dressed in black clothes, as he said, just as good as those worn by the President. Being of a thrifty turn of mind, he had stripped them off and sold them at a pulperia, when he had dried them in the sun.

It seemed to him fortuitous, that a black rascal who in all his life had never done a stroke of work, but walked about just like a gentleman, making a lot of silly rhymes, at last should be of use to a white Christian such as he was himself, white, as the proverb says, on all four sides.

He added, as he stood beside his half-wild colt, keeping a watchful eye upon its eye, and a firm hand upon his raw-hide halter, that as a negro's skin was of no value, he pushed the body back into the stream, and had no doubt that it would soon be eaten up by the caimáns.

Neil M. Gunn

THE OLD MAN

HE was the Old Man of the gipsy tribe, and his work consisted entirely in settling the disputes of the upcoming generations. Any evening – or morning, for that matter – he could be found sitting on a dry log smoking his pipe and looking meditatively and pleasantly at whatever was or was not before him.

His advice was most frequently sought after a Saturday's night bout of methylated-spirit drinking, mixed fights and a night or two in the cells. His dispensing of justice followed the invariable practice of never inflicting any penalty beyond his own speech. And his speech rarely began until they had talked themselves hoarse and sometimes into a fight on the spot.

But when he began speaking, he kept going. No mere verbal interruption, however explosive, stopped him. And he talked 'like a book'. It was even said that he had read old books in his young days, just because he was descended from a ditchside poet in the year one. More than once opposing sides had combined to call him a windbag and other uncomplimentary terms, and had retired, in new-found harmony, shouting at him as he still went on talking. But such derision would be short-lived. Presently they would splutter and laugh among themselves and say, 'Did anyone ever hear such an ould fool?' If the money could run to it, they would bring him a sup of whisky, or a finger of black twist tobacco. For long enough the camp would be a scene of harmonious endeavour, bounded on the right side by horse-dealing and on the left by begging.

However, every now and then he had to arbitrate on difficult matters. A single person would come with a deep personal grievance, touching theft, or hatred. It was not always easy. As each and all came voluntarily, they felt entitled to the advice or backing they specially desired.

But sometimes a man came when his mind was a dark whirl, and then he would not put his point, but talk round about it or remain gloomily silent. This was the most difficult case of all. It gave the Old Man scope. Dan's was a case of this sort.

The snout of his cap well down over his left eye, Dan looked gloomy and raven-dark. His petulant mouth, too, was bitter. When he spat explosively, he turned his nose away at once from the spit as from his own thought or the other fellow's argument. He had white teeth, a brown rich skin, and was just turned thirty. In the way he would often not look at you there was something of a spoilt boy or a warped criminal.

The Old Man said nothing.

In the silence, Dan wriggled and kicked the rotten end of the log, not hard, but persistently.

'I feel every kick in me,' said the Old Man at last.

'Ye won't feel it much longer,' said Dan. 'I'm for off.'

'Indeed,' said the Old Man politely. 'Are you going soon?'

'I'm going at once,' said Dan savagely, and he stopped kicking and looked away.

'If you have now finished what you are going to say and want my opinion on it, I'll give it to you.'

'What d'ye think ye're talking about?' asked Dan with brutal sarcasm.

'It's a very difficult situation,' nodded the Old Man, 'very difficult. But it has this to it that it's not new. Accordingly, I can make a few remarks on it in a general way to begin with, for I have found that nearly every trouble in life lifts like a mist once the understanding understands and shines into it.'

'Horn spoons!' said Dan.

'Take a case, for example, of a man and his wife. They fall out.'

'Who fell out?'

'They fall out more than once. Until the time comes when they are in a continuous state of having fallen out. It is one of the queerest states in the world, that, and one of the most critical. Now the word critical has two meanings. For instance, take the rotten old swing-bridge down there before it broke under you last week. When you were on the middle of it, it was in a critical condition, and – listen, now – you were critical of it being in that critical condition.'

'Are you trying to make a fool of me, or what?' asked Dan threateningly.

'So it is with marriage. The two supports of the bridge, as you would say, are in a critical condition, and so are critical one to another. The female support or wife will become critical of the male support or husband. As he moves about in his bad nature, she will see all the nasty things in him that she missed before. She will see first of all that he is ill-tempered, and then she will see that he is mean-spirited, and then she will see that he notices little things like any miser, and then she will see that he is a bully, and finally she will see that he is cruel. Everything, in fact, that she thought he hadn't got, she now sees that he has got. She thought him always a good cut above other men, now she sees that he is below them, for they are manly to their wives whatever else. When she grows ashamed of him in company –'

'What the blazes –'

'Hsh,' said the Old Man. 'There's your wife coming round the quarry.'

At that, Dan's expression grew so vindictive that it was clear he would gladly have smitten the Old Man out of existence if he could have done it in time. He spat, stubbornly held his ground, and did not look round. When next he gathered sense in the Old Man's words, they were flowing: '... so he becomes critical of her. He had thought her a good-looker, and he wonders to himself bitterly where his eyes could have been. He had thought she had spirit and was full of fun, and now she goes about more silent than a funeral, with an expression of misery that if you could get it in a bottle would do for rennet. He bawls at her and she does not answer, and that is enough to drive a lively man to murder. And then she will say something that is worse than saying nothing. When he cannot eat from anger the small noises she will be making eating steadily like a blind cow will make him want to vomit, and then he gets up and kicks the bottom out of the stool he was sitting on.'

'Who the hell told you I kicked the bottom —'

'Then he begins to notice ...'

'Will ye listen to me?'

'... little things that he would be ashamed to tell anyone he noticed. But I can explain that better if, first of all, I compare this wife of his with a young woman he saw singing a ballad song at the horse fair at Knockfalish. The sound of her voice would draw the heart out of you, and she had a shy dark eye more impudent than a bad woman's kiss. When you would be standing there looking at her, you would think to yourself that the whole world could roar to hell in the glory of a dozen or maybe thirteen fights, if —'

'Will ye stop yer gab?' roared Dan, and he caught the Old Man by the whiskers.

'Well,' said the Old Man calmly, 'have you thought of your complaint yet?'

'Complaint!' When Dan got back his breath he laughed — and roared, 'Has my wife been talking to you?'

'No. She is the kind who would never talk to me.'

Dan glared at him and threw his whiskers aside. 'Begod, ye're right there. What the hell then have ye been talking about?'

'I have just been filling in time till you could put words on your complaint. And surely the relations between a man and a woman are interesting at any time. For the first time in six months my egg was boiled hard as a stone this morning, and I can only take it soft.'

Dan gave a roar of laughter, and took off his bonnet and put it on again. 'You, who haven't done a stroke of work in twenty years! You, whose wife has never stopped working for ye in twenty years! You're the one to know about marriage!'

'Well, don't you think I am?' asked the Old Man.

'Ye ould hairy amadan, you!' cried Dan, swaying on his feet. 'This is as good as a fair!'

'As I was saying —'

'Oh, shut yer mouth,' said Dan, 'and tell me this.' And when he had stopped the Old Man, he bellowed derisively, 'D'ye mean to tell me that is the way of it between people and them married?'

'That is the way,' said the Old Man.

'Between all people?'

'Between all people, everywhere, high and low. To every married couple, from the king and the queen on their thrones to the horse-dealers at Knockfalish Fair, a time comes when that is the way, for better or for worse, for longer or for shorter.'

'And who told ye about the kings and queens? Eh?'

'In the old histories of our country . . .'

'Stop now, will you? Stop!'

'. . . the ancient kings and queens would be quarrelling in a way that was known to every story-teller that slept in a ditch. Moreover they —'

'I believe ye there,' said Dan. 'I've heard the stories myself.' He marvelled for a short time, his eyes in a bright humour; then he forcibly stopped the Old Man once more.

'Tell me this,' he said, looking at him narrowly, so that he should not escape him. 'Tell me this. How d'ye know the exact things they would be thinking of one another? Tell me, now. Come on!'

'How should I know but out of the wide experience I have gained from life? Do you think when I am sitting here alone that I am doing nothing at all? Is it for the like of you —'

But Dan got him stopped by shouting into his ear, 'If it is the same with everyone, then it must have been the same with yourself?'

'Manifestly,' said the Old Man.

At which great word, Dan roared afresh and tweaked the grey beard in sport. 'Are ye telling me!' he cried.

The Old Man smoothed his beard calmly. 'I don't like anyone,' he said coldly, 'to touch my whiskers.'

Whereat Dan doubled up.

The Old Man remained silent.

'Is it offended ye are now?' asked Dan, pausing in his laughter to enjoy this new delight.

But presently he said coaxingly, 'Ach, now, what are ye

offended about? Aren't ye the wisest man in the world? Don't
we all know it? Come, now, don't ye be offended with me. I'm
going away off to the town this night and bedamn if I won't
take back as nice a drop in the heel of a flask for you as ever
you tasted. Only, tell me this now, and it's all I'll ask. Tell me.'
His voice lowered confidentially. 'When ye were in that state
with herself – how did ye get out of it? Wait! One minute!
First of all, was the state ye were in with one another as bad as
you have made it out to be? And look!' added Dan threateningly. 'If ye tell me a lie I swear on my soul I'll pull the whiskers
clean out of you.'

'It was worse,' said the Old Man calmly. 'Much worse.'

'Good,' said Dan. 'Go on.'

'It was the end. The only thing that was worse than seeing
her in my sight was thinking of her out of my sight. And every
time I had a look at her out of the corner of my eye, I saw
something that made me worse than ever. Sometimes it would
be no more than a drop to her nose, or hair sticking out over
her ear, or lines in her neck, or a bunch in her clothes, but each
small thing would be the last hay seed. Do you know, when I
would be going back to her sometimes there would be a reluc-
tance on me like a sick pain. And the way that would make me
stop and use words enough to commit my soul, and I would
smash my heels in the ground and walk round myself in a
small circle ...'

'Whist!' said Dan, taking a turn round about himself. 'That
will do for that.' He was lost in wonder for a minute and then
gave a small chuckle.

'... so there we were in the wood ...'

'What wood was that?' asked Dan. 'Begin that bit again,
will you?'

'... and the words spoken. I walked away from her. She said
nothing. She did not ask me to stay. She did not plead. It was
all over. It was finished. Before you can say words of parting
like that you have to work yourself into a great rage. I had
worked myself so high that a fear got hold of me that she
might do harm to herself. For it is never the women who

threaten to take their own lives who do take them. It's always the quiet women who have never said cheep.'

'Are ye telling me that?'

'Yes. You watch them, Dan. Watch the quiet women.'

'Go on,' said Dan thoughtfully.

'It may be difficult for me to get you to understand, for in that wood a queer thing happened to me. Thinking, as I told you, that she might do harm to herself, I stopped in my tracks, and turned, and went back quietly to the wood. I stole from tree to tree until at last I saw her again, all alone by herself, in that quiet place, with the trees like gallows, where she could do to herself what she might be in the mind to do and no one to say her no.'

'And what was she doing?' asked Dan.

'She was gathering sticks,' said the Old Man.

'Gathering ...' A gust of laughter choked the words in his mouth. Twice he looked at the solemn Old Man and twice he laughed. Then he asked, 'What did ye do?'

'I sat down and watched her. She went slowly from tree to tree gathering the sticks. She broke them, as she gathered them, into lengths, and made a heap of them. And it was while she was doing this with no one to see her in that lonely wood but my own eyes – it was while she was doing this that the true vision of her came to me. I saw her like the mother of generations, the gatherer and the provider; and I thought to myself that this is the greatness of great women, that this is what remains when all the tempers and vanities of great fools of men have passed on the wind.'

'Did ye now? God, and weren't you the great ass! You'll be telling you wept next.'

'I wept,' said the Old Man.

'Jehosaphat!' said Dan, and his breath went from him. It came back in a gulp of derision at this old fool of a woman before him. 'And to think that we would be wasting time on getting advice from the like of that!'

But the Old Man protected his beard with a smoothing hand. 'Time is never wasted,' said he.

'Isn't it now? And what advice d'ye think you have been giving me?'

'If I haven't been giving you advice,' said the Old Man, 'I have been giving your wife time.'

'What's that ye say? Giving her time for what?'

'When she passed out by a little while ago, going towards the Quiet Wood, I noticed that she had a rope hidden on her. I noticed it because of an end which hung in sight with a loop on it.'

'What ...'

'What would she be wanting with a rope and a tree and her married to a man like you? It's very difficult for me to answer you that, Dan, but, as I told you before, she is a quiet woman.'

Dan swole up with the wrath that was in him, and drew back his fist to clout the Old Man a blow that would finish him. But the other fist, intending to push the Old Man straight, tipped him heels up over the log. After Dan had said a few words, he began to hurry towards the Quiet Wood.

He was in time, thank God! for she had not yet got the rope fixed. From behind the trunk of a tree he watched her, and had great trouble to keep himself from laughing, for she had tied a small stone to one end of the rope and was trying to throw the stone up over a branch; and not only that, but as any fool could see, the branch was rotten!

The shapes she made at throwing the stone convulsed him, for he could have shot it from his thumb-nail; but she was persistent, never losing her temper; she was like doom; and when, at the fourth throw, she got it over, Dan stopped laughing. She lowered the stone towards her. She's got it now! he thought. But she was in no hurry. She took her breath for a little, standing quite still; then she stirred and looked up at the branch. Would it be strong enough? She tried it; she tugged at it; she tested it with her full weight from a little jump. Crack! and the branch, snapping, fell on top of her fallen body.

Dan fell too and stuffed his mouth. The fun of it was too much for him. And when she sat up and began rubbing her head like a clown in a circus, he turned on his belly, rooting in

the friendly earth. 'Are ye seein' her?' he asked the earth.
'Whist! for God's sake!'

When he looked again she was on her feet, dragging the
branch over to a big stone. And then he perceived the reason
and purpose of all her acts. She was not hanging herself at all:
she was gathering sticks!

He was speechless for a long time, seeing only what a fool
he had been, what an ass. The ass swole up and went stalking
through all the air to heaven. He clenched his fists in wrath, he
began to laugh at himself in derision, in unholy mirth, and
then just to laugh inwardly.

At last she had so great a bundle tied round with the rope
that she couldn't lift it to her back. He watched her like a man
with a bet on a horse, but she couldn't do it.

'Blast ye!' he said, for his mind had put his money on her.

But was she beaten? She dragged the pile to the top of a
little bank and got below it. Straining heavily at the neck, she
heaved upward, steadied herself and her bundle for a moment,
then, bent double, began to stagger away. The end of a stick,
jutting from the bundle, grazed a tree and swung her round,
and the bundle fell. She looked at it dumbly, then began dragging it back to the little bank.

The sight of her doing this was more than flesh and blood
could stand. He jumped up and strode down upon her. 'What
in the name of little frogs are ye thinking ye're trying to do? Is
it ye have lost yer senses entirely? If the thing was too heavy
for you, couldn't ye take a stick or two out?'

Her young face looked grey and ancient. There was a dumb
misery upon her like the weight of all the world.

'Can't you speak?' he shouted.

'I am tired, Dan,' she said. The last shred of fight had gone
from her voice. It sounded small and thin, and haunting as a
child's.

'Mother of God.' he cried harshly and pulled her against him
so that she might not see whatever happened to his eyes, for a
wild gush of feeling had started up behind them.

Margaret Hamilton

CHOICE

WITH the others Anna blundered out of the coach.

On a gravel drive, sharpened by sunlight, their hostesses were waiting. Slim beside the heavily-clad foreigners, they both had silver hair with pale blue auras. In the hall behind them, in bowls and vases and converted jam-jars, were flowers with golden auras against the dark wood panelling.

'It's a daffodil year,' they murmured apologetically.

'It's a daffodil year,' the guide on the coach had explained, using the same voice as when he had said, 'There is Big Ben' or 'We are approaching Westminster Abbey.'

They were approaching daffodils which stormed cottage lawns and gatecrashed gardens where a sedate few had been invited.

That morning, going to the other airport, the students had seen snow, almost ready to melt and yield up a seven months' store of empty cigarette packets, dead cats and lost galoshes. Now, by a leap in space, not time, they were with the daffodils: a flower which most of them had never seen.

Botanists among them aired knowledge as they crowded upstairs. 'Member of the *Amaryllidaceae* family –' 'Native to southern Europe and brought to England by sailors in the eighteenth century –'

Then friends were claiming beds beside friends and saying careful English *Senk yous* before chatter leapt out in their own tongue like the fresh clothes they were unzipping from bags.

Only Anna remained in the hall. A student of English, she was intoning dutifully, *Ten thowsend sor I et a glentz, Nodding zare heads in spraitlee dentz*. But in fact she was bemused by the daffodil scent. Such an odour, clean and insipid like all the English – as you knew, of course, from your studies – ought to be confined to one bloom or a small bouquet. Instead it attacked

84

you in a strength more suited to the perfumes used by some men at home because, living in a room with female in-laws, they could not wash very thoroughly.

At last, feeling light and almost brittle because a day had been hollowed from her by air travel, she wandered up the shallow stairs. They were painted a dull white as if the wood beneath had been dark-stained for years, and the long dormitory had the same whitened-over look.

There was no bed left for her. 'Stupid, I couldn't keep it any longer,' hissed Katya, her friend. The next bed was being solidly sat on by a physics student, frisking her perm with a comb till she deemed it safe to stand up.

Then Mrs Carter, one of the blue-haired ladies, led Anna to a little room, left empty by the others because they thought it was not for them. 'I do hope you won't mind being on your own,' she smiled.

'*Mind!*' Anna smiled back, her face breaking free of the heavy plaits piled on top of it. Alone. She ran to the window, standing for a moment in what must be ecstasy.

Never since she was conceived had she been alone. Always there had been the envelope of other people's presence: her mother's body, then the flat where all the time people were thinking, if not actually talking, of facts, figures, percentages, equations. Only she had turned her back on science as a career. Later she would teach or translate, but meantime she was allowed to lose herself in the world of English literature. A world which had seemed rather like the view from this window. Smooth grass leading to the river, a silver snake between college buildings. On the other side a garden, its near edge banked with daffodils whose colour was being enamelled by the slow English twilight.

Suddenly she tore herself away, uneasily, as if she had been caught staring in instead of out.

Next morning she woke early, feeling rested, as if last night's unease had been shed like her padded winter coat, hanging unneeded behind the door. She dressed, and experimentally pushed up the lower sash of the window. Yes, she could step on to a porch roof and from there drop to the ground.

Daffodils, hugging the blinded house, were unspritely now, dew-draggled. She crossed the wet lawn, leaving footmarks, briefly, on the grass. In the river was a small boat beside a wooden landing-stage.

Mrs Carter had said, 'Do use the equipment.' Perhaps she had meant only balls and racquets, but she was not there to object as Anna rowed out to meet the sunlit world of English literature.

At the other side she tied up the boat and climbed a sloping path between daffodils which here were briskly shaking off the night.

The garden was filled with flowers which she could not name – coming as she did from a land where spring to atone for its lateness leapt at once into lilac and cherry-blossom.

Behind a clump of tall, deeply golden daffodils she found, scarcely to her surprise, a man. He was sitting on a rug beside a canvas chair and at first she thought he was that actor, he who played Nelson in the film which she had seen so often. Evening after evening she had sat in the crowded cinema, needing no subtitles but improving her English as she waited for the time when she and all the other women would weep for battle-scarred English love.

This man was not Lord Nelson, although he had the same strong chin and brows which seemed arrogant but were only watchful. His hair was touched with silver, but not (she gravely noted) blue-haloed like Mrs Carter's. He sat looking at her with dark eyes under those defensive brows.

Anna took a deep breath before enunciating slowly: 'Excuse – me – please. I wish to know – the correct Greenwich time.'

Rather to her surprise, he did not produce a large gold pocket-watch. He shot out his wrist and frowned over a thin dial, pulsating among the tawny hairs on his arm. 'The correct Greenwich time is ... twenty-nine ... and ten seconds.'

'Oh, s – thank you.' Having adjusted her chugging chrome watch, she turned away.

'Please don't go.'

Obediently she sat beside him in the chair with its faded canvas seat. He frowned again and she half-rose, thinking that she ought to have waited for an invitation. A movement of his hand gave it to her.

'My name is Anna –' she began.

'But of course ! ...'

So he knew her. His country's spies must have found out that Uri, her brother, was concerned with atomic research. She must escape before the torture began, the merciless probings after things which she did not know ...

'You came before, you know,' he said. 'Your name was Anna. You had the same hair, the same overburdened little face. You'd come *over there*' – he nodded towards the house across the river – 'to be nursed.'

Absurdly now she was concerned less with what he was saying than with phonetics. The accent, the vowels, were as she had been taught, but the emphasis on *r*'s was not wholly English.

'They gave you a small room where you could see my garden, and sometimes they rowed you over here. In the end you stayed with me.'

'*Of course!*'

'They told you about her – about my wife?' He looked almost angry, but it was that same thing, a defence of himself.

'No. I did not mean to interrupt, but your voice puzzled me. Now I understand it was because of someone who was not English, who pronounced her *r*'s in the continental way. Someone who was close to you –'

'For a few years only. Each year I planted more flowers to take away the smell of the concentration camp. But it was in her mind, not her nostrils, and nothing I could do was enough. She died.'

'Here in this garden?' Anna stood, dutifully, just as at home you would give an older person your seat on that part of the Metro train where a notice said you must.

He shook his head. 'No – in hospital. So' – with a sad but charming little smile – 'the chair is yours now, if you wish.'

Every morning, he said, in good or bad weather he came out here for an early hour of peace. 'Often I think it's the only reality. Inner peace ... contemplation.'

She had a sudden vision of something that she had never seen, but had been told so often that it was like part of her own memory. Of an estate at home where her grandmother used to go for picnics when she was a girl. Its owner, a little old man, had been friendly to students and others who had too little money to enjoy life, but did. All day they would run about, playing games, making a lot of noise. And all day, oblivious of their presence, the old man would sit contemplating a rocky pool where he kept a couple of penguins. He loved birds and these would not, in the course of nature, fly away from him ... But the old man had been dead for many years and his estate was farmed collectively.

'You sound ... *old*,' Anna said to this man who liked to contemplate his flowers.

'Suppose I choose to be ... old!' He was laughing at her and she blushed, but stood up facing him.

'You can't choose a thing like that.'

'Why not? Choice is a wonderful thing. Men die for the right to choose instead of obeying. And you —' Again he was laughing at her. 'You think you must go back now, but really you could choose to have breakfast here with me and meet your friends later. Perhaps some day you will ...'

Almost every morning she found herself crossing the river to join this man, Robert, in his garden. It was, of course, a splendid chance to improve her English. They talked of Anna's life at home, her crowded student days, and the country village where she had been evacuated during the war; often she went back to keep her memories of broad summer fields and a man-made river flowing over the place where old Aunt Marya had as a girl gathered mushrooms.

They talked of Robert's wife, the other Anna, who, he said, had been like her: 'Among people but always apart, alone ...'

88

The fine weather continued and sometimes they sat for a long time saying nothing. There must be something in this contemplation business, for Anna, getting through the sight-seeing, note-taking days, felt remote from the others, as if she were wrapped in a cellophane envelope of the kind they sold stockings in.

Each morning, breathing the queer scent of daffodils, she thought that the scents of home were far away and all, by comparison, undesirable. Decaying vegetables in the peasant market, sunflower seeds chewed by workers in the crowded trams, Ivan's breath after he had eaten garlic.

She told Robert of Ivan, who hoped to marry her when they both had finished their studies and one of them might qualify for a flat or a room.

'And you, Anna – do you share Ivan's hopes?' Robert spoke lightly, but he was not laughing.

Gravely she answered: 'I think – that I shall study for many more years ...'

He laughed now, but she had learned not to mind his laughter. In a few moments he asked her again to have break-fast with him.

'But –'

'It's your last day, Anna. Please choose to stay.'

There was no choice, really. Because of all the contemplation they had shared, because he had lost the other Anna and soon would lose this one, she followed him to the house.

All the time he was making coffee, serving orange and boiled eggs, her eyes wandered about the little room: furniture pale all through with no suggestion of darkness covered up – the lack of any ornament except the bright pattern of curtains and rug. She would remember this.

Quietly, as if answering her, he said: 'Why don't you stay here?'

'Stay?'

'This morning you thought you must go back for breakfast. Instead you chose to stay here. Choose to stay always, Anna.'

'How can I?'

89

'These things can be arranged. If you married me, it would be easier. But afterwards you would be quite free. Free to choose.'

At home you did things because you had to, or because they meant more money, better food and clothes. But to do something for no other reason than that you wanted to ... She was silent, uneasy again in this strange, apparently undemanding country.

The other students were non-committal when she appeared, breathless and with colour in her cheeks, so that it was silly to say she had not felt well and had gone for a walk because she didn't want breakfast.

At lunchtime Katya contrived to sit beside her and afterwards they strolled away from the soaring cathedral which they had just visited. Fields, rolling from the edge to the town, reminded you a little of home.

'Ah, how good to think we'll soon be back,' Katya sighed. 'In time for spring – real spring with rivers of melted snow in all the streets ...'

Anna said nothing and Katya was suddenly pleading: 'Anna, those daffodils – I think they must have drugged you. Their genus name is *Narcissus*, you know – from the Greek, *narke*, meaning "stupor" – because some of the species have a narcotic quality. They've made you forget about home and work and ... Ivan.'

The sturdy competent Katya had always been fond of the sturdy competent Ivan. The two of them would do well together if Anna chose to stay here, chose not to resist the demure enchantment of daffodils.

If instead she chose to go home, she would take Robert with her: not in the flesh but as a legend to set alongside the man who contemplated penguins. *With this one it was daffodils. He had a garden full of them, brought at great price from distant lands to sweeten his nostrils against the stench of beggars at his gate.* (She would have to sneer and lie to wipe out her guilt at having left him.)

This last day, as a climax to the brilliant weather, grew more and more thunderous, dark grey clouds appearing and settling immobile like the hair of an ageing, mannish woman. Like Katya some day when she had written her thesis and done all the valuable work which assuredly she would do ...

That night as Anna lay for the last time, sleepless, in her little room, the thunderstorm broke. Rising to close the window, she saw the freak hailstones battering the lawn, stripping young leaves from the trees, beating down the daffodils.

In the morning, looking out, she felt calm. She was not drugged and her mind was made up: she could not leave Robert with his slaughtered flowers.

Crossing the soaked lawn, she thought her little boat was missing, the boat which she needed to take her to him. But she found it upside down on the grass – having been drawn up, she supposed, for safety.

Then she saw them. Two rather squat young men in over-coats and cloth caps, a little way downstream. On this side, Katya or one of the others must have reported her morning out-ings and these two had been sent to watch her: strong-arm men of the type that she had seen wandering aimlessly in public buildings at home.

Luckily they were not looking towards her and she could slip back to crouch, trembling, beside the porch.

Waiting among the now-blurred flowers, she remembered that other, older poem: *Fair daffodils, we weep to see You haste away so soon ... We have short time to stay as you, We have as short a spring ...*

But sometimes, by a rare chance, you got an extra spring, a *buckshee* one as people here would say. An English spring which for the rest of your life would sweeten every spring you knew.

Soon after a maid had opened the door and Anna had gone into the house, the two young men walked slowly away. English students, they were going to face the music at their college, where they had arrived last night very late, and in no condition to climb the walls.

Dorothy K. Haynes

VOCATION

She was alone in her cell, praying. It was so still that her fidgeting fingers made little noises, dry noises like crickets in the grass. Tomorrow she was to make her vows, and as she prayed, she let her mind go back to the start of it all, seeking a sign to show her that the way she had chosen was the answer to her prayer.

It had happened two years ago, when she was on holiday.

'Put your two fingers on the glass, dear,' Miss Mather said. 'Lightly. Just make your mind a blank, and let the spirit guide you.'

They were alone in the lounge, bent over the coffee table with its tumbler and its ring of letters. Miss Mather had put the light out, and the standard lamp, with its shade tilted towards them, covered them in a parchment-coloured glow. It was silly, Susan thought. She didn't believe in it, but in these small hotels one had to be sociable.

'Don't think of anything,' Miss Mather said, coughing over her cigarette. 'Just relax, and It'll do all the work.'

The clock ticked, and the woman opposite breathed hard through her nose. She was like a man, Susan thought, with her tie and her striped shirt and her smoker's cough. She looked at the fingers, square nailed, and the sleeves with the pearl cuff links, and suddenly the tumbler lurched and jigged erratically. 'You pushed,' Susan said, watching it slither and pause.

'No, I didn't. Hush. Concentrate and see what It says.'

The glass was stubborn again, poised in the centre of the circle. Throwing away her cigarette, Miss Mather spoke in a firm, masculine voice.

'Who are you? Tell us your name or your initials.'

Slowly, the glass veered over to the letter C, touched it, and slid across to V. Susan raised her eyebrows, and Miss Mather

93

frowned for quietness. 'C' it said again, and 'V, CV, CV, CV" over and over again.

'Two names,' said Miss Mather. 'Let's ask for more information. Have you a message for anybody?'

'SU-S-' The glass faltered and stopped.

'You. You ask It, my dear. It's you It wants.'

'Oh, but – all right, then.' She laughed suddenly, letting her disapproval go. Enter into the spirit of the thing ...

'Male or female?' she said, edging a little nearer.

'S-I-S-T-E-R-S.'

'Well! You must have the gift, Miss Simpson. Ask their proper names. See if they'll tell you.'

'C-H-R-I-S-T-I-N-A V-E-R-O-N-I-C-A.'

'I bet they're nuns,' said Susan, and then she started, scared at herself. What had made her think of that? It was not even a question. But –

'Y-E-S,' said the tumbler definitely.

'You're sure you're not cheating, now?' asked Miss Mather, lighting another cigarette. 'You mustn't decide on the answers beforehand, you know.'

'No, I didn't. It just came to me, somehow, that they might be nuns. I don't know why. You ask the next question, and see.'

Miss Mather thought for a moment before asking, 'Where are you speaking from?' as if she were dealing with a deaf person on the telephone. There was a clatter as the glass careered in circles, scattering the letters out of place. 'Mischief,' said Miss Mather, removing her fingers. 'Too much noise. Find out which one's talking.'

Strange how easy it was to be serious about it. Susan waited, as Miss Mather took over again. 'CHRISTINA', said the glass, and then, without a pause, 'HELL.'

'Good Heavens!' gasped Miss Mather, affronted and a little afraid. 'There's no need –'

'Let me, now.' Susan was eager, a great power and curiosity surging inside her. 'Are you in Hell? You must have done something wrong. Tell me what you did.'

There was a long pause, and then the glass faltered slowly, as if in shame. 'L-O-V-E . . .'

'What . . .?'

'That's enough now,' barked Miss Mather, sweeping up the letters and setting the tumbler upright with a bang. 'You've a vivid imagination, you know. Too vivid. I don't think we should do any more of this tonight.'

Next evening, however, they started again, with an audience grouped round the larger table in the middle of the room. 'Don't pay any attention to them,' Miss Mather whispered. 'Concentrate. Just forget about yesterday and concentrate.'

She was serious about it, serious and rather perturbed, but to Susan it was still nothing more than a joke. Miss Mather had been cheating. It had been easy to feel the pressure of her fingers on the glass. But when the glass started its C-V careering all over again, Miss Mather frowned and said, 'Don't push, dear. Don't anticipate what It wants to say.'

'H-E-L-P,' it spelled, without any prompting. 'S-U-S-A-N HELP.'

There was a murmur all round the table. 'That's what It meant yesterday,' said Miss Mather, with relief. 'Got Its spelling wrong.'

'How can I help?' Susan asked, speaking coaxingly. 'What can I do?'

'C-O-M-E.'

'Come where?'

The tumbler went berserk in an orgy of communication. 'WHERE I BURN.'

'I don't like this,' said Susan. 'If you're playing a trick —'

'I wouldn't dare.' Miss Mather looked sickly in the parchment coloured light. 'Do you want to stop? It's up to you.'

'Ask It — no, I'll do it. How did you die? What happened?'

'W-A-L-L . . .' The tumbler faltered and stopped.

'Walled up!' Miss Mather's voice was almost shrill, pushing the tumbler away as if it were a reptile. 'I knew it! Love,' she said. 'That's how they punished them . . .' She looked at Susan, then round at the watching audience. 'Just keep out of this,' she warned. 'You don't know what you're playing with.'

Had she tried it, pulling the answers from the wish of her sub-conscious mind? It was easy enough. The glass spelled Y-E-and the fingers pushed automatically toward S. But what had started the story? Veronica and Christina had come unbidden. The nuns were her own idea, but who had put the idea into her head? And she had never thought of them as being in Hell. Were they both in Hell, or was it only Christina? She tried one night, after she was home, sitting at the kitchen table with her sister, but the glass would not co-operate. Not, that was, to the extent of anything new. 'Who is Christina?' she asked, and got the answer, 'NUN'. But when she asked about Veronica, she got nothing but a jumble of phrases, SUSAN HELP, DAMNATION or COME . . .

Sometimes, she laughed at it. Sometimes it worried her. The game cropped up at parties, and she played it, joking dread-fully. 'Let's see what Christina's got to say today.' The answers were all the same, her finger pushing out the letters with too much assurance. It was only with Veronica that she drew a blank.

'Leave it alone,' her mother told her. 'It's enough to make anybody daft.' But her mother could not know how it obsessed her. In bed, with the light out, she would go over and over the nun's last hours. She lay with the agony dragging through her own mind, far too vivid and detailed, the bricks earthy brown, damp looking, and the trowel going lick, lick like a grey tongue. At first the doomed one would stand quiet, contemptu-ous, knowing that a step could mount the structure. Suppose she struggled . . .

But it would not happen that way. The wall would mount brick by brick, and there might be prayers from the mouth which could still breathe and articulate. Breast high, the hands might forsake the rosary, and rest a moment, almost lovingly, on the soft mortar; and then a brick would bruise the nails, and the hands would retreat in quick pain; and soon the wagging, trembling chin would thrust forward in a last look, and the mouth scream in sudden realization . . .

But it was when the light went that the cries would be most anguished. They would ring out, astonishingly loud, beating and fluttering in that small place, the narrow place without air; and the other nuns would listen, a sickness sucking at their hearts, and thinking, in death she will still be upright. There was no room to fall; and how did she keep silence so long, knowing the dread death only an hour away, and the more dreadful judgement to follow?

'Damnation,' Christina had said, and Susan would not follow her that far; but in dreams she hung over a Biblical Hell, the steep-sided pit with its sulphur fumes and fathoms of searing fire. She could see the nun there, tossed in the tide, a small triangular face and a shorn head not yet burned away. It took eternity to burn. The face pleaded, tortured, above the white hot flux of the body; and there was a piteous beauty about it, pain and a twisted innocence . . .

But she kept her conscious thoughts away from it. Hell, to her, was a tumbler sliding, the black letters being nosed out of place. She brooded, and refused her food; the man who used to call on her had gone away long ago. When her mother, worried, showed irritation or dismay, she sprang into a ghastly sprightliness, but she found the effort more tiring than it was worth. Gradually, she was beginning to lose touch with her mother, her sisters, her friends. The girls in the office were growing tired of her moods, and she didn't care. All she wanted was to be left alone.

Prayer soothed her. Sometimes at the dinner hour she would slip out to a church, and come back late for work. Her fingers fumbled in the typewriter, her lips muttered, and peace was already slipping from her soul. So quickly . . . there was never enough time to store up peace . . .

There was a convent near her home, a small place with a tower rising over the high encircling wall, and sometimes the sisters let visitors in to look round the grounds and the less private parts of the building. She went in one day, with a handful of people. Strange how she had never been interested in it before. How quiet it was, quiet and narrow and peaceful! It frightened her, the stern discipline moulding the peace. The faces seemed all the same, like masks ...

The sister who was guiding them smiled perpetually. She smiled even in the graveyard, among the worn crosses with the names, Sister Benedicta, Vocation 21 years, Sister Martha, Vocation 15 years, Sister Perpetua, Vocation 10 years –

'You hadn't – you hadn't a Sister Christina here?' asked Susan. 'Or do you not ...?'

She had not wanted to say it. The words had come out unthinkingly, before she realized that this was the name she had been seeking all the time. 'I just wondered – maybe long ago ...?'

The nun did not answer. Only, her smile faded a little, and a closed look came into her eyes, as if she were seeing with dread, and almost with satisfaction, the horror of justice which comes to a woman breaking her vows. 'It was nothing, really,' Susan murmured, sick at the mute confirmation. 'Only a name I heard ...'

'You see all the graves here,' the nun answered.

She visited the convent again and again. The place fascinated her. She did not want to become a nun. She had a horror of eternal renunciation, the boredom of penury and penance; but at least there would be peace, time to meditate, to let her mind go till it reached the mind lost and damned – She forsook prayer, and consulted the tumbler again. Her mother, sceptical but resigned, went out of her way to help her, one worn finger on the glass, and the letters moved in little nudges, 'COME,' and more slowly, 'W-H-E-R-E I B-U-R-N.'

'It's wicked!' The woman scattered the letters, and left the glass upturned among the little cards. 'You'll have to get rid of these notions. Are you *listening*? How long is this going to last?'

'I don't know,' said Susan. 'I don't know.'

She became a novice. There was no love, no joy in her decision. All she wanted was time to meditate, to bury herself in her vision and so sate herself into peace. But there was no rest at all. The body suffered and shrank a little, and the soul was steered into paths even more strait. Work and prayer loaded the hours, and her sleep was at the mercy of bells which dragged her from her pallet to pray again. In the boredom of eternal obedience, her purpose weakened. How had she been trapped into this? She should have confessed her fantasies, had them explained away and exorcized. Her belief in them was fading; and so there was now no point in her dedication.

But she could not draw back; and now, making her last prayers before the bonds were tightened and the body tethered to the dominant soul, she went over it as if she were memorizing an old story. 'Put your fingers on the tumbler dear ...' The laughing acquiescence became the cancer-like growth of her dread. The dread had borne fruit now. She was here, swaddled and shapeless, and tomorrow the keys would turn on her.

And what good would it do? In the tight bitterness of relinquishment, she prayed for an understanding of her sacrifice. All through the long months there had been no sign, nothing to help her; and now, only half resigned, she repeated her plea.

It was so still, as she knelt, that she could hear her blood pounding out eternity. Her hands sweated, and there was sweat on her brow, and the haggard runnels of her face. If there is any purpose, show it to me, she prayed. Make Thy ways plain, O Lord ... !

She was still kneeling when the old nun came in, shuffling on chilblains, and more than half blinded with cataract. So that was how it ended, a name on a tombstone, the modest boast, Vocation – how many years? Strange how she had thought of them all as young ... but one renounced youth here. One even renounced one's name. The old nun placed a slip of paper on the bed, and went shuffling away without speaking, and the novice reached out her hand and unfolded the paper, still on her knees. It was there now, the sign, the direction, she had

pleaded all night; and as she read the two words, she knew
that prayer could no longer help her. There, in black letters,
like the letters the tumbler had chosen, was her new name,
and her destiny; her obituary, and her only epitaph,

SISTER VERONICA.

J. F. Hendry

THE CAVES OF ALTAMIRA

'Dee!'

Remote, powerful as a lioness, she gazed through him without recognition.

Again he called through the room.

'Dee!'

Her hair was a wild mane forbidding his impotent whimper.
'I am not Dee!'

Her voice felled his decision like a tree. Blind as a wrecked lighthouse, he stood empty, not daring to listen.

Out of the cyclone fell the still chair dead. Out fell the nest of tables, crackling sudden sticks. The lampshade flapped, a rag, and the whispered blankets huddled together in their leprosy.

Out fell the foul heart of her face in web. Out fell identity like a spider crawling in the distorted vision of one eye. The rear wall bulged and the carpet was sick with crumbs. Down loveless corridors aflame with the presence of dark hosts burning history, their two small rooms ran amok.

Starred in her shameless atoms she stared straight through his breast with eyes that held no mirror. Their visions settled on the furniture and on his face, like prisms, or round as the white scales on underwater stones. A strange crab there stirred two claws and shut all things in time between them. Within the pools of the pupils waters in great caverns coiled and uncoiled through the room immensities of evil.

This was happening far away. Between him and the bed rode mile upon mile of the most proud distance. He took her hand lying anchored on the cover. Remembrance in its frozen touch was ice. In the burned-out glance her knowledge glared, consumed.

Within three feet a torrent roared he could not cross. It

drowned his voice. Its foam obscured them from each other's sight. Through it they fought like enemies.

Lost he rose to light a cigarette. At once her high scream hit the silence.

'Don't light that!'

He stopped still. Another scream rang round him. Appalled, he put the cigarette down, still moist.

'You'll be burned to death!'

She was weeping. So. She was concerned. Somewhere in the recesses of her mind, memory lurked and was alive. Somewhere the life they knew stretched out its fingers into the dark and felt toward him.

In the terrible still afternoon a dying light preserved for them the city's doubtful balance. By it the man could see that though the windows shuddered in mad kaleidoscope, somewhere in their fragments constant pattern lingered, so he mirrored none of their monstrous arbitrary shapes, nor shivered when they shivered, nor wept their broken crystals.

Instead, he went over to her. She was farther than the horizon outside, yet he could touch her shoulders. He raised her hand and stroked it. It was like stroking the dead. London shrivelled. The room was suddenly as empty as a coal-bucket.

She covered her lids, turned away upward again in horrid agony.

'Go away! Go away!'

She shrieked and hid her ears from her own pathetic sound.

Over their exiled shores ebbed again the gulls of his childhood.

Stepping back he heard her moan: 'Duty! ... Duty! ... Uniform ...' and softly tiptoed into the next room. There he changed out of khaki into a grey suit.

She was not Dee. She was not his wife yet he was still her husband.

Truth lives or dies on bitterness of philosophy, he felt through tears now all the luxury of his disaster in marriage cracked in huge, mad, carnival. As he watched, she nodded a monstrous puppet head heavy with grave joy.

If he were a soldier no longer, if now he were Michael, might she not be Dee again? Had she believed to be real the terrible joke that was man's prancing pantomime – history? Would she ever return from the circus of its Hell?

As he was putting on his jacket, her voice, long and full with consciousness, sang through the doorway a fearful hymn: 'Michael! Michael! Michael!'

Running in, he saw her sit up with arms outstretched toward him, wild as love pleading for deliverance. Kneeling he embraced her and stroked her hair, kissed her forehead. Was she really Dee again? Looking in her face he wondered for how long.

'Michael, Michael, now you are Michael.'

She was sobbing with happiness.

'You don't have to go away again, do you?'

'Darling,' he asked, 'why did you say just now you were not Dee?'

'Did I, Michael? I didn't mean to. Have I been talking rubbish?'

He made no reply. In his cowardice the air was singing. The rear wall leapt back into place and the pictures smiled again bright sunlight from the captured cornfields of France.

'If you only knew all I've been through. If you only knew, Michael.'

Her grey-blue eyes were swamped with merriment.

'I've never read Kafka but I know exactly how he felt.'

A carelessness in her laughter alarmed him.

'Dear Dee, lie back and I'll make you some toast. Then, if you feel like it, we can sit together on the balcony in the sun and talk.'

'Don't bother, Michael. I'm all right, honestly I am.' She rose and began to dress, nervous and precise.

'I only need a little rest, and now you're here I can have that. Let's go out for tea, shall we?'

Suddenly they were living forward and backward, smoothly, like the pendulum of the clock . . .

2

She was wearing the fur-cape he had first seen in the little single cab as they sped over the cobbles and through the lilac in Gorizia. On the side of her head again perched the challenge of the black toreador cap. She was gay, showing all her teeth in a smile, and it might have been peace, even here in London, in the middle of a war, except for the frayed edges of other lives outside, roads paved with dust and dung, shutters sealed as coffins, blind beggared windows set in shops, wrecked ships, their locked and battered hulks battened down in crazy hope.

Here commerce was blood, crime was philosophy, business a bartering of conscience.

He crooked an arm in hers to come closer to his wonder returned.

'Dee, even if this should all go, don't let it influence you. The people who will suffer are those to whom reality is this block of flats, that cinema, the department-store, and the "Green Man", as they are and where they are. If these crumble, their minds crumble for they have none of their own. They depend for their living upon unconscious oppression. Darling, be independent of all this. Ignore it as anything but man's creation and be free . . .'

She stared at the flower-shop.

'Shall we go in here? They have teas here.'

'What's been happening, Dee?' he asked inside, in the hope of hearing a hidden clue.

'Oh, Michael, I've done some terrible things.'

He could not take his eyes off hers. They were sparkling with wit and mischief.

'What, for example?'

'I told Mrs Wax she was superficial.'

'She probably is.'

They both laughed, dancing on a bright playground in a new

communion of spirit. She had never been like this in all her life before.

'It wasn't tactful to say so, though. Don't worry over it, darling.'

They drank their coffee by a lonely drooping palm. Saccharine made it over-sweet.

'What's all this in your letter about being able to read her mask?'

'I can!'

'That's a strangely sybilline remark for you to make!'

'And do you know what I said to Miss Price? That if she were married and had a child she'd be the most perfect woman!'

'Now that was cruel, Dee! Miss Price is a wonderful person. It's cruel because it's true. You never used to say things like that. What possessed you?'

'Isn't it terrible?'

She was smiling again, tantalizing, brilliant, glancing in challenge round her now and then, mistress of this and all possible situations. What *possessed* her?

Michael grew more and more uneasy.

They walked back through the dark, talking streets and she was very happy.

'Michael,' she said, laying her hand on his arm as if it were the thought itself, 'let's go to Hampstead!'

'What? Now?'

'Yes.'

'Oh Dee, it seems so silly. Soon it will be dark, and the raid will be on.'

'I must, Michael, I must. I'll go alone then.' She stopped.

Her face hardened, a Hallowe'en mask.

Sudden dread seized him. She was moving away from him again even whilst she stood there.

'I must see the flat and the cafe where we spent the first night of the black-out. I have to face it, Michael.'

There was a battle in her face.

'Dee, don't fall into the trap of rushing around in the streets or in your mind. Excitement brings panic. I'll help you. I'm with you. Please don't go to Hampstead!'

Theories of thaumaturgy, symptoms of mental disorder, Blake's Vala, spun through his brain in dizzy rout. What were names? What could sieze and halt this horrible blight? Were the great days over? Were love and art and living no more valid now than bombed-out villas, like whores defaced by vitriol? Was she doomed by all this death and he by hers?

Surely men had made these things great and would do so again? Not the great days were over – they would never be over – but the small days were, and they knew it, therefore they wept and cursed and spat in her eyes and committed the deepest ignominy.

She was more beautiful and more heart-taking than ever. 'How would you like to go to Scotland tonight, Dee? If we rush off to Hampstead now we can't go up there. Think of seeing David?'

'It would be lovely, Michael!'

'We'll think about it, shall we?'

We'll think about it. The 10.30 p.m. out of Euston, tight as a cigarette-packet, teddy-bear soldiers, jack-in-the-box sailors, the gesticulation of iron women hiding fear in shrill laughter, mad quadrilles on the darkened platform, during a raid and in the midst of all these circles of Inferno, Dee, clinging delicately to the banisters of sanity on her steep stair.

She might have to leave the train before it crossed the border say in the Black Country. That would be all hell let loose. Questions tore at him like dogs. How could he care for her in a swaying, shouting train?

She said nothing. Together they picked their way in silence among fallen branches of blossom and scattered sand in oil, toward a grappling restaurant.

Uneasily he held her round the upper arm in futile guidance, in dumb misplaced encouragement. The place was a wilderness of white dishes, where cutlery clashed interminably like swords. Absently he chose a table. Food, all the formality of sitting and rising and paying suddenly grew ridiculous beside this grim struggle of hers.

'Please eat,' he said. 'Miss Price said you had had nothing since yesterday at noon. You're almost exhausted, Dee. Why not eat now?'

'Poor Miss Price!' Again she smiled reminiscence, as if she were living on the strangest planet, or in the lovely moon, tranquil and inspired. She seemed to shower over others so much love and interest that her own identity was gone.

'Did I tell you she was in love with the milkman?'

He stared, only half-listening.

'It's true Michael. And she can't marry him. Isn't it awful?' The terrible concern in her eyes held and tortured him. Was it a tale or a projection?

'I suppose it's just possible, even if Miss Price is sixty. God knows anything is possible these days, but how you found out I don't know.'

Her hand quivered over the tea-cup. She said nothing. She watched him hungrily until he wept for the little he could give. 'I'll fight it Michael,' she said, smiling a smile that was no smile.

Oh God, he felt, now Scotland's out. It's worse than I thought. Heart and hope sank like stones. The thing was to be normal.

He rose. 'Let's go!'

He loved her. She was his world. It seemed years since he had spoken to his world.

3

The nightly trek was ending. A few stragglers laden down with bundles of blankets and food were pulling their way along to bury in the catacombs of the tube their last and most immediate desires.

'Michael!' She turned in the dim lighting. 'Why can't we go to Hampstead?'

The old wound opened up again.

'Darling, it's much too late. Don't you see? You need lots of sleep. Let's go back and rest.'

'What time is it?'

'A quarter to seven.'

'We'd better hurry.' She quickened her step. He felt her whole rhythm change. Her breathing was less deep, less assured.

'Why?'

'The raid will begin soon.'

In clustering darkness they wound their way through hopeless streets, shrunken as home.

Back in the room he drew the pall of curtains and switched on the light. As he did so a gun boomed like a clock and the air was torn by the droning tick of time that was a bomb.

'Michael!' She started up. 'Don't you think we'd better go along to the shelter?'

'It would do me good. I could sleep in peace without these thoughts.'

Her voice was calm, but weak, like that of a convalescent. It frightened him.

She pointed to the bundle of blankets and mattresses stuffed with cushions and lying trussed on the floor like a straitjacket.

'You said a moment ago you wanted to face things. Can't we face everything here?'

'It's not that, Michael. I only need sleep.'

She was pleading now. In a second she would be abject. He picked up the bundle and they groped their way together downstairs into a darkness lit with flashes of uninspiring fire and barred with searchlights. Acrid, a furnace hung over the docks.

Three times a Bofors quick-firer barked woof, woof, woof. It seemed at his elbow. A high wasp hummed over the screaming sting. He pushed her into a doorway and knelt on one knee, staring out.

'Do what I say,' he said. 'Flat down if necessary.'

The earth sobbed twice. Gulping into the murderous lungs of air bush and flower and brick and man, the wide jaws overhead closed. The air cleared. The wasp was gone. They were at the gate now. A few yards and they saw the red light by the shelter. She stepped gratefully down the shaft into the human wine-cellar.'

'Don't let's go with the others, Michael,' she said, and whisked along the corridors to the right instead. This section was deserted, whilst the other was crowded. In it was A.R.P.H.Q., where wardens brewed tea, received reports and held the various corridors free in case of street casualties.

She sat limply on the wooden bench running along the wall. A saw outside buzzed again and the barrage in the park opened up with a sound like the kicking of colossal footballs. The walls shuddered. Dee looked at him in soft wonderment and giggled.

'I'm not frightened, Michael, honestly I'm not.'

'Now listen, Dee, lie down. I'll tuck you in and you must go to sleep. I'll read now, and make you tea later.'

She was smiling contentedly as they made the wooden bed by pulling down the extension to the bench and laying out the blankets. Then she lay down quietly and snuggled under the clothes, closing her eyes in sleep and now and then opening them to watch him and make sure he was still there.

He patted her hand. It was hot. 'Sleep Dee!' and ran his thumb over her tired lids.

'Come here!' shouted a sudden voice from the foot of the corridor. He stood up. 'Be quiet!'

'Come here!'

'Shut up!' he said, making his way angrily down.

It was a tall, trim figure in blue A.R.P. overalls and steel helmet.

'I'm the warden in charge,' he said, 'Lord Potter, and I want to know what you propose doing about the lady.'

'Speak softly, please, she's almost asleep.'

He was angry now.

'I am her husband. I can do nothing if you keep interrupting. She has been very excited recently. I hope to calm her now I'm on leave.'

He suddenly felt hate for all these people with so little understanding, or even human tact.

'Oh, very well, you'll be responsible for her?'

'I'll be responsible.'

Dee was awake when he went back, and laughing. 'I'm Lord Potter,' she said. 'This is my shelter.'

'Go to sleep, darling,' he insisted. She closed her eyes again.

The raid grew in intensity. From the next trench came a snore. Now the guns were bounding about like dogs, baying at the raiders in the moon.

She laughed in her sleep and opened her eyes. 'I'm not afraid,' she repeated. 'I'm only thinking of Uncle Peter. He used to snore like that. Isn't it funny, Michael?' She smiled and her eyes wrinkled up in such delight that his heart was torn between pleasure at her loveliness and fear for her existence.

She was leading, not he.

More thuds shook the riveted trench, and he saw terror, like a robin, perch in her eyes. They were far away and listening. As the barrage opened up again she trembled. Shells became indistinguishable from bombs in the screaming chaos outside. 'Dee,' he said, 'that's Charlie up there, you know. All our R.A. friends are up there on the predictors and height-finders and 4.7s, all the men from the Dragon Battery.'

She came back and smiled at him. 'I know.'

The light flickered as he dozed. He was aware that it was very cold. The world was an oblong box. There was nothing anywhere but Dee, and he could not find her.

He opened his eyes, and there she was across the narrow corner, staring at him again, inscrutably, as if puzzled, as if not knowing whether to be hostile or not, with a terrible objectivity, almost like a cat.

'Sleep, Dee?' he whispered, but even as he whispered she was slowly rising. 'Let's go,' she said. Terror struck him, but she was still all right, still in the dimensions of his world. 'It's too cold here. There's a stove in the next trench.'

For a moment she looked at him and then laughed. 'Poor Michael,' she said, laying her hand on his again, 'You shouldn't worry so much, I'm all right. Tomorrow we'll go to a psychologist together, shan't we, Michael? Take me to a good psychologist.'

'I'll take you, Dee. You're a little run down, that's all, a little restless. Don't allow the restlessness to win, darling. I need you as much as you need me, you know. Think of that.'

'Let's see Mrs Wax,' she said. 'We mustn't disturb them, though.'

Together they crept through the silent corridors and down the alleys of no thought, he with the mattress, she with the basket, toward No 3 Shelter. The shells were still thudding outside in far-off lobs, and an occasional bomb pierced the distance, whining against the police-whistles.

In No 3 they were all asleep: girls, old women with shawls, youths, old men with sticks, teapots, baskets, paper-bags, sandwiches, gloves, rouge, powder and dust, all stilled in the long mercy.

She picked her way over the outstretched feet and chairs toward a free space on one bench. There she lay down, but now she was more concerned with him, as if a battle was about to begin in her, or was over. She put her hand out from the blankets and touched his as he lay across the passage.

'It's lovely to have you here, Michael,' she breathed, eyes wide with happiness. 'You're losing sleep because of me, though. Goodnight, dear Michael!'

He could not sleep with any comfort. Always now he was waiting for something. The spaces in the bench imprinted their pattern on his back.

The oil lamp flickered and threw heavy tongues of shadows over the sleeping figures. The raid grew in intensity, loud as gongs, a veritable inferno of explosion and shuddering, rocketing, pivoting, thud and counter thud, menacing all life.

Yet the people slept on. Down their several layers of concrete peace and slabs of comparative apathy they slept on.

He rose to go to the latrine bucket behind the curtain of sacking at the end of the cold stone corridor, and returning, almost tripped over the feet of an affluent Jewess with the expression and breast of an owl. Surprisingly she flashed hatred up at him.

'You're back! Well, I hope for your sake, your wife will be all right.'

What had happened while he was away? Christ, if war could strip people like that and reveal their 'real' selves there would always be wars, until everybody was stripped. That false old whore was a root cause. He could have slapped her for her cruelty, the bad taste, the rudeness, the sheer spite in her face, but he walked on instead, torn, without a word.

Just as he was getting under the blankets Dee screamed twice and rose up in her bed, eyes dismantled with horror, and arms outstretched, barriers against fearful despair. 'This is a tomb. Let me out! Stop the war! It's a tomb.'

He jumped forward to take her in his arms, but she fell back unconscious.

The battle was on.

'Dee,' he called, 'Dee! My darling!' On one knee, forgetful of everybody. Ungraciously the Jewess handed him some smelling-salts. He waved them under Dee's nostrils. To his knowledge she had never fainted before. They had no effect.

He prised open her lids. The pupils were turned upwards back into the head. She was gone, he knew. This was her body. 'Dee, Dee,' he called in urgent agony. 'Trying to escape me, eh? Well you won't, not that way!' Saying anything that came into his head to hurt, frighten, shock or love her into living.

There was a faint flicker in one eye. She was staring at him. She knew him. 'Michael,' she said, and her whole face melted into a compassionate smile.

'Darling, sniff this.' He held out the bottle. 'I think we'd better go. The raid's over, and it's not cold any more. A walk through the park would be nice as the light is coming up.'

'Yes,' she said, 'we'll do that, Michael, we'll do that.' He kept her busy tying up the wretched bundles, so that she should not fall away again into the pit of heaven. 'This is a horrible place,' he said. 'There's no peace here.'

4

Together they walked back along the paling moonlight into the appalled town. It was too early for anyone to be astir.

No one wore newspaper aprons at the corners of the street. No one trundled milk in trays of white shells, there was no whistling or singing in the panting city. Instead, the red lamps burned low as anger keeping the blood lit, and policemen stood about lost. Roads irrelevant as ribbons stretched into speechless distance.

Together they walked past the disembowelled house over the way from the gardens. Into its empty heart wound a tumbled path of ruin paved with the bricks and rubble of disordered mind. Man builds the world in his own image. This was the Catacomb of murder once suspended in some brain like a sick cell, upside down like the bat of history.

Together they passed down the lane of the boulevard that had no turning and came to catacomb No 2. This was the crater under the pastry shop, a gaping hole tearing at the sunken water-pipe as if it were a jugular vein. 'Wait for me,' she used to say, 'I want to buy some bread!'

It was delicious and French. Now she did not want to buy any bread. The whole building was rent in two and sagging like a wedding-cake shorn of icing. This was the Catacomb of Appetite.

By the pillars of a store they came to the 3rd, scarcely visible and most terrible of all; a rent between pavement and glass where a bomb had fallen at an angle of 45 degrees. Inside lay drowned 14 people, caught in the burst of a water-main and drenched in the once hidden flood. This was the Catacomb of Fear in tears dropped from an airman's eye.

How many more mailed fists of urgent bombs would punch high caves in the moonlit streets? How many more fiery catacombs lay hidden in the cheek of the clouds? How many more nights would blot the memory, the people, the skies, and the jagged shop-face shored up with wooden sticking plaster?

'Isn't it lovely, Michael?' Dee breathed. She was looking at the hanging sky, pin-pointed still with stars, her arm crooked in his.

'Oh, Dee,' he said as they turned into their own street, where the floors rose like waves and the bank was nowhere ...

'Are you all right? Look at me! Answer me!' She was staring rapt at the moon, almost on tiptoe, seeing nothing – or a vision.

As they moved toward the house her body slowly went rigid. Her head fell back. 'I love John!' she gasped, and swooned in his arms.

For a moment he stood like a statue, unable to realize what had happened. Then he propped her against the wall, slapped her cheeks, intending to fetch a glass of water. Instead, light dawned in her face. Languidly she moved. Wearily she made for the gate.

'Dee, are you all right?'

She looked up, not at him, no, at the early morning sky again, and her whole face cleared. 'There's nothing to worry over, Michael,' she said, still watching the moon.

Mercy was in her face, more glorious awareness than his. He did not exist in that world.

He saw the railings round the house all rimmed with tears. 'Let's go in,' he muttered, feeling for the key.

It was afternoon when she awoke.

'How are you?' he asked, going to and fro, preparing tea and hoping she noticed.

Her teeth were tight, Her eyes glared in anger. A deep and husky voice he had never heard before said, sitting in her throat:

'I AM RENATA!'

There was the strength of a leopard in her face. He was too stunned to speak. All the theories he had ever listened to were useless. This madness was an 'Anfall,' a fall, an occurrence, a happening that had to happen, an apparition, natural as an avalanche. Now he could see, and desperately strove with it. His mind raced. Forty-eight hours leave. Time to take her to a clinic. They would not know her story. They would take weeks, months, to discover it if left alone. And how good would they be? How sympathetic?

He began to jot down her remarks. It might help. Now he must think of nothing but 'the case'.

Could he get her to Scotland? Would it be better to apply for an extension of leave and take her into the country? They could lease a cottage. His sister, perhaps, could come down. He could beat back the attacks, calm her, make her the Dee he once knew or the Dee she wanted to be, if he had time, though it took years.

Now the voice was different.

'I am Helen,' it said mincingly. 'Don't you know me? Helen!'

Affected though the accent was, it was yet more of an incarnation than an imitation.

She moaned, then suddenly shouted in her own voice, 'I'll help you, Michael! I'll help you!'

Despairingly, in tears. 'Take this down!' she said, seeing him make a note, and began a long rambling account of her trip two years before through Jugoslavia, full of innuendoes, intended to shock and wound.

'In Skoplje I was arrested as a spy. The officer took me into his office and locked the door.'

'Well?'

'He kissed me!'

'Oh Michael, Michael, there was a man in Cleveland once at a party. He was waiting for me upstairs. They were all drunk. He seized me and forced his kisses on me. He was a brute ... I liked it ...'

His heart was wrung like a wet cloth. Mad she might be, but she was taunting him. The width of death in these eyes was reasoning him out of his wits. She became soft, sympathetic.

'What would you say, Michael, if I became a prostitute?'

'What do you mean, Dee?'

'What I say. If I went out now and picked up a man in the street?'

'Which man?'

'Any man?'

She was watching him narrowly, beating the frightened

reason out of him with a flail, and yet, surely he must retain it if he were to help her.

'Oh Dee,' he said. 'You're trying to test me, aren't you?'

She suddenly relaxed, went limp, turned away. 'I suppose I am.'

The sun fell through the window. The fire glittered dim, as if going out. He rose, poked it, heaped on coal, and then went through to the desperate kitchen to light the stove. Water dreared hopelessly into the kettle. Dust ground the shelves like slag. He dared not leave for a minute. He was fearful of the window.

Now he collected the Copenhagen cups on to a tray and took them in. She sat up almost brightly.

'Michael, this is lovely!'

'Isn't it?' He tried to smile.

Her swift amnesia, visions and transformations, blinding and buffeting, still cuffed him dumb.

He poured out the tea, gave it her, and was pouring out his own when he felt rather than noticed, her pause. Looking up he saw her staring in horror into the bottom of the cup.

'It's terrible!' she shouted, and raising her arms high as she could deliberately dashed cup and saucer on the floor. They broke into jumping fragments, and lay jagged in his heart.

'Oh Dee,' he said, gathering then up. 'Oh Dee!'

These were her cups. She had chosen them and loved them for their curving lips and cool green shade. They had been comely and peaceful Sunday mornings of sun and coffee together, and perhaps the dusty trees of Duino.

Now he knew indeed that it was all over.

'Mama quel vino è generoso!' she sang, in a tragic rant.

The tones, deep and unbound, were seeking for their ghost. Loud were all the evenings she had spent at the opera, and the gestures of Rosa Ponselle twisted into pathetic caricature. The caps and the gowns and the taxis and the music tumbled over each other in waves discordant and uncontrollable as New York honkey-tonk.

Through them shone the bloodshot orange groves of Sicily and the wrecked smacks of Santa Lucia Luntana. All the folk-songs and the trumpets and the cries and consolation of man for his lost liberty tumbled down to meet the sea's green jealousy. The Arch of Trajan lay strangled in myrtle, the broken spinal column of Europe.

Swiftly he leapt up and ran downstairs to Miss Price. She stood at the door, precise, cool, awake as a heron. 'Now she's worse, Miss Price,' he said. 'Much worse. I must go to the doctor and find out what he has to say. Can you look after her? I'm afraid to leave her now for a second!'

'Certainly.'

Miss Price's face shone in a reassuring smile, like the sun appearing from behind a cloud.

'She'll be all right, Mr Mason.'

He rushed out.

5

The afternoon was still. The streets deserted. Everywhere all that had been living was coming to a halt. Only the trees still budded and the birds still sang, either unconscious of hazard or from their long conquest of it.

As he passed through the streets he scarcely felt the bomb crater at the corner of the gardens, which had maimed the railings like limbs and dug its fiery metal in the rhododendron's heart. That was the one that had almost blown up the floor of the cinema when he and Dee were there one Sunday – in a terrible fountain of sympathy. He missed the long Moscow Road, ripped across from door to door like a rag. These were old friends and old wounds. It was the doctor's street that really appalled him. The sense of desolation there and in his mind was absolute. Nothing lay beyond. Nothing, nothing.

In a row five houses, one after the other, lay broken and crumbled like teeth that had been cut by a careless dentist. The gardens, limp and pock-marked, were a breeding-ground for blowflies and the torn cobbles, tongueless as old boots, shouted flight.

Most of the remaining homes lay empty and barred in grime. Nothing mattered in these wastes, neither wealth, nor hope, nor pity, nor even life.

What if the doctor were out? Or indifferent? It was his duty to remain! This was the front-line! Indifference to life was graver than looting! Yet he wasn't in the army. Why should he bother? We have armies because obligations are fulfilled only under compulsion.

He might be gone, or dead. The house was still standing. He ran up the path and rang the bell. It jangled in his ears among the ruins.

As was to be expected, the doctor was distant, even un-friendly, matter-of-fact, that is never a fact. He remembered Dee. 'She is neurotic,' he said, with an air of final dismissal, guarding in that knowledge his own sanity.

'She is more than that now, doctor. What can I do for her?'

'It's up to you. If you think she should go to a hospital, send her there.'

'Is there hope for her there?'

Again the jangling bell among the ruins. 'Oh yes, many are cured nowadays. Oh yes, ohyes, oyez, oyez ... blah ...'

'You will be responsible for her,' said the warden. 'Yes, I'll be responsible.'

'You are responsible for her,' said the doctor.

'I'll be responsible.'

RESPONSIBLE!

As he turned down the shattered street, he saw a raid was in progress. Wardens stood at corners, less like shepherds than awkward mothers.

Thunder was coming out of the sun. Soon a machine-gun crackled, like something being broken to pieces. He hurried home, oblivious to the larger, less real storm. Even its violence was a kind of vulgar jazz.

Fearfully again he opened the door and stood still a moment. The stairs were quiet, and the thick walls of the building seemed to seal it off from the outside. Rushing to meet him before she herself could hope to do so, often he had heard her voice sing out as she came up.

'Michael! Michael!' In two clear notes.

All was silent now. All the steps and doors and handles and windows and banisters were casting off and saying time's up, and we never were part of you anyway, though we had no objection to assisting to this little dénouement of yours. He stood looking at them for a moment and listened, as if something of the past might help to restore the present, then went in. Dee glanced up fixedly, with determination and some unimportant kind of recognition (it's only Michael!), as if looking through him, puzzling over something. Her face twisted into an expression of distaste.

'Who am I?' she asked.

He dropped on one knee again.

'You're Dee. Your name is Ussai.'

She thought it over and could not place it, so glorious, so great was her mind.

'Where was I born?'

'In Gorizia.'

She tried to remember, as if she had been asked 'Where were you at 3.35 last Monday?' It was no good. She couldn't.

He drew the black-out curtains.

The problem now was to – what? Clinic? Hospital? She would have 'attention'. She would have people to bring her tea at the wrong times, a bed to lie in, other people to stare at, sedatives from those who would not share or fight or influence her thoughts and emotions. Tomorrow might be too late.

He stroked the fire as the first bomb fell. The flames fizzled slowly and drowsily. The one important thing was that she should have some sleep. Her eyes appalled him. They were wild as hydras. Her weakness turned him to water. He gave her a dose of bromide.

In a few minutes she sat up in bed and looked at him sorrowfully. He realized as he had not done before that she was still real, she was still Dee. Her lovely shoulders bunched under his hands like ripe apples, her arms and her body, still firm and brave against his, were sane, and not the limp patient he had thought. She was Dee. For that he must save her. Consciousness and love swept over him as he seized and kissed her, embracing her all over. 'Darling Dee!' he said. 'You *must* be all right! How can I bear anything to happen to you? Tell me what it is!'

She smiled, and he could not say if she knew him or not. 'I like the way you kissed me,' she said.

It was almost ten o'clock. He half-undressed and slipped into bed beside her. Not to sleep, no, to lie awake, to watch her, to comfort her if possible, to reach her with his touch, hand, arm and body, with his mind and voice and lips. In spite of himself he dozed, lost all sense of time and urgency, drifted. Then suddenly he leapt awake, to see her struggling from the clothes, to hear her shouting. For a split second he thought it was a horrible dream. No. He had *awakened* this time into nightmare. He saw this for the crisis it was.

'What's the matter?' he rasped. Too much sympathy here was dangerous. She looked lost, uncomprehending, hostile.

'I am waiting,' she said.

'Waiting? For whom?'

'For Landini!'

'Who is Landini?'

'I love him!' she cried, backing up against the wall.

For a moment he felt a pang of jealousy. Then, remembering she had said she also loved John, he wondered if it could be a real name.

'You must save him, Michael! You must! ... He's deaf! You must go back to Trieste and save him ... He's the naval man there ... remember?'

'You never met him!' said Michael, caught out. 'Besides, why should I go back and save him if you love *him*?' This again to see the effect on the possible illusion.

She was nonplussed.

'Oh, I'll stay with you, Michael. I won't leave you, but you must go, otherwise I'll never be able to see you again,' she went on, almost in a frenzy.

'Never be *able*?' So it was *himself* she wanted to see? And who was he?

'All right,' he promised, 'but you'll have to help me. Let me have some names.'

He began to write them down again to quiet her, make her feel something was being done for these oppressed and murdered friends and relations of hers, shot, exiled, press-ganged into fascist armies of ignorance, those, the masses of loved ones who somehow also were the despised and neglected hopes and desires of her own unconscious being.

The list became long and dreary. Raving slightly, she lay back. Then in a corner of her eye tilted the sunlit Piazza del Duomo. She saw again the pigeons, and in the distant blue the Sabotino and Monte Grappa, the Isonzo, stretching up into old Austria, and fell asleep again.

He could not sleep. Instead, very quietly, in the small room, he listened to the raid, and leaned forward to poke the fire gently. The black-out was not quite perfect at the top, so he could not switch on the lights, but the fire could be fed so that the flames cast enough dim light to see her, and no more.

He hated the raid for its attempt in pandemonium to obscure this far more fatal struggle. He knew no falling bomb would damage the house in the least, however fierce grew the 'blitz', for it was but the background set to her despair. That was his enemy, since he loved her, her despair. He hated that too, and all the mournful brood and death of despair outside. To fight one must know one's enemy. Who was the enemy?

'I am the enemy,' he said.

How much of all this was his own fault he was well aware. Egotism affected 'beliefs'. Too facile acceptance of conventional unfaith had at least partly caused this reaction in one who loved him and found only destruction in stupid reason.

She opened her eyes again. They were no longer shut with terror. They were smiling. Her whole face was youthful. It was a child's innocent, delighted and shy face. Was she a child? She pulled the blankets round her chin and kept on smiling as if just awakened from a long, refreshing sleep. It was a miracle, it was not natural. She was living acres of experience he could never enter.

'Who is Landini?' he asked suddenly, hoping to startle her into telling him. She laughed. 'Oh, that's a name I made up!' He wondered. That might be an explanation and a way out. If she loved someone else and yet could not tell him, it might well cause such a conflict in her mind that death or madness seemed the only escapes. Could he give her up to someone else? To John? If he knew it would make her whole and happy again? The mere thought of it was a terrific wrench – like having one's arm torn off. She and John. Yes, he decided, he'd risk facing even that to have her well. She'd have been far better with someone like that, anyway. A regular life, a regular income, a settled and distinguished future to which she might look forward. What could such a man as he offer a woman? Hazard, neglect, often 'failure', deliberately elected by him in his mono- mania. He had no right even to look at a woman. Now he even hoped she was in love with John! Anything to break up this night and this chaos. He'd see John in the morning. An- other thought struck him. 'Can't you see Dee? I am Landini! I love you, and you're trying to struggle through to me. Can't you see? You've made a figure out of London – I'm that figure!' He pressed her hands.

'Yes!' she breathed, eyes almost glassy. 'You are. You are Landini!'

'And I'm all the others as well!' he cried in his happiness. 'I'm John, and the milkman Miss Price loves and can't marry, and Reg, whom Miss White loves but can't marry. Don't you see? I'm all these people! I'm Michael and you *can* marry me, darling. You're my wife. We *are* married!'

'I'm tired, Michael,' she said, 'so tired. And I'm weak. My poor arms. I can scarcely raise them!' Sitting on the floor by the bed. 'Oh, Dee darling!' He broke into tears. 'What can I do for you. I was away too long, darling. I should have been looking after you. You've had nothing to eat for days! I'll make you something now.'

As he rose a circle of guns all round him flamed and boomed. The room was lit for a second in a ghostly light by a flare as her stranded face looked up at him. 'Why do I hate black?' she asked. 'I hate it! I hate it!'

She was staring in horror at the black-out curtain. 'You hate it because it is dark, Dee, and because it is where fascism and repression and fear and the proud tyranny of Venezia Giulia lie hidden.'

'Yes,' she said. 'I hate it, ugh, I wouldn't touch it.'

'Sleep, Dee,' he said. 'Go to bed and sleep.'

She lay down, still preoccupied, and turned her face to the wall.

He put more coal on the fire so that it would not go out during the night, and switching off the light went to bed, not to sleep though, to lie awake and yet asleep all night long if necessary in case she should suddenly start up or do something dangerous, even homicidal. Nevertheless he was so tired that he dropped off in spite of himself.

6

When he awoke it was to see her rising in crisis to ward off some gigantic enemy only she could see, and to hear a shower of bombs falling around the house. Flames from the fire cast shadows on the wall that licked hungrily.

'What is it, Dee?' he asked.

Face contorted with suffering, she was an alien wild being again.

'I am the Devil!' she shouted at him.

'Dee,' he said gently, pleadingly, 'sit down, darling, in the chair!'

He wrapped a dressing gown about her shoulders, while she continued to stare at him balefully, menacingly.

Then he stirred the fire and sat down opposite.

'What is it, Dee?' The flames must not be too high or they would show over the black-out and invite a bomb. The guns still boomed and flared in Bayswater. The attacks were constant. The house shook.

'I am the Devil,' she said, glaring at him, face ashen grey, rent with weariness and wax with evil.

'There is no devil,' he said. For a moment the atmosphere was electric, tense. She was following every word, the least mistake in logic, the least insincerity, would lead to any desperate absurdity.

'There is a devil!'

'Dee, the devil does not exist. He is always trying to exist, but he does not exist, he can never exist, that is his doom. As soon as he appears, he withers. Say it, Dee. There is no devil.' The words came mechanically. 'There is no devil.'

The suffering went from her face. She was inert, motionless, the picture of despair, as she looked without expression into the fire.

He watched. Suddenly she stared again.

'I am a prostitute!' she shouted.

'Yes,' he said, 'like the devil. What is a prostitute, Dee? You are Dee. Prostitutes don't exist either. They are dead people trying to exist, but they don't, not as prostitutes.'

He jumped forward and looked at her.

'Dee.' She looked down and slowly her face changed again. She smiled in commiseration.

Twice in ten seconds her whole face had changed as completely as if the whole personality were different. She was a different person.

For a long time she looked into the fire, and when he saw her look at him again, it was as if she knew everything, as if in ten minutes she had seen his whole future, and aged thirty years. Her eyes were full of pity and tears and understanding for him, her face drawn and grey with disaster. She sat motionless and old, like a Sybil. There was nothing more to be said. He helped her to bed. She was utterly worn out. Her face was more terribly pitted than all the craters in the streets. She was turning into ash before his very eyes in a Catacomb of Terror.

7

In the morning it was all over. She was trembling and she was beyond aid.

'My husband is not a soldier,' she said to the nurse who came to fetch her. 'He's an admiral and the best of admirals. Oh, you're so kind. Take that grin off your face, Michael. Look at it, that grin at the side of his mouth, like an Epstein Christ. I like you,' she said to the warder, and winked. – 'You see my husband was nothing but reason, reason, reason, we should all be like little dwarfs. Oh, I know where we're going. I can take it.' She kicked her heels in the air like an overgrown schoolgirl.

The woman, the books, the furniture he loved, were bidding him good-bye without a word. There was no friend, no relative, no smile, no belief, or even purpose at this white funeral. 'This is her story,' he said to the nurse. 'Please give it to the psychiatrist. I shall be writing him, and I'll tell him anything I can.'

She was gone. He saw a book on the floor. It was Russell's *Principles of Philosophy*. Blindly he kicked at it, through tears. More in heaven and earth than dreamt of in your philosophy, said Shakespeare to him, but her face was cold as the bust of Lawrence, and everything was full of silence, and everything had begun to grow dust, and everything had begun to hide its head. He would never again find anything to touch and be alive because things would never again be friendly. Always they would flee from him.

It was night again when he telephoned the blue hospital where the mad and wounded fought for the white life of the ghosts of the warders, but he knew the answer before it came, he felt the answer in his face.

Through the disinherited city the gale was blowing all before it. It blew all the lights into flickering pin-heads of hope, or prancing columns of slow ghosts. It blew houses into eroded hills. It raised mountains of wreck where the ore of the universe hid in a corpse.

It blew whole streets into fountains and littered their dumb seas with the frozen waves of brick. It shuffled the docks like cards.

Through her face and through her eyes it blew the purple lilac and the lovely windings of the Sava under Ljubno. Along the paths of mountainous cheeks in Europe barefoot she ran to stir the belfry in Slovenia with its jester's jangling cap and bells.

Turbulent invisible mountains, raining down all belongings on her appalled ears, spent her childhood on the orphaned pavement. Her shadow exploded. – 'I'm sorry,' said a voice at the other end of the city, – 'Mrs Mason died this evening at seven o'clock.'

– 'I know,' he said, still listening.

What was there to do? The carpet would never have anyone to walk on it again. No one would ever sit on the ridiculous chair. There would never be anything on the little tables of the law.

The stove was stiff with the beard of tea. The matches froze in fat. The curtain flapped in sympathy with the gale.

Where were the snows of the Great Lakes and the long rains of Lombardy? Feeling blindly in the cupboard he found a still bottle. It was champagne. Pouring it into the glass was like opening the cage of a canary, a freeing, not a celebration.

He drank it up.

Then, spinning the glass in his fingers, he looked round at the room. They were the same.

The world had come to an end – in the Catacomb of Love.

Robin Jenkins

CHRISTIAN JUSTICE

In Kalimantan there are secondary schools where more than half the staffs are Tamil Indians, both men and women. Science and mathematics departments are staffed almost exclusively by them. They are said to know their subjects well enough, and to be conscientious in teaching them, particularly the women, who would really have to be dedicated seeing that at the end of each month, according to Indian custom, they hand over their salaries to their husbands, without deduction or demur.

The majority of these Indians are Christians, of the first or second generation; in very few cases does the connexion with the Western faith go back far. This may be the reason for their curious lack of understanding of it, their preference for many Hindu customs such as arranged marriages and dowries, and their adoption as their own surnames of the Christian names of those Scots or English missionaries who converted their fathers or grandfathers. Thus they are known rather abruptly and truncatedly as Mr George or Mr John or Mr James, and so on, with nothing at all to come after. But a rather more serious shortcoming, as a result of this belated embracing of the faith, is their naive but absolute inability to appreciate that the words of Christ, read in the Bible and heard from pulpits, were supposed by Him to be guidance for one's conduct in one's daily life, and not simply sonorous reiterations. They do not, in short, have the sophisticated hypocrisy of centuries to hide behind. Therefore the contrast between what they smile at in church and what they actually do outside it is often as conspicuous as their women's bright saris. Sin, in the Christian sense, is for them newly minted.

To Api had come from a small town in Madras State Mr and Mrs Kishan, he to teach science and she mathematics. They were not young when they first arrived, he being fifty-four, she five years less; that had been six years ago. With two sons in England, one studying law and the other medicine, they had to live quite carefully, in order to be able to send the necessary allowances every month. If Mr Kishan had any serious failing it was gluttony: he could consume a whole chicken and a heap of rice twice as large as it at a sitting, and yet be interested in his next meal. To compensate, however, he neither smoked nor drank. As for his wife, small, stout, and grey-haired, addicted to drab saris, her big fault, if it could be called a fault, was a tendency to go down on her knees there and then if she heard of a friend's trouble, and pray aloud for him or her, invariably bringing more embarrassment than solace. Still, since he was not living in starving India, where six could have been fed from his plate, and since her impromptu prayers did no harm that anyone could prove, they had become well-established and respected in the Indian community. It could have been said, and indeed was said, by the vicar of All Saints for instance under whom they worshipped, that, considering their newness to the faith, they were exemplary Christians.

It would be hard to say therefore what came over them that set them off on their amazing persecution of young Mrs Kumar. It could scarcely have been because she was a Hindu, for the Kishans had several friends who were Hindus. She was a young Indian woman who came to teach biology in the school where Mrs Kishan taught mathematics. Her husband, who had gone to India to fetch her, without ever having seen her before, was an Education Officer with a job in administration. Unfairly, according to Mr Kishan, he had recently been promoted into Division I, whereas Mr Kishan, almost twice his age, had applied three times for similar upgrading and three times had been refused. But it could scarcely have been this professional jealousy, though bitter enough, that caused the Kishans' vendetta against Kumar's pretty young wife.

Nor could it have been her prettiness, her pale good skin, and her neat figure that did not need to be hidden under saris. Mrs Kishan, now a very mature woman of fifty-five, had long ago given up being disappointed with her own swarthiness, her pocked cheeks, and her corpulence. Moreover, though she had herself never worn anything but saris, and dull ones at that, she had no objection in principle to young Indian women occasionally wearing dresses or even, on picnics, slacks or jeans. Perhaps the young couple were less religious and more sporty than the Kishans thought seemly in Indians, playing tennis not only on weekdays but also on Sundays, with Mrs Kumar wearing a very short white skirt that revealed far too much of her slender legs. But since the vicar himself played golf on Sunday, and since his wife played tennis on that day wearing shorts shorter than Mrs Kumar's skirt, with less beautiful legs to display, it would have been absurd for the Kishans to have hated Mrs Kumar on this account alone, and up to this point they had never been absurd in all their lives, having on the contrary a reputation for sense and propriety.

Above all, thickening the mystery, Mrs Kumar, as befitted a newcomer to the staff, was quiet, humble, deferential, willing to take advice, pleased to sit and listen to her more experienced elders, and, if noticeably vivacious, careful to curb it. She was really everything that an Indian woman of Mrs Kishan's generation and background would have wished for in a daughter or even a daughter-in-law. Yet within a month of Mrs Kumar's coming to the school Mrs Kishan, abetted by her husband, had embarked upon a persecution of her, endangering their own reputations and careers in an attempt to ruin hers.

The Kishans of course thought, and said, that there was no mystery at all. It was very plain. They simply suspected, or rather they knew, for they had no doubts, that Mrs Kumar was being paid on a scale (incidentally higher than Mrs Kishan's) to which she was not entitled. She, or her husband, for like all Indian wives she was under his domination in all things, had falsified her qualifications, claiming to be a graduate of a certain University when, according to the Kishans, she had no degree at all. Therefore she was being paid more than her due because of a lie. As a good Christian Mrs Kishan considered it her duty not to allow this falsehood and dishonesty to flourish; and her husband considered it his to assist her.

It was Mrs John, who rather innocently started it off. A buck-toothed, cheerful, little woman, she was herself more amused than shocked by Mrs Kumar's duplicity. In her laughing sing-song voice she had said, 'Yes indeed, it is true, Mrs Kishan. I was at the same University, you know. But I was some years older. My sister was in her same year. My sister writes to me to say she did not sit her degree examination. I understand she was sick. But how could she pass if she does not sit? It is not possible. What do you say, Mrs Kishan?'

Mrs Kishan could say nothing. A voice roared in her ears. There was suddenly a great pain in her belly as if someone had kicked her there. A hand or iron seemed to have her by the throat. Afterwards, when telling her husband, she was to suggest humbly that it must have been the Lord letting her know what He wanted her to do on His behalf.

'It is very true, Mrs Kishan,' said Mrs John, taking Mrs Kishan's gasps and chokings to be caused by incredulity or by indignation at Mrs John herself for having said such a dreadful thing about pretty young Mrs Kumar. 'And it is wrong, I think, to say you have a degree if you have none. My husband says to me, "Be quiet, woman; it is not your business. If she wishes to lie and risk disgrace for the sake of money then it is her affair, not yours or mine." But of course he is a man, and Mrs Kumar is pretty.'

'It is a terrible sin, Mrs John,' whispered Mrs Kishan.

Mrs John was the kind of Indian Christian who giggled at the word 'sin', she hurried to say, still giggling a little, 'Yes, yes, it is a sin. To lie is always a big sin. What a bold woman she must be though she does not look very bold. My husband says it is Kumar her husband who is the guilty one. He is a man who loves money. Yet I must say he lets her buy many beauti-ful saris: nylex saris, made in Japan.'

Mrs Kishan was not listening to that nonsense. 'Is this true that you have said?' she whispered.

Mrs John took in her hand the gold wedding chain round her neck. 'I would swear it on this chain.'

'Would you swear it on the sacred book?'

'Do you mean the Bible?'

'Yes, the Bible.'

Mrs John shook her head. 'No, Mrs Kishan, I am a Christian, as you know, but I am afraid of such swearing. Also, my husband would not permit me.'

'He should permit you, for he is a Christian himself. But it does not matter. I shall look for other proof.'

Two days later, Mrs Kishan was knocking at the principal's door.

'Come in, come in, whoever you are, or else the devil will catch you, as we use to say in Ireland when I was a boy. Ah, it's your own good self, Mrs Kishan. How wrong I was then. The devil hasn't got the legs to catch the likes of you.'

Father Duffy was from Dublin. Shrivelled and yellow-faced after twenty years in the tropics, he was still alert and cheerful in mind. Dressed in white cassock, he was standing with a book in his hand. He had a cigarette in his mouth. Often he spoke without removing it. He regretted this, as a rude habit, but refused to agree that the Anglicans on his staff, such as the lady now before him, were justified in denouncing Rome because of it.

'And what can I do for you, dear lady?' he asked. 'If you're thinking you've interrupted me in reading the life of a saint, have no worry. This is merely a good old-fashioned murder yarn. You look troubled. What's the matter this time? Have the Lower Sixth been playing pranks again? These Chinese youths have the weirdest sense of humour, I must say.'

'It is not about the Lower Sixth I wish to speak to you, Father Duffy. It is about a member of your staff.'

'Nothing serious, I hope.'

'Very serious indeed, I am sorry to say.'

'I'm sorry too, Mrs Kishan. But shouldn't we have her here to hear what you've got to say? I'm taking it she's one of the ladies.'

'She is a woman, Mrs Kumar.'

'Yes. I've noticed you don't seem to approve of her for some reason. I've been surprised, because she strikes me as a pleasant well-intentioned young woman who wouldn't hurt an ant.'

'You do not know her if you say such things.'

'I didn't think you knew her all that well. She's only been here a month. You didn't know her before she came here.'

'She is a liar and a cheat. She must be dismissed and punished. Immediately. It is very urgent.'

'Good God. What are you saying, woman? That's a slanderous statement, you know.'

'It is a truthful statement. She has no degree, but on her papers she has said she has. She must be exposed without delay. It is bad for your school, Father. It is bad for us all.'

'Now hold on. Aren't we jumping over too many streams here? What proof have you got?'

'Plenty. Three ladies, including Mrs John of your own staff, who were at the same university, say Mrs Kumar did not gain a degree.'

'Do they, by God? All Indians?' And all as plain as broomsticks, he wanted to add.

'All Christians, Father. One of them is a Roman, like yourself. You are right to say God is offended.'

'I wasn't aware I had said anything of the kind. I should think Our Heavenly Father has rather more to bother Him, what with this Vietnam War and the hunger in your own country, Mrs Kishan.'

Mrs Kishan had not listened to that rebuke. She was like a lioness that, with one deer by the throat, had no interest in any other.

'First she must be exposed, then she must be dismissed, and finally she must be punished.'

He came over and laid his hand on her shoulder. He was not surprised to feel it trembling. Her face and voice indicated great stress. He could not understand why. He knew she was supposed to be devout, in a superficial kind of way, but she was about the last woman he would have expected to show fanaticism. He wondered if there could be some purely Indian reason for her hatred. She had two sons. Was it possible Mrs Kumar had been promised to one of them? No, it couldn't be that, for Mrs Kishan herself had said she hadn't known Mrs Kumar previously.

'With all respect to your Christian principles, Mrs Kishan,' he said, 'I'm perplexed as to why you should let this distress you so much. I'm supposed to have Christian principles too, professionally you might say, but it doesn't distress me at all to think she may be getting a dollar or two more than she's strictly entitled to. All teachers are underpaid, if it comes to that.'

'It is forty-five dollars per month, Father Duffy. But even if it was only one cent it would be a sin.'

'Ah, there you're on my ground. Yes, even if it was one cent.'

'I agree.'

'But, God help us, sins of that sort are all round us like mosquitoes in the evening. Have you consulted your husband, Mrs Kishan?'

'He too wishes to see this liar and cheat punished.'

'All our lives we are surrounded by liars and cheats. Man is born sinful, you know. But that's never a very helpful thing to say. Look at it this way, Mrs Kishan. If it turns out you're making a bad mistake it could have very serious consequences for you and your husband.'

'There is no mistake. We shall have proof. Luckily my husband's cousin is at present registrar of that university. We have written to him to look up the records.'

'I see. You are a woman who prays, Mrs Kishan.'

'Yes, I pray.'

'Are you praying that this young lady's name is there in the records, or are you praying that it isn't?'

'Praying would make no difference now. It is not there.'

'How can you be so sure?'

'From the first moment I saw her I knew she was a bad, lying woman.'

'Good God, madam, I would have thought the very opposite. Everybody takes her immediately to be the pleasant sweet young woman she is. The children love her.'

'She deceives men, because she is pretty, and because she smiles sweetly. You are a man, Father Duffy, therefore you are deceived.'

'I'm also a priest, please remember. Your husband is a man. Why is he not deceived?'

'He has been fortunate to see her through my eyes.'

'Are you saying you've put your husband up to this? Are you saying you've deliberately infected him with your own hatred? That would be wicked, Mrs Kishan. That would be a great sin.'

'My husband and I serve Christian justice, Father. If you will not help we shall do it alone. Good morning.'

'Good morning.' He went with her to the door. 'Take care. Hate is a poison that could destroy you.'

'She is the one who must be destroyed. She is the guilty one.'

He was left not knowing what or whom to pray for.

Mr Kishan's cousin, Mr William, the registrar, was a man prompt but verbose in his replies. Days earlier than expected his letter came, causing in Mr Kishan a grave smile of pleasure as he took it out of his P.O. box. It was good to have relatives on whom one could depend. But when in the car beside his wife he read it his smile slowly gave way to a sorrowful frown. It was written in English, as he had asked; but in an English so contorted, so thick with long words, and so interlarded with complimentary phrases that flattered but also confused, that the kernel, the information about Mrs Kumar's degree, was difficult first to detect and then to understand. After the third reading they thought that what he was saying was what they had wanted him to say: that though she had indeed attended the degree course she had not sat for the examination. But a fourth reading raised doubts again. What was indubitable was that the letter as it stood could not be submitted to the Director as proof. Cousin William would have to be written to again, and given clear firm instructions: he would have to be told exactly what it was they wanted him to write.

An obliging amiable man, who felt that doing people prompt favours put him in a position of superiority over them, he again replied speedily, curbing his verbosity a little, and stating categorically that Mrs Kumar, so far as the records showed, was never awarded a degree by his university.

The Kishans had their own letter of explanation ready. In it they informed the Director that in the interests of fairness to all other teachers they felt he ought to know about Mrs Kumar's dishonesty. They pointed out respectfully that they were enclosing a letter from the registrar of the university in question. Without consulting anyone they posted it and waited confidently and patiently for the answer. Often they assured each other they did not look for gratitude for having exposed an impostor. But if gratitude was shown, as it ought to be, they would reply that as good Christians they felt well enough rewarded with the knowledge that they had done their duty. If, however, the Director insisted on a reward of some sort they would respectfully suggest that he support Mr Kishan's application for a renewal of contract, made months ago and so far not even acknowledged.

Sustained by these hopes, they waited for two weeks, smiling at each other often, patting each other's hand, reading passages from the gospel every night, and feeling in their hearts that peace which God bestows on those who have unselfishly done His work.

They waited for still another week. The smiles went on, alternating now with rather puzzled stares. The pats were less frequent and briefer. The readings were shorter, followed by long silences. The feeling of peace was fretted at the edge with anxiety.

By the fifth week smiles, pats, readings, and peace in the heart had all been driven away by righteous resentment. It pervaded their whole lives. The grace they said before meals was saturated with it. It filled up every letter to their sons in England, and their relatives in India. In bed it made them stiff and loveless. They both felt, without having to mention it, that while this dirty thing hung over them, polluting their lives, they could not join their bodies in marital affection.

Holding hands, they considered in bitter whispers what they

should do now. Obviously the Director, a friend of Kumar's, was in the plot: it was necessary to get past him somehow. Approach must be made to the Minister himself, but since he was a Muslim with three wives and a fondness for pretty women, it might be difficult to convince him a serious crime was being committed by a woman whose beauty was almost certain to seduce him from his duty.

More than once Mrs Kishan, perplexed beyond endurance, crept sighing out of bed, in her long white gown, and with her grey hair flowing down over her back knelt on the floor and prayed. Her husband, though sleepy and tired, nevertheless felt that if he remained snug in bed the efficacy of her prayers might be weakened, so he too got up, in his red-and-white pyjamas, and knelt beside her, leaving her to say all the words which he, and God also to tell the truth, had already heard fifty times.

Whether with God's guidance or not, they decided the next move should be for their cousin to write direct to the Director, on official university notepaper. He was instructed to make it clear and concise, and utterly leave out all flowery greetings to the Director who, a Tamil from Malaya, he claimed to have met once during an educational conference in Madras.

He replied at once, with rather diminished enthusiasm, to say he had written as instructed, and enclosed a copy of his letter. While it would not have been true to say he had eschewed greetings these were not quite as flowery as they might have been. So his cousins pronounced it satisfactory, and again began to wait, though this time with damaged confidence.

The summons came, so smartly as to startle them, and so curt as to strike them as rude. Only Mr Kishan was summoned, but this they had expected, since no Indian in authority would wish to deal with an Indian woman on a matter of any importance.

The appointment was for three o'clock, a time when Mr Kishan usually had his afternoon nap, without which indeed he felt tired and listeness for the rest of the day. But it could not be helped. Wearing a tie, he drove to the Secretariat in good time. His wife accompanied him; she would wait in the car while he was upstairs with the Director. Afterwards they would go into town and have tea in a restaurant to celebrate.

Tall, dignified, his sparse silver hair and his ample bald brown scalp gleaming, he slowly climbed up the stairs of the Secretariat. The Education Offices were at the top. A little breathless when he got there but still dignified, he was pleased rather than huffed when the Director's secretary, an elderly Malay, asked him to wait in the ante-room for a minute or two, as the Director was busy at the moment. But half an hour later he began to feel he was being discourteously treated.

'My wife,' he murmured to the secretary, who was busy with some papers at a desk, 'is waiting for me below in my car.'

'She will wait.'

'Yes, she will wait,' agreed Mr Kishan, after a pause. Then he went on waiting himself.

'You must understand the Director is a very busy man,' remarked the secretary, ten minutes later.

'I am sure he is,' replied Mr Kishan politely.

Twenty minutes later a bell rang. The secretary, peeved himself now, for it was after four, his hour of release, went into the inner office, and returned in a minute or so to tell Mr Kishan the Director was now free to interview him. Mr Kishan entered, feeling hurt. He had assumed the Director was engaged with, say, the Minister or a Deputy Director or even the Commissioner of Police. Instead here he was quite alone, in a lilac shirt with a blue-and-white bow-tie; and no one had come out. He was looking furious too.

'Sit down, Kishan,' he said.

It was not friendliness that dropped the Mr, but rudeness. Surely as the younger man, though the one in authority, he should have shown more respect.

More noisily than was necessary, he opened a drawer and took out Mr William's two letters and the one the Kishans had sent. With a grimace of disgust he threw them on to his desk.

'What the devil do you mean by pestering me with this stuff?' he demanded.

Mr Kishan, taken aback, could find no ready answer.

'I'm warning you, Kishan, any more of this and you'll find yourself in hot water.'

'But it is true. What is written there is true.'

'Are you trying to teach me how to do my job?'

'No. I am acting as a good Christian.'

'Now please don't make me sick as well as angry. This is not the work of a good Christian. This is the work of the devil of envy. I've been making enquiries. I have discovered you have a reputation for this sort of thing: not minding your own business, trying to make fools of your superiors, always applying for this or for that. You have been doing it all during your career. No, please be quiet, for your own good do not say anything. I shall tell you what I am prepared to do. I'm prepared to hand these back to you, if you promise to take them away and burn them. Concentrate on your own work, Kishan. Are you so convinced that your own work is so good that you can afford to interfere in other people's work? You have sent in an application for a renewal of contract. Is that not so? Yet you are nearly sixty. You should be humble, man, instead of writing impertinent letters. Why are you getting up? I haven't finished yet.'

Mr Kishan remained standing. Thinking of his wife waiting devotedly, depending on him as she had done from the day of their wedding, he was able to feel resolute, although his heart sank at the remembrance of that gibe about his age, and at the threat not to renew his contract.

'I am sorry, sir,' he said. 'My wife and I –.'

'Yes, she's the one who started all this, so I have heard. Doesn't the foolish woman realize she could ruin you?'

'My wife is not a foolish woman.'

'Utterly foolish. I could say worse, but foolish will do. Everybody else is satisfied, why the devil aren't you and she? Go home, burn these, and forget the whole thing.'

'We have prayed for guidance.'

The Director stared at him in amazement. 'I'm beginning to think you must be mad, Kishan. You stand there in my own office and tell me to my face you have prayed for guidance in a matter that is none of your business, but is very much my business. I would like to remind you that it is usual when one prays to seek good for others, not harm. Speaking as a man in authority myself I should think God would be very angry indeed to be asked to do your spiteful work for you.'

'We are not spiteful. This woman is not innocent. Those letters prove it.'

'Are you going to take them away and destroy them?'

'I cannot. They are now official documents. Neither you nor I have any right to destroy them.'

'Go, Kishan, for God's sake, go. But no more of this. There's not a cent being taken from your pocket, so why all the fuss?'

'You insult me if you are saying it is the money that is troubling me.'

'No, I would not be insulting you. On the contrary, I would be accepting you as a normal man. My last word must be a warning. Take this no further. Good afternoon.'

'Good afternoon.'

In the outer office the little secretary was bitterly peeved. He muttered that he was late for a golf match. Mr Kishan had to smile, sorrowfully, at this concern over a triviality in a world where important matters were contemptuously and sinisterly neglected.

His wife saw at a glance that the interview had not been successful. Briefly, with pity in his voice for her, he told her what the Director had said.

She put her plump hand on his. 'What do we do now?' she whispered, in their native Tamil.

To him then it was the language of surrender. In English he replied, 'We must fight on. I shall talk to Patel.'

'He will take a fee,' she said, still in Tamil.

'I shall not consult him professionally.'

'His fees are high.'

'Please speak in English. I shall consult him as a friend. There will be no fee.'

'He is not very friendly,' she said, persisting in Tamil. 'And he is cunning. He knows there is talk of all foreign lawyers being told to leave the country.'

'That is not quite true. The new law is to prevent any more foreign lawyers from coming into the country.'

'Work permits can be taken away. Should we not write to the People's Forum?'

That was the correspondence column of the Kalimantan Gazette.

'We could use a pen name. No one would know. We could sign it: Christian justice.'

'We would have to give our real name too. But it is not because we are afraid that we must not do it.'

'And what is the reason, husband?'

'I have said it before. The people who write those letters are mean people, foolish people. They are not seeking Christian justice; they are seeking only revenge. We are not seeking revenge.'

'No, husband.' Her voice was at its fondest and proudest. He looked so distinguished, much more so than the Director, in spite of the latter's coloured shirts and bow-ties.

Patel, the lawyer, was regarded by his fellow Indians as a renegade. Born in Bombay, that city of vice, sophistication, and lack of principle, and trained in London, centre of imperialism, he had married a blonde Englishwoman and loved to make it known that she had brought him in dowry exactly three shillings and sixpence or two and a half rupees, which was all she had left on their marriage day out of her week's wage as a typist. He would follow up this revelation by challenging those listening to say how much their wives had brought. Usually proud to tell, for the sums were flatteringly large, twenty thousand rupees, fifty thousand, even one hundred thousand, they hesitated now, because of the utter absurdity of the amount he had mentioned. When they had muttered the sums he would then say, with a leer, 'But of course I got something worth more than a million rupees.' When they asked uneasily what that could have been he whispered, his lips gleaming with whisky of which he was too fond, 'Love.' Of course they would then protest that love, that trifle really, had been thrown in along with the multitude of rupees; but he would shake his big clever head, put his finger to his lips, and whisper, 'Didn't your mothers choose your wives for you?' They could scarcely deny it, since it was true, nor could they really be so unmanly as to claim that their mothers were surely the best judges of what kind of girls would suit them. It was known what answer Patel had made to one simpleton who had made that claim. He had said, with a sneer, 'As a cook, as an ironer of your shirts, as a fetcher of your slippers, as the mother of your kids, as the warmer of your bed, as a receptacle for your cock. (He was very coarse.) But as a lover, no, a hundred times no.' In spite of his coarseness and his sneer, what he had said was true in many cases, for if you were able to boast that you had got as much as fifty thousand rupees then, alas, it inevitably followed that your wife was buck-toothed, or skinny or fat or pimply or puny-breasted or stupid, certainly never very exciting in bed, as Patel's tall, fair-haired, laughing, beautifully-bosomed Englishwoman must be.

Mr Kishan was too old to be tormented any more by regret that he had not married a beautiful woman. At the same time, he still did regret a little that the dowry paid with her had been so low, only ten thousand rupees, which, even taking into consideration the fall in the value of the rupee since then, had been below average. Her parents had pointed out, sensibly enough, that they had spent a lot of money on her education, at a time when few Indian women were educated at all, and they had no doubt that in the course of her life she would earn for her husband a considerable sum. This had turned out to be true. As a mathematics teacher, she had made the calculation herself; after thirty years it amounted to one hundred and eighty thousand; and she would be able to work for at least another five years.

Therefore there was no need for him to feel cowed in Patel's presence. Yet he could not help it. Even when the unprofitable but lovely Englishwoman was not there. Even when speaking over the telephone.

'Good evening, Patel, Kishan here.'

'Oh. Good evening. What do you want?'

'How are you, Patel?'

'Now you haven't rung me up at this inconvenient time just to ask me how I am. What is it?'

'It is rather a private matter.'

'Perhaps you'd like to make an appointment to see me at my office?'

'No, no, that is not necessary.'

'Look here, Kishan, I'm going to be blunt. I have a living to make. You don't teach for nothing, do you? Well, I don't hand out legal advice for nothing.'

'But this matter does not really concern me.'

'It's you that's telephoning, isn't it? My God, don't tell me it's this Mrs Kumar business.'

'Have you heard?'

'Mosquitoes buzz it in every ear. It's rumoured you have gone mad, Kishan, you and your wife. Your senses have flown away, like birds, and left only dry sticks behind.'

'Nonsense. Nonsense.'

'Well, nonsense or not, I want no part of it. I happen to like Mrs Kumar. I think she's got enough to put up with being married to that mercenary bastard without you or anybody else persecuting her. So I shall give you some advice *gratis*. Give it up. Good night.'

Mr Kishan found himself with a dead telephone in his hand. In wonder he saw his wife's face, not pretty, not young, not happy, and not confident in him any more.

'So he will not help?' she whispered.

'He said our senses have flown away, like birds, and left only dry sticks behind.'

'What impertinence,' she murmured, seeing in her mind the nests of childhood, in the tall trees of home, far away and long ago, in a village on an Indian coast.

'I did not think he would be of help.'

'No one is of help.'

'Are we alone in the whole world in wishing Christian justice to be done?'

'Yes, husband, we are alone.'

'Even our sons.'

'Yes, but they are in England, they do not understand.'

Their sons' advice and support had been sought, but both of them, the doctor to be and the student lawyer, had given the same counsel: do not meddle with what is not your business. It had been sad to learn that one's own sons had become so worldly.

She spoke in Tamil. 'What do we do now, husband?'

He answered in the same language. 'We must go on.'

'Yes, we must go on, of course.'

'We shall write to the Minister.'

'Yes.'

'If he will not do anything then we shall write to the Chief Minister himself.'

'Yes, husband.'

They gazed at each other, marvelling that they two alone, out of the whole world, were concerned about Christian justice.

A day or so after the letter to the Minister had been sent off Mrs Kumar had the audacity to stop Mrs Kishan in the corridor of the school. Classes were changing at the time, so that children and other teachers were passing noisily to and fro. Pale enough for her blush to be seen, Mrs Kumar was wearing a pale blue sari trimmed with gold, and a blouse of gold, much too low at the neck so that the cleft between her breasts could be seen. It was a sari too gaudy and bold for any teacher to wear. Only a brazen woman like Mrs Kumar would have worn it. Her blush did not deceive Mrs Kishan, who knew that it was guilt which caused it, not shyness.

'Mrs Kishan,' she said softly, in Tamil, either because she was nervous or because she did not want the pupils, almost all Chinese, to hear, 'what harm have I done you?'

'I have nothing to say to you,' said Mrs Kishan, in English, and walked on. Before she had gone six steps she turned. Mrs Kumar was gazing after her, very pale, almost in tears. Mrs Kishan came back. 'Resign,' she said. 'Please resign.' It was almost an entreaty though she spoke harshly. If Mrs Kumar resigned, she and her husband had decided, they would drop the whole thing, even if she went unpunished.

Mrs Kumar shook her head. 'My husband would not let me.'

'Then expect no mercy.' This time Mrs Kishan did not turn back.

It was not a letter from the Minister that came, but one from the Public Service Commission. It stated in very few words that no renewal of contract could be granted, nor any extension. Mr Kishan's service therefore would end on 19 December, in accordance with the terms of his present contract.

'But that is so unfair,' said Mrs Kishan. 'Where will we go for Christmas? Will they expect us to leave on the next day?'

'That is the regulation.'

'But this has been our home for six years. After you have given such excellent service for so long. And I am the chairman of the Church's Children's Christmas Party Committee.'

'I am the chairman of the K.T.S.A.,' he said, sadly. That was the Kalimantan Teachers' Science Association. 'As you know I have called a meeting for the 21st of December. They will meet, it appears, without a chairman.'

'They will laugh,' she said. 'They will all laugh.'

'Yes, they will laugh, but in the end it is we who will laugh. We are not defeated. If the Minister does not reply, we will write to the Chief Minister. If again there is no reply, or a reply that does not satisfy us, we shall write to the House of Lords in London. That institution, you understand, is still the highest court of appeal in the Commonwealth.'

'Yes, husband,' she said, quietly and proudly.

Eric Linklater

SEALSKIN TROUSERS

I AM not mad. It is necessary to realize that, to accept it as a fact about which there can be no dispute. I have been seriously ill for some weeks, but that was the result of shock. A double or conjoint shock : for as well as the obvious concussion of a brutal event, there was the more dreadful necessity of recognizing the material evidence of a happening so monstrously implausible that even my friends here, who in general are quite extraordinarily kind and understanding, will not believe in the occurrence, though they cannot deny it or otherwise explain – I mean explain away – the clear and simple testimony of what was left.

I, of course, realized very quickly what had happened, and since then I have more than once remembered that poor Coleridge teased his unquiet mind, quite unnecessarily in his case, with just such a possibility; or impossibility, as the world would call it. 'If a man could pass through Paradise in a dream,' he wrote, 'and have a flower presented to him as a pledge that his soul had really been there, and if he found that flower in his hand when he woke – Ay, and what then?'

But what if he had dreamt of Hell and wakened with his hand burnt by the fire? Or of Chaos, and seen another face stare at him from the looking-glass? Coleridge does not push the question far. He was too timid. But I accepted the evidence, and while I was ill I thought seriously about the whole proceeding, in detail and in sequence of detail. I thought, indeed, about little else. To begin with, I admit, I was badly shaken, but gradually my mind cleared and my vision improved, and because I was patient and persevering – that needed discipline – I can now say that I know what happened. I have indeed, by a conscious intellectual effort, *seen and heard* what happened. This is how it began ...

How very unpleasant! she thought.

She had come down the great natural steps on the sea-cliff to the ledge that narrowly gave access, round the angle of it, to the western face which today was sheltered from the breeze and warmed by the afternoon sun. At the beginning of the week she and her fiancé, Charles Sellin, had found their way to an almost hidden shelf, a deep veranda sixty feet above the white-veined water. It was rather bigger than a billiard-table and nearly as private as an abandoned lighthouse. Twice they had spent some blissful hours there. She had a good head for heights, and Sellin was indifferent to scenery. There had been nothing vulgar, no physical contact, in their bliss together on this oceanic gazebo, for on each occasion she had been reading Héaloin's *Studies in Biology* and he Lenin's *What is to be Done?*

Their relations were already marital, not because their mutual passion could brook no pause, but rather out of fear lest their friends might despise them for chastity and so conjecture some oddity or impotence in their nature. Their behaviour, however, was very decently circumspect, and they already conducted themselves, in public and out of doors, as if they had been married for several years. They did not regard the seclusion of the cliffs as an opportunity for secret embracing, but were content that the sun should warm and colour their skin; and let their anxious minds be soothed by the surge and cavernous colloquies of the sea. Now, while Charles was writing letters in the little fishing-hotel a mile away, she had come back to their sandstone ledge, and Charles would join her in an hour or two. She was still reading *Studies in Biology*.

But their gazebo, she perceived, was already occupied, and occupied by a person of the most embarrassing appearance. He was quite unlike Charles. He was not only naked, but obviously robust, brown-hued, and extremely hairy. He sat on the very edge of the rock, dangling his legs over the sea, and down his spine ran a ridge of hair like the dark stripe on a donkey's back, and on his shoulder-blades grew patches of hair like the wings of a bird. Unable in her disappointment to be sensible and leave at once, she lingered for a moment and saw to her relief that he was not quite naked. He wore trousers of a dark brown colour, very low at the waist, but sufficient to cover his haunches. Even so, even with that protection for her modesty, she could not stay and read biology in his company.

To show her annoyance, and let him become aware of it, she made a little impatient sound; and turning to go, looked back to see if he had heard.

He swung himself round and glared at her, more angry on the instant than she had been. He had thick eyebrows, large dark eyes, a broad snub nose, a big mouth. 'You're Roger Fairfield!' she exclaimed in surprise.

He stood up and looked at her intently. 'How do you know?' he asked.

'Because I remember you,' she answered, but then felt a little confused, for what she principally remembered was the brief notoriety he had acquired, in his final year at Edinburgh University, by swimming on a rough autumn day from North Berwick to the Bass Rock to win a bet of five pounds.

The story had gone briskly round the town for a week, and everybody knew that he and some friends had been lunching, too well for caution, before the bet was made. His friends, however, grew quickly sober when he took to the water, and in a great fright informed the police, who called out the lifeboat. But they searched in vain, for the sea was running high, until in calm water under the shelter of the Bass they saw his head, dark on the water, and pulled him aboard. He seemed none the worse for his adventure, but the police charged him with disorderly behaviour and he was fined two pounds for swimming without a regulation costume.

'We met twice,' she said, 'once at a dance and once in Mackie's when we had coffee together. About a year ago. There were several of us there, and we knew the man you came in with. I remember you perfectly.'

He stared the harder, his eyes narrowing, a vertical wrinkle dividing his forehead. 'I'm a little short-sighted too,' she said with a nervous laugh.

'My sight's very good,' he answered, 'but I find it difficult to recognize people. Human beings are so much alike.'

'That's one of the rudest remarks I've ever heard!'

'Surely not?'

'Well, one does like to be remembered. It isn't pleasant to be told that one's a nonentity.'

He made an impatient gesture. 'That isn't what I meant, and I do recognize you now. I remember your voice. You have a distinctive voice and a pleasant one. F sharp in the octave below middle C is your note.'

'Is that the only way in which you can distinguish people?'

'It's as good as any other.'

'But you don't remember my name?'

'No,' he said.

'I'm Elizabeth Barford.'

He bowed and said, 'Well, it was a dull party, wasn't it? The occasion, I mean, when we drank coffee together.'

'I don't agree with you. I thought it was very amusing, and we all enjoyed ourselves. Do you remember Charles Sellin?'

'No.'

'Oh, you're hopeless,' she exclaimed. 'What is the good of meeting people if you're going to forget all about them?'

'I don't know,' he said. 'Let us sit down, and you can tell me.'

He sat again on the edge of the rock, his legs dangling, and looking over his shoulder at her, said, 'Tell me: what is the good of meeting people?'

She hesitated, and answered, 'I like to make friends. That's quite natural, isn't it? – But I came here to read.'

'Do you read standing?'

'Of course not,' she said, and smoothing her skirt tidily over her knees, sat down beside him. 'What a wonderful place this is for a holiday. Have you been here before?'

'Yes, I know it well.'

'Charles and I came a week ago. Charles Sellin, I mean, whom you don't remember. We're going to be married, you know. In about a year, we hope.'

'Why did you come here?'

'We wanted to be quiet, and in these islands one is fairly secure against interruption. We're both working quite hard.'

'Working!' he mocked. 'Don't waste time, waste your life instead.'

'Most of us have to work, whether we like it or not.'

He took the book from her lap, and opening it read idly a few lines, turned a dozen pages and read with a yawn another paragraph.

'Your friends in Edinburgh,' she said, 'were better-off than ours. Charles and I, and all the people we know, have got to make our living.'

'Why?' he asked.

'Because if we don't we shall starve,' she snapped.

'And if you avoid starvation – what then?'

'It's possible to hope,' she said stiffly, 'that we shall be of some use in the world.'

'Do you agree with this?' he asked, smothering a second yawn, and read from the book:

'The physical factor in a germ-cell is beyond our analysis or assessment, but can we deny subjectivity to the primordial initiatives? It is easier, perhaps, to assume that mind comes late in development, but the assumption must not be established on the grounds that we can certainly deny self-expression to the cell. It is common knowledge that the mind may influence the body both greatly and in little unseen ways; but how it is done, we do not know. Psychobiology is still in its infancy.'

'It's fascinating, isn't it?' she said.

'How do you propose,' he asked, 'to be of use to the world?'

'Well, the world needs people who have been educated – educated to think – and one does hope to have a little influence in some way.'

'Is a little influence going to make any difference? Don't you think that what the world needs is to develop a new sort of mind? It needs a new primordial directive, or quite a lot of them, perhaps. But psychobiology is still in its infancy, and you don't know how such changes come about, do you? And you can't foresee when you *will* know, can you?'

149

'No, of course not. But science is advancing so quickly –'

'In fifty thousand years?' he interrupted. 'Do you think you will know by then?'

'It's difficult to say,' she answered seriously, and was gathering her thoughts for a careful reply when again he interrupted, rudely, she thought, and quite irrelevantly. His attention had strayed from her and her book to the sea beneath, and he was looking down as though searching for something. 'Do you swim?' he asked.

'Rather well,' she said.

'I went in just before high water, when the weed down there was all brushed in the opposite direction. You never get bored by the sea, do you?'

'I've never seen enough of it,' she said. 'I want to live on an island, a little island, and hear it all round me.'

'That's very sensible of you,' he answered with more warmth in his voice. 'That's uncommonly sensible for a girl like you.'

'What sort of a girl do you think I am?' she demanded, vexation in her accent, but he ignored her and pointed his brown arm to the horizon: 'The colour has thickened within the last few minutes. The sea was quite pale on the skyline, and now it's a belt of indigo. And the writing has changed. The lines of foam on the water, I mean. Look at that! There's a submerged rock out there, and always, about half an hour after the ebb has started to run, but more clearly when there's an off-shore wind, you can see those two little whirlpools and the circle of white round them. You see the figure they make? It's like this isn't it?'

With a splinter of stone, he drew a diagram on the rock.

'Do you know what it is?' he asked. 'It's the figure the Chinese call the T'ai Chi. They say it represents the origin of all created things. And it's the sign manual of the sea.'

'But those lines of foam must run into every conceivable shape,' she protested.

'Oh, they do. They do indeed. But it isn't often you can read them. – There he is!' he exclaimed, leaning forward and staring into the water sixty feet below. 'That's him, the old villain!'

From his sitting position, pressing hard down with his hands and thrusting against the face of the rock with his heels, he hurled himself into space, and straightening in mid-air broke the smooth green surface of the water with no more splash than a harpoon would have made. A solitary razorbill, sunning himself on a shelf below, fled hurriedly out to sea, and half a dozen white birds, startled by the sudden movement, rose in the air crying 'Kittiwake! Kittiwake!'

Elizabeth screamed loudly, scrambled to her feet with clumsy speed, then knelt again on the edge of the rock and peered down. In the slowly heaving clear water she could see a pale shape moving, now striped by the dark weed that grew in tangles under the flat foot of the rock, now lost in the shadowy deepness where the tangles were rooted. In a minute or two his head rose from the sea, he shook bright drops from his hair, and looked up at her, laughing. Firmly grasped in his right hand, while he trod water, he held up an enormous blue-black lobster for her admiration. Then he threw it on to the flat rock beside him, and swiftly climbing out of the sea, caught it again and held it, cautious of its bite, till he found a piece of string in his trouser-pocket. He shouted to her, 'I'll tie its claws, and you can take it home for your supper!'

She had not thought it possible to climb the sheer face of the cliff, but from its forefoot he mounted by steps and handholds invisible from above, and pitching the tied lobster on to the floor of the gazebo, came nimbly over the edge.

'That's a bigger one than you've ever seen in your life before,' he boasted. 'He weighs fourteen pounds, I'm certain of it. Fourteen pounds at least. Look at the size of his right claw! He could crack a coconut with that. He tried to crack my ankle when I was swimming an hour ago, and got into his hole before I could catch him. But I've caught him now, the brute. He's had more than twenty years of crime, that black boy. He's twenty-four or twenty-five by the look of him. He's older than you, do you realize that? Unless you're a lot older than you look. How old are you?'

But Elizabeth took no interest in the lobster. She had re-treated until she stood with her back to the rock, pressed hard against it, the palms of her hands fumbling on the stone as if feeling for a secret lock or bolt that might give her entrance into it. Her face was white, her lips pale and tremulous.

He looked round at her, when she made no answer, and asked what the matter was.

Her voice was faint and frightened. 'Who are you?' she whispered, and the whisper broke into a stammer. 'What are you?'

His expression changed and his face, with the water-drops on it, grew hard as a rock shining undersea. 'It's only a few minutes,' he said, 'since you appeared to know me quite well. You addressed me as Roger Fairfield, didn't you?'

'But a name's not everything. It doesn't tell you enough.'

'What more do you want to know?'

Her voice was so strained and thin that her words were like the shadow of words, or words shivering in the cold: 'To jump like that, into the sea – it wasn't human!'

The coldness of his face wrinkled to a frown. 'That's a curious remark to make.'

'You would have killed yourself if – if –'

He took a seaward step again, looked down at the calm green depths below, and said, 'You're exaggerating, aren't you? It's not much more than fifty feet, sixty perhaps, and the water's deep. – Here, come back! Why are you running away?'

'Let me go!' she cried. 'I don't want to stay here. I – I'm frightened.'

'That's unfortunate. I hadn't expected this to happen.'

'Please let me go!'

'I don't think I shall. Not until you've told me what you're frightened of.'

'Why,' she stammered, 'why do you wear fur trousers?'

He laughed, and still laughing caught her round the waist and pulled her towards the edge of the rock. 'Don't be alarmed,' he said. 'I'm not going to throw you over. But if you insist on a conversation about trousers, I think we should sit down again. Look at the smoothness of the water, and its colour, and the light in the depths of it: have you ever seen anything lovelier?

Look at the sky: that's calm enough, isn't it? Look at that fulmar sailing past: he's not worrying, so why should you?'

She leaned away from him, all her weight against the hand that held her waist, but his arm was strong and he seemed unaware of any strain on it. Nor did he pay attention to the distress she was in – she was sobbing dryly, like a child who has cried too long – but continued talking in a light and pleasant conversational tone until the muscles of her body tired and relaxed, and she sat within his enclosing arm, making no more effort to escape, but timorously conscious of his hand upon her side so close beneath her breast.

'I needn't tell you,' he said, 'the conventional reasons for wearing trousers. There are people, I know, who sneer at all conventions, and some conventions deserve their sneering. But not the trouser-convention. No, indeed! So we can admit the necessity of the garment, and pass to consideration of the material. Well, I like sitting on rocks, for one thing, and for such a hobby this is the best stuff in the world. It's very durable, yet soft and comfortable. I can slip into the sea for half an hour without doing it any harm, and when I come out to sun myself on the rock again, it doesn't feel cold and clammy. Nor does it fade in the sun or shrink with the wet. Oh, there are plenty of reasons for having one's trousers made of stuff like this.'

'And there's a reason,' she said, 'that you haven't told me.'

'Are you quite sure of that?'

She was calmer now, and her breathing was controlled. But her face was still white, and her lips were softly nervous when she asked him, 'Are you going to kill me?'

'Kill you? Good heavens, no! Why should I do that?'

'For fear of my telling other people.'

'And what precisely would you tell them?'

'You know.'

'You jump to conclusions far too quickly: that's your trouble. Well, it's a pity for your sake, and a nuisance for me. I don't think I can let you take that lobster home for your supper after all. I don't, in fact think you will go home for your supper.'

Her eyes grew dark again with fear, her mouth opened, but

before she could speak he pulled her to him and closed it, not asking leave, with a roughly occludent kiss.

'That was to prevent you from screaming. I hate to hear people scream,' he told her, smiling as he spoke. 'But this' – he kissed her again, now gently and in a more protracted embrace – 'that was because I wanted to.'

'You mustn't!' she cried.

'But I have,' he said.

'I don't understand myself! I can't understand what has happened –'

'Very little yet,' he murmured.

'Something terrible has happened!'

'A kiss? Am I so repulsive?'

'I don't mean that. I mean something inside me. I'm not – at least I think I'm not – I'm not frightened now!'

'You have no reason to be.'

'I have every reason in the world. But I'm not! I'm not frightened – but I want to cry.'

'Then cry,' he said soothingly, and made her pillow her cheek against his breast. 'But you can't cry comfortably with that ridiculous contraption on your nose.'

He took from her the horn-rimmed spectacles she wore, and threw them into the sea.

'Oh!' she exclaimed. 'My glasses! – Oh, why did you do that? Now I can't see. I can't see at all without my glasses!'

'It's all right,' he assured her. 'You really won't need them. The refraction,' he added vaguely, 'will be quite different.'

As if this small but unexpected act of violence had brought to the boiling-point her desire for tears, they bubbled over, and because she threw her arms about him in a sort of fond despair, and snuggled close, sobbing vigorously till he felt the warm drops trickle down his skin, and from his skin she drew into her eyes the saltness of the sea, which made her weep the more. He stroked her hair with a strong but soothing hand, and when she grew calm and lay still in his arms, her emotion spent, he sang quietly to a little enchanting tune a song that began:

'I am a Man upon the land,
    I am a Selkie in the sea,
And when I'm far from every strand
    My home it is on Sule Skerry.'

After the first verse or two she freed herself from his embrace, and sitting up listened gravely to the song. Then she asked him, 'Shall I ever understand?'

'It's not a unique occurrence,' he told her. 'It has happened quite often before, as I suppose you know. In Cornwall and Brittany and among the Western Isles of Scotland; that's where people have always been interested in seals, and understood them a little, and where seals from time to time have taken human shape. The one thing that's unique in our case, in my metamorphosis, is that I am the only seal-man who has ever become a Master of Arts of Edinburgh University. Or, I believe, of any university. I am the unique and solitary example of a sophisticated seal-man.'

'I must look a perfect fright,' she said. 'It was silly of me to cry. Are my eyes very red?'

'The lids are a little pink – not unattractively so – but your eyes are as dark and lovely as a mountain pool in October, on a sunny day in October. They're much improved since I threw your spectacles away.'

'I needed them, you know. I feel quite stupid without them. But tell me why you came to the University – and how? How could you do it?'

'My dear girl – what is your name, by the way? I've quite forgotten.'

'Elizabeth !' she said angrily.

'I'm so glad, it's my favourite human name. – But you don't really want to listen to a lecture on psychobiology?'

'I want to know *how*. You must tell me !'

'Well, you remember, don't you, what your book says about the primordial initiatives? But it needs a footnote there to explain that they're not exhausted till quite late in life. The germ-cells, as you know, are always renewing themselves, and they keep their initiatives though they nearly always follow the chosen pattern except in the case of certain illnesses, or under special direction. The direction of the mind, that is. And the glands have got a lot to do in a full metamorphosis, the renal first and then the pituitary, as you would expect. It isn't approved of – making the change, I mean – but every now and then one of us does it, just for a frolic in the general way, but in my case there was a special reason.'

'Tell me,' she said again.

'It's too long a story.'

'I want to know.'

'There's been a good deal of unrest, you see, among my people in the last few years: doubt, and dissatisfaction with our leaders, and scepticism about traditional beliefs – all that sort of thing. We've had a lot of discussion under the surface of the sea about the nature of man, for instance. We had always been taught to believe certain things about him, and recent events didn't seem to bear out what our teachers told us. Some of our younger people got dissatisfied, so I volunteered to go ashore and investigate. I'm still considering the report I shall have to make, and that's why I'm living, at present, a double life. I come ashore to think, and go back to the sea to rest.'

'And what do you think of us?' she asked.

'You're interesting. Very interesting indeed. There are going to be some curious mutations among you before long. Within three or four thousand years, perhaps.'

He stooped and rubbed a little smear of blood from his shin. 'I scratched it on a limpet,' he said. 'The limpets, you know, are the same today as they were four hundred thousand years ago. But human beings aren't nearly so stable.'

'Is that your main impression, that humanity's unstable?'

'That's part of it. But from our point of view there's something much more upsetting. Our people, you see, are quite simple creatures, and because we have relatively few beliefs, we're very much attached to them. Our life is a life of sensation – not entirely, but largely – and we ought to be extremely happy. We were, so long as we were satisfied with sensation and a short undisputed creed. We have some advantages over human beings, you know. Human beings have to carry their own weight about, and they don't know how blissful it is to be unconscious of weight: to be wave-borne, to float on the idle sea, to leap without effort in a curving wave, and look up at the dazzle of the sky through a smother of white water, or dive so easily to the calmness far below and take a haddock from the weed-beds in a sudden rush of appetite. – Talking of haddocks,' he said, 'it's getting late. It's nearly time for fish. And I must give you some instruction before we go. The preliminary phase takes a little while, about five minutes for you, I should think, and then you'll be another creature.'

She gasped, as though already she felt the water's chill, and whispered, 'Not yet! Not yet, please.'

He took her in his arms, and expertly, with a strong caressing hand, stroked her hair, stroked the roundness of her head and the back of her neck and her shoulders, feeling her muscles moving to his touch, and down the hollow of her back to her waist and hips. The head again, neck, shoulders, and spine. Again and again. Strongly and firmly his head gave her calmness, and presently she whispered, 'You're sending me to sleep.'

'My God!' he exclaimed, 'you mustn't do that! Stand up, stand up, Elizabeth!'

'Yes,' she said, obeying him. 'Yes, Roger. Why did you call yourself Roger? Roger Fairfield?'

'I found the name in a drowned sailor's pay-book. What does that matter now? Look at me, Elizabeth!'

She looked at him, and smiled.

His voice changed, and he said happily, 'You'll be the prettiest seal between Shetland and the Scillies. Now listen. Listen carefully.'

He held her lightly and whispered in her ear. Then kissed her on the lips and cheek, and bending her head back, on the throat. He looked, and saw the colour come deeply into her face.

'Good,' he said. 'That's the first stage. The adrenalin's flowing nicely now. You know about the pituitary, don't you? That makes it easy then. There are two parts in the pituitary gland, the anterior and posterior lobes, and both must act together. It's not difficult, and I'll tell you how.'

Then he whispered again, most urgently, and watched her closely. In a little while he said, 'And now you can take it easy. Let's sit down and wait till you're ready. The actual change won't come till we go down.'

'But it's working,' she said, quietly and happily. 'I can feel it working.'

'Of course it is.'

She laughed triumphantly, and took his hand.

'We've got nearly five minutes to wait,' he said.

'What will it be like? What shall I feel, Roger?'

'The water moving against your side, the sea caressing you and holding you.'

'Shall I be sorry for what I've left behind?'

'No, I don't think so.'

'You didn't like us, then? Tell me what you discovered in the world.'

'Quite simply,' he said, 'that we have been deceived.'

'But I don't know what your belief had been.'

'Haven't I told you? — Well, we in our innocence respected you because you could work, and were willing to work. That seemed to us truly heroic. We don't work at all, you see, and you'll be much happier when you come to us. We who live in the sea don't struggle to keep our heads above water.'

'All my friends worked hard,' she said. 'I never knew anyone who was idle. We had to work, and most of us worked for a good purpose; or so we thought. But you didn't think so?'

'Our teachers had told us,' he said, 'that men endured the burden of human toil to create a surplus of wealth that would give them leisure from the daily task of bread-winning. And in their hard-won leisure, our teachers said, men cultivated wisdom and charity and the fine arts; and became aware of God. — But that's not a true description of the world, is it?'

'No,' she said, 'that's not the truth.'

'No,' he repeated, 'our teachers were wrong, and we've been deceived.'

'Men are always being deceived, but they get accustomed to learning the facts too late. They grow accustomed to deceit itself.'

'You are braver than we, perhaps. My people will not like to be told the truth.'

'I shall be with you,' she said, and took his hand. But still he stared gloomily at the moving sea.

The minutes passed, and presently she stood up and with quick fingers put off her clothes. 'It's time,' she said.

He looked at her, and his gloom vanished like the shadow of a cloud that the wind has hurried on, and exultation followed like sunlight spilling from the burning edge of a cloud. 'I wanted to punish them,' he cried, 'for robbing me of my faith, and now, by God, I'm punishing them hard. I'm robbing their treasury now, the inner vault of all their treasury! – I hadn't guessed you were so beautiful! The waves when you swim will catch a burnish from you, the sand will shine like silver when you lie down to sleep, and if you can teach the red seaware to blush so well, I shan't miss the roses of your world.'

'Hurry,' she said.

He, laughing softly, loosened the leather thong that tied his trousers, stepped out of them, and lifted her in his arms. 'Are you ready?' he asked.

She put her arms round his neck and softly kissed his cheek. Then with a great shout he leapt from the rock, from the little veranda, into the green silk calm of the water far below ...

I heard the splash of their descent – I am quite sure I heard the splash – as I came round the corner of the cliff, by the ledge that leads to the little rock veranda, our gazebo, as we called it, but the first thing I noticed, that really attracted my attention, was an enormous blue-black lobster, its huge claws tied with string, that was moving in a rather ludicrous fashion towards the edge. I think it fell over just before I left, but I wouldn't swear to that. Then I saw her book, the *Studies in Biology*, and her clothes.

Her white linen frock with the brown collar and the brown belt, some other garments, and her shoes were all there. And beside them, lying across her shoes, was a pair of sealskin trousers.

I realized immediately, or almost immediately, what had happened. Or so it seems to me now. And if, as I firmly believe, my apprehension was instantaneous, the faculty of intuition is clearly more important than I had previously supposed. I have, of course, as I said before, given the matter a great deal of thought during my recent illness, but the impression remains that I understood what had happened in a flash, to use a common but illuminating phrase. And no one, need I say? has been able to refute my intuition. No one, that is, has found an alternative explanation for the presence, beside Elizabeth's linen frock, of a pair of sealskin trousers.

I remember also my physical distress at the discovery. My breath, for several minutes I think, came into and went out of my lungs like the hot wind of a dust-storm in the desert. It parched my mouth and grated in my throat. It was, I recall, quite a torment to breathe. But I had to, of course.

Nor did I lose control of myself in spite of the agony, both mental and physical, that I was suffering. I didn't lose control till they began to mock me. Yes, they did, I assure you of that. I heard his voice quite clearly, and honesty compels me to admit that it was singularly sweet and the tune was the most haunting I have ever heard. They were about forty yards away, two seals swimming together, and the evening light was so clear and taut that his voice might have been the vibration of an invisible bow across its coloured bands. He was singing the song that Elizabeth and I had discovered in an album of Scottish music in the little fishing-hotel where we had been living:

> 'I am a Man upon the land,
> I am a Selkie in the sea,
> And when I'm far from any strand
> I am at home on Sule Skerry!'

But his purpose, you see, was mockery. They were happy,

together in the vast simplicity of the ocean, and I, abandoned to the terror of life alone, life among human beings, was lost and full of panic. It was then I began to scream. I could hear myself screaming, it was quite horrible. But I couldn't stop. I had to go on screaming ...

Neil McCallum

A HOUSE IN SICILY

THE house stood on the north side of the courtyard. It was pleasantly neat and the door was closed, locked, and painted green. The shutters were folded quickly over the windows. A yellow mat of plaited grass hung on the parapet of a well. Beside the well a bucket and a coil of chain shone with a clean pewter colour. The portico, which stretched along the front of the house, was shaded by a wooden trellis on which purple bougainvillea grew thickly. Tall trees framed the entire house as a hat frames a face.

Once every morning and once every evening Fortunato Sacco came down from his room above the stables, holding the large key of the green door. After breakfast and after supper, with Mario, his grandson, he unlocked the door and examined each room of the house. Little Mario, eleven years old, enjoyed these caretaking duties enormously. He loved the passageways, bright with light from the small unsealed windows. He loved the rooms, mysteriously dark, vast in the sombre light that seeped through the joints of the shutters.

The old man and the boy were the only two left at the house. The other workers and servants had gone when the padrone Signor Francesco, had packed his young wife, his year-old baby, and two suit-cases into the car, and vanished over the hill-crest where the road turned towards Catania.

Old Fortunato had refused to go. 'I will stay,' he had told the padrone gravely. 'I have been no further than Enna and Catania in all my years. A war cannot uproot me. I have become old here and here I will die in God's time.'

At that short speech the padrone had looked nervous. He had glanced from Fortunato to the polished car. He had wiped his large fleshy face with a silk handkerchief. 'I should like to stay,' he had said, looking now only at the car, 'but it will be nothing. Soon it will all be over and peace will be back.'

This evening, the fourth since the red car had gone, Fortunato and the boy walked through the house. It was of two storeys. The ground floor was a series of store-rooms. When the first door was opened the floor looked like heaped gold, till, in the gloom, the eyes saw a sea of grain held back against the walls by wooden boards. In the cheese-room the small round cheeses were laid on the floor like checkers. Another room was thick with the vinegar smell of maturing wine.

Mario liked the coolness and the smells of the store-rooms, but it was upstairs that he preferred to go, looking over the arm of his grandfather as the doors were held open. He was fascinated by the solemn furniture, faintly shining in the dark, the warm smell of clothes and fabrics, the quick sparkle of glasses and the gleam of plates. The odours that came from the rooms were rich and dizzying, like the scent of the signora when she used to sit in the shade of the portico.

Mario sniffed and his eyes stared. He wondered if his grandfather enjoyed it as he did.

'Everything is all right, small one. Let us hope the padrone will soon be back.'

'Yes, grandfather.'

They went downstairs and locked the green door and then climbed the outside staircase to the small room they lived in above the stables. Before it was quite dark they went to bed. From his bed Mario could see the smoke of Mount Etna become red in the evening sun and then golden, like a long flat plume.

When the sky was lightening with dawn they were awakened by the crackling of rifle and automatic fire. It was not very near. They went down to the courtyard where the cobbles were still warm from yesterday's sun. In the west there were small spurts of flame.

It grew lighter. The firing continued, moved behind the house and up to the top of a long hill where three olive trees grew in a triangle. On the hill there was an indistinct movement of men.

The answering fire was far away. They told it by the duller, quicker rattle of automatic weapons. Stray bullets whined far above their heads and twice something smacked sharply into the slates of the house.

'Are you afaid, young one?'

'No, grandfather.'

'That is good. There is nothing to fear unless they have big guns.'

It was very light. Soon the sun would rise.

The firing worked into a crescendo and six times there was a swelling burst of mortar bombs, muffled by the hill with the olives. Then silence, so sharp that when a cock crowed behind them they started.

'Boy,' said the old man. 'We have forgotten the horses. The cock doesn't forget to crow because there is a war. Let us look to the horses. They may be nervous.'

They went to the stables and found that the two horses were quiet, indifferently chewing their fodder. The old man then went upstairs to prepare breakfast. Mario watched the hill where everything was now plainly visible. There were soldiers digging. He could hear the sound of their picks biting into the hard brown earth. As he watched he saw a few people leave the hill and come towards the house. A tall man walked in front with a revolver in his hand. Two of the others had rifles and there was one with a short weapon, like a very small shotgun.

'Grandfather, the soldiers are coming.'

They both stood in the courtyard as the small party arrived. Sicilians and soldiers looked at each other, unsmiling, but without hostility.

The tall man, an officer, tried to open the green door. Fortunato hurried up to him and explained he would bring the key. The officer was impatient and did not understand. He spoke to the man with the small gun and the man fired into the lock. The officer burst open the doorway and the soldiers went in, their boots ringing on the stone passage.

The boy looked at his grandfather, expecting him to be angry. 'They are very tired,' said the old man.

The shutter of an upper window was flung back and a white handkerchief was waved as a signal. More men, nearly twenty, came down from the hill and when they arrived the officer placed them round the house where they began to dig small trenches under the trees. Then the well was discovered and all the men swarmed round it. For five minutes there was no more digging till everyone had drunk his fill and the portico was wet with water spilled from the bucket.

Mario had never seen anyone with so much energy as the officer. One minute he was in the house, peering from the windows. Then he was rushing through the garden, talking to the men. Then he would go back to the house again and place a machine-gun to point to the main road. Out in the garden again he stationed a man under a tree to watch the countryside through binoculars.

At last the officer relaxed. He came up to Fortunato and smiled.

'*Guerra. Finito,*' he said, and then he pointed to his mouth.

'*Mangiare?*' said the grandfather.

The officer nodded.

'Mario. Bread and wine and cheese for the soldiers.' Mario ran off to gather the food.

In the cheese-room the officer sat at a table. The men came in by twos and threes and were given food and drink. Outside they had finished their digging in the soft garden earth and they lay on the ground, resting. A few wandered into the house, opened the drawers of the furniture, pulled out sheets and rugs and fell asleep on the beds. They were all tired, but felt a sense of well-being now that the fighting was done and they had eaten.

The officer called the sergeant into the cheese-room.

'Let the men use the house for resting. Keep a couple of sentries on duty. I'm going to snooze for half an hour, then I'm going to see the company commander. Waken me in time.'

The officer went upstairs. On the passage walls there were prints and small pictures. He paused to examine them and yawned, then he looked into the rooms. Heavy carpets made him aware of his dirt-encrusted boots. In one room he found silk fittings, on wrought bronze rails, hanging over a silver crucifix on the wall. The shutters had been opened and the room was filled with a soft light.

Everything was in perfect taste, he noted, and for a moment the thought struck him that he himself was the cause of the occupants fleeing from this house to which they had given so much care. He felt himself a strange intruder. Then he yawned again and took off his equipment and was going to place it on a small fragile table. He paused and with a weary smile he put his kit under the bed. Without removing his boots he lay on the pink silk bed-cover. How uncivilized we are, he thought, stretching luxuriously, and then he fell asleep.

His sergeant awakened him.

'Have you seen the house, sir? Some place.'

'Pretty good, isn't it. Everything quiet?'

'Not a sign. Must have spent a pretty penny on this place. Sort of gets you, a place like this.'

'You feel that way,' said the officer, wondering at his sergeant who had been a butcher and looked like a prize-fighter. 'Gets all of us,' he told himself, 'when you haven't known what a home is for umpteen years.'

'That furniture's good stuff, sir.'

'D'you know about furniture?'

'My father-in-law was a cabinet-maker – old-fashioned man but a craftsman. Don't find the like of him nowadays. He taught me a lot about furniture. Made his own coffin, too. Wonderful heavy oak it was. And polished. It was a shame to think of the worms getting it.'

They went round the other rooms, cool inside the thick walls. A few of the men were rummaging in drawers, pulling out coloured fabrics, handling suits and dresses.

'No fountain-pens or watches?' asked the officer. The men smiled. 'No, but we're still trying.' One of his men appeared with a woman's hat on and a frock bunched round his waist. He looked like a ploughman in ballet dress.

They need this sort of idiocy, the officer thought. It is as good as being out of the line for a spell.

In one of the bedrooms there was a cradle with a cascade of white lace falling from the high carved back.

'Jesus!' said the sergeant. 'They didn't ought to let us see things like that. Makes you think. Oh, what about the Sicilians, the old man and the boy?'

'What about them?'

'D'you think they're all right? They're hanging around watching everything.'

'They're all right, I suppose. They don't seem to worry one way or the other. If they're not all right the only thing to do is shoot them. D'you want to shoot them, sergeant?'

'Why ... Oh no.'

'I'm going to see the company commander now ... my god! what in hell ...'

There was no need to ask what it was. The familiar scream was followed by the familiar explosion. Inside the building everyone ran downstairs. The officer went outside. The shell had landed in a field, fifty yards short of the garden.

'Tanks. They're hull down about a mile away.'

The next shot went over the roof. The officer lay flat behind a low wall. Out of the corner of his eye he saw the old man and the boy climb the staircase to their room. Wonder if they know what's coming, he thought. Probably they feel safe there; no one can picture the inside of his own home as a battle-ground. At the same time he wondered how long their own guns would take to range on the tanks. Maybe the guns had not yet arrived in support. What a bloody picnic, and meantime they had to lie down and be shot at.

He had counted on a quiet day and resented the unannounced tanks, as though they had deliberately fired to shatter the harmony of the house and the garden and the memories evoked by the furniture in the cool rooms.

The next shot went clean through an upper window, and

just after it there came the whine of the first artillery shell in reply, high above their heads.

A tank shell screamed into the garden. Shrapnel slashed the trees and made bright cuts in the stonework of the house. A rain of clods and earth and stone pattered heavily to the ground.

'Anyone hurt?'

A muffled voice replied, 'No.'

Then the air was loud with the shriek of their own shells passing overhead and the ground around the tanks erupted in smoke. A vague hysterical cheer came from the garden. 'That'll fix the bastards. That'll fix 'em.'

In five minutes all was quiet again. A column of black smoke came from the area of the tanks.

The men came to fill their water-bottles. 'Gives you a thirst, don't it!'

The officer saw the old man and the boy come down to the courtyard. The man was dignified and quiet. The boy was smiling. He made a whooshing noise. 'Boom, boom,' he said. The soldiers looked at him and winked. 'The little bastard thinks he's been to the pictures.'

'I'm going off. Keep a look-out,' said the officer to the sergeant.

When he came back, an hour later, no one was about. He saw a few people lying in the garden, and the lookout with the binoculars was behind a tree, scratching his head.

He went into the house. The shell that had gone through the window had exploded on an inside wall upstairs, blowing a hole in the wall and filling the upper passage with plaster and bricks. An ornamental chandelier lay like a metal octopus, sprawling on the floor.

He looked for the sergeant. In the first room there was no one. An indescribable mess littered the floor. Drawers had been ransacked and the contents strewn wildly. The door of a cupboard hung awry on one hinge.

What in hell has happened, he muttered, growing angry. He scrambled through plaster and broken glass to the next room. Paper and clothes and scores of snapshots lay on the floor beside upturned drawers. The air was heavy with the smell from a broken scent bottle. Curtains had been wrenched from the rails. In one corner he saw two of his men asleep. On the bed, fat flesh lax in sleep, was the sergeant, wrapped in the lace net from the cradle. Two flies buzzed over his face.

'Sergeant, wake up. What in God's name has happened?'

'Ugh ! Wassamarrer. Eh ! Oh, I've been taking forty winks.'

'Yes. Yes. But the house. It looks as though a horde of lunatics have been running wild.'

'I know, sir. It's bad. I tried to stop it but I was too late. I was in the garden talking to the N.C.O.s and a lot of men came from the other companies for water. I didn't know what they were doing ...'

'All right. They've gone through the place like savages. But it's not so important as some other things, I suppose.'

He went into the third room and his heel came down on something hard. It was a rosary. A bundle of letters lay on a chair, spilled from the ribbon that tied them. A jumble of clothing was strewn across the bed. Books were scattered in the fireplace. Picture frames were smashed.

Damned ruffians, he muttered. He felt slightly sick and he wondered why he should be so moved by this petty destructiveness in the midst of war's normal carnage.

'Sergeant, I don't like this. The men are bloody ruffians. Have the two Sicilians seen it?'

'Yes. The boy started to cry. The old man said nothing. Just walked away.'

I should like to apologize to them, he thought, but I can't. I'd like to tell the old man that these soldiers have been far away from their homes for so long that they have become barbarians, that their own homes are so far away and they have been away for so many years they have forgotten many things, that doing this was maybe a kind of revenge for their being away. But I can't explain it, nor can I explain that it is better to do this than take a man's guts out with your bayonet. I can't explain anything. The shell, yes, that would merit the usual formula, *la guerra*, or whatever their word is. But this hooliganism, even though you understand it, it makes you angry, because it is wild and berserk and outside the pattern of behaviour even in war.

'Sergeant, we're leaving in half an hour. Battalion is advancing. Get the men ready.'

Alone, he sat in a chair, surrounded by the debris of the household. He was surprised at his own anger, that out of the vast destruction of lives and places in which he took part every day he should single this one act of riot. The absurdity of it amused him and he started to laugh, rocking in his chair like a madman, as the spasm of humour gripped him and the tears rolled down his cheeks.

When he joined the men in the courtyard they were ready to leave. The sergeant shouted. They moved off, marching in files to the road.

The midday sun burned hotly on the house. The shutters lay loosely open. One was broken by a splinter of shell and the yellow wood was like a wound. Bits of branches and rubble lay in the portico.

Fortunato and Mario walked slowly into the house. When they came out some minutes later they pulled the broken door behind them. Fortunato dangled the useless key from a finger. Mario sobbed, rubbing his knuckles into his eyes. His grandfather patted his head.

'This afternoon, my boy, we must start to work. The soldiers will not come back and there will be no more fighting here. We must tidy and clean. Even the shell hole we can try to mend with bricks and mortar. Soon we will put things to rights. The war has passed. Look, Mario, away there.'

On the foothills below Mount Etna tiny puffs of smoke were born like young clouds, exploding suddenly into existence. Mario stopped sobbing as he watched.

On the roads the files of soldiers, already minute, marched steadily towards the shell-bursts.

Moray McLaren

A TRIFLE UNNECESSARY

I HAD not been in Edinburgh for some years; and it was with pleasure mingled with a not wholly disagreeable melancholy that I had been wandering through those familiar streets and squares. How little the place had altered! In the New Town my eye recalled many half-forgotten beauties of form and line. I even discovered in my heart an affection for some of the uglier nineteenth-century solid excesses. I was glad that they had, with all their ponderousness and lack of economy, not been removed. They had been the circumstances of my childhood.

Then I turned towards the Old Town, that straggles down the hillside on the other side of Princes Street Gardens. Someone had told me that a good deal of 'improvement' had been going on there. I was interested to see what had been done. The person who had told me had been Roy Crann, the president of the St Ninian's Society of Edinburgh. Roy, whom I had known for years, was an earnest, pushful young man, who would probably remain unchangingly earnest, pushful and young from the age of twenty-five to fifty-five. What would happen to him after that one could but guess. He was now, I suppose, about forty. I had run across him in my club in London and he had spoken most earnestly, and indeed eloquently, of the work the St Ninian's Society was doing in cleaning up Edinburgh architecturally.

'I hope you are not being too drastic,' I had said at length.

'No, no,' he assured me. 'Our aim is to strip Edinburgh of its Victorianism –'

'A formidable task,' I interrupted. But he went on as if I had not spoken.

'To strip it of its Victorianism and get down to the eighteenth-century form and the medieval quality which is still there, but so terribly overlaid.'

'It sounds good, Roy. I wish you luck.'

'You should come up and see what we are doing,' urged Roy.

'I will. I have to come north next month. And I hope to spend a few days in Edinburgh.'

'Come and call at our offices in George Street and I'll show you round. Or if I'm not there I'll get someone to take you.'

Roy's eyes, behind his powerfully lensed glasses, glistened eagerly.

'Really, Roy, I don't need anyone to lead me on a conducted tour of my native city. I'll have a look round by myself first. Then I'll come and call on you.'

It was, therefore, with the vague idea of seeing what Roy and his St Ninian's Society had been doing in the Old Town that I turned into the High Street. I decided to make first for Mac-Gregor's Close. Roy had told me that this was one of their most notable improvements. Moreover it was a corner of Edinburgh which had made a deep impression on me in my youth. I cannot say that I had visited it often. But in the old days, just after the War of 1914, it was a place which, once seen, was not easy to forget. It had been one of the most noisome corners of Edinburgh slums. It had also been the most picturesque remnant of Edinburgh's medieval domestic architecture. Its atmosphere combined a sense of the decay of the past with the rottenness of the present that was truly startling. In its macabre way it was one of the show-places of the town.

When I entered the Close from the High Street and saw the reformation that had been achieved I was compelled, perhaps a little reluctantly, to admit that Roy had done an effective job of work. The old scarred and peeling walls had been stripped and cleaned, and were now attractively white-harled. The outside stairs had been mended or tastefully rebuilt. The original line of the rooftops against the sky to the north had been carefully preserved. And a sixteenth-century sundial had been dug up from somewhere and placed in the centre of the court. Its appearance was certainly in harmony with its surroundings. But I could not help wondering what use it served. Very little sunlight could ever penetrate to the centre of MacGregor's

Close, however much 'improved'. There was only one thing that remained unalterably the same – the smell, that peculiar rancid, sweet sour smell of an Edinburgh Close.

Still, as I have said, it was an effective job of work. And who was I, from the seclusion of my fairly comfortable existence, to allow even a shadow of regret for the old romantic squalor to cross my mind? If such a thought did touch me I instantly rejected it. In doing so I felt myself warming a little towards Roy Crann. People might say that he was pushful, earnest and professionally young, but at least he did the job. While other people had spent decades in talking about improving Scotland and Edinburgh, Roy in one lustrum had, in one practical direction, achieved more than all of them put together. I knew that this was only one specimen of his and his society's efforts.

'Ay, it's a bonny sicht, is it no?'

The words, uttered in a cracked old female voice, broke in upon my thoughts. I turned to see who had spoken them. They came from a figure strangely out of keeping with the improved MacGregor's Close. Huddled in a corner of the Close hard by its entrance was an old woman, with a shawl of faded and filthy tartan round her head and a tray of shoe-laces, which she was presumably offering for sale, upon her knee. Here was a living revocation of the past, a creature of the Edinburgh of my childhood.

'Yes,' I agreed, 'they've certainly cleaned the old place up.'

'Ay, they have that.'

'Do you like it better as it is now?'

'Weel, Ah ...'

Seeing that I was inclined for conversation the old woman beckoned me closer to her, and said in a lowered voice:

'D'ye want tae see the sichts o' Edinburgh? I can show them tae you, sir.'

'No, no, Mother,' I laughed. 'I know them as well as you do. I was born here – in Edinburgh, I mean.'

'Ay, ye micht hae been. But I wis born here long afore you, sir.'

'How old are you, Mother?'

'Ah'll no be seeing seventy-fower again. Ah can show you sichts ye hae never seen in all your born days. Ah can tak ye –'

'No, no. I don't think I'll bother you to stir your old bones.'

'Then gie me a shilling for my auld banes, and Ah'll tell ye things, sir, aboot Edinburgh that'll mak yer hair staun on end.'

'What can you tell me, Mother, that I don't know already?' I asked her, as I handed her a florin. She clutched it in her claw-like hand and raised it quickly to her mouth. For a moment I thought she was going to swallow it, but she was only readjusting her teeth, which had come loose in her excitement at seeing the coin. As soon as she had regained her composure she spoke.

'Weel, tae begin with ...'

And here I may say she used a Scotticism much more vigorous and crude than the English words which I am compelled to write.

'Tae begin with, I was the mistress of Lawrence MacMarr.'

It was enough. This was a statement to which I could not bear the thought of additions or decorations. It was complete in itself. I wished to do no more than to have heard it, believed it and leave it. I gave her five shillings and hurried out of the Close.

Lawrence MacMarr. What, I wondered, would have been the effect of the statement I had just heard on other Edinburgh folk of my acquaintance. Some of the older people, those of my parents' generation, would, I think, have been profoundly shocked; not so much at the old woman's voluntary defamation of her long-defunct chastity as at the thought that Lawrence MacMarr could have ever had a mistress, let alone one drawn from such a class. Some of my own generation, or those a little bit younger than I am, would have been, in an equally tiresome way, delighted. They would have cross-questioned the old woman, worried the last detail out of her, and have written the whole thing up in a psycho-analytical way in some up-to-date journal devoted to denigration of the idols of the past. And what about the very young? The sad thing is, I think, that they would just not have been interested at all. But they would have been wrong; and I am fairly sure that those who come after them, in a hundred years or so, will agree with me.

As I walked up the High Street I wondered whether the old woman could possibly be speaking the truth. I made a rapid calculation of dates. Yes, it might be true. MacMarr had left Edinburgh about the middle nineties, and had died just after the turn of the century in the South of France. And from what one knew of his life in Edinburgh it was not improbable that ... I hesitated, and almost turned round to go back and talk to my old friend in the Close. But no, it was better to leave things as they were. If ever a statement was self-sufficient hers was. I walked on in the direction of Roy Crann's offices in George Street.

Lawrence MacMarr. What a stir his memory had made in the Edinburgh of my youth! What a conflict of opinions had raged about him in the years that had passed since then! He died in the year before I was born, but I have the fancy that I am one of the not very large number of his fellow-citizens who understand him, appreciate him at his true worth, neither idolizing nor contemptuous of him. I rather think that my view of him is the one that posterity will take (if it takes one at all), for, by the accident of my birth, childhood and youth in Edinburgh during the early part of this century, I became aware of Lawrence MacMarr just between the two waves of opinion about him – adulation and denigration.

Lawrence MacMarr was one of those strange freaks that are thrown up by the Scottish genius once every hundred years, freaks that now and again touch the hem of the garment of international greatness. He really was an astonishing and fascinating creature. Born of an Edinburgh middle-class family, and intended by his parents for the pursuit of some ordinary Edinburgh profession, he had early displayed a remarkable versatility and industry in the arts, and, so one is led to believe, to a lesser degree in the sciences. It was this versatility that, in the high noon of his post-mortem popularity, had earned him, amongst his most reckless Edinburgh admirers, the ridiculous soubriquet of 'The Scottish Leonardo da Vinci'.

It is true, however, that like Leonardo he is, and probably will be, most remembered by his paintings. Apart from those in private collections, there are two of his paintings in the National Gallery of Scotland, two in the Tate, and a number in galleries in the United States, where, twenty years ago, there was a great vogue for him. He was much under the influence of the French Post-Impressionists, but if his style derived from them there was something not only in his subjects but his manner that was highly individual and national. You feel, when you look at even one of his least significant works, that it is painted by a Scotsman and that that Scotsman is undoubtedly Lawrence MacMarr.

It is the same, but only more so, with his poetry and verse. Here, too, the influence of Baudelaire, Verlaine and the rest of them is felt. But there is something about the delicate vigour in his choice and use of English words and rhythms that shows that it is a Scotsman who is using them. Now and again, too, he bursts out into the use of the Scots tongue in his lyrics with an effect that is almost, but not quite, Burnsian in its quality.

His prose, by which he is less well known, has for me a little too rigid and Latin a flavour about it. It was in the lyric, expressed either in paint or verse, that he was at his most successful. I have heard that he was a skilful musician, but have no more evidence of this than the existence of two or three quite pleasant settings of his own verse. He studied science at Edinburgh University. And the scientists, in their own arid phraseology, tell me that some of his post-graduate work there was 'quite useful.'

Despite all this, Edinburgh did not think very much of him when he lived there; and it was only after he had left Scotland, had died in France, and had through his paintings achieved a measure of international reputation, that the people of his native city woke up to the fact of Lawrence MacMarr. Once having woken up, they certainly made up for their neglect. Articles, criticisms, reminiscences and imitations filled the Press and Journals. Halls were crowded to hear lectures on him and his works. For a brief period it might have seemed that Raeburn,

Scott, Stevenson and Burns were all cast into the shade. And Edinburgh took all the credit.

Then, after the War of 1914, the reaction set in. His very talents were selected for derision. In an age of specialization his versatility was dismissed as superficial. His industry, at a time when slipshod writing and slapdash painting were the fashion, was sneered at by clever writers from London as being more craft than art. And Edinburgh sat back, a little shocked and surprised.

As with his work, so with his private life. MacMarr, like many men condemned to die early, had a strong gusto for life. He took it where he found it. Mingled with his native puritanism was a powerful dash of what it was then fashionable to call *La nostalgie de la boue*. The public-houses, dance halls and places of less savoury reputation in Leith Walk had known him well at one time. All this was conveniently forgotten as soon as he was dead and famous. Humanity has a passion to model its heroes of the moment after itself. It makes its gods in its own image; and there is no use complaining about it. It is the inevitable fate of any artist to be made, if only temporarily, into a plaster saint as soon as he becomes popular. Be that as it may, there must have been some who smiled to hear Lawrence Mac-Marr's sayings quoted with approval from a dozen Edinburgh pulpits and his less felicitous 'verse prayers' collected together into a volume that practically amounted to a manual, of devotion. I do not say that these utterances and writings of his were not genuine: they certainly represented one side of the man. All I do say is that there must have been some who perhaps excusably smiled when they heard or saw them.

The reaction to this too set in. For my part I found it much more irritating and tiresome than the process of whitewashing, which was, at least, an innocent if muddle-headed pursuit. With truffle-nosed industry the C.I.D. of the post-1918 literary world plunged into Leith Walk, London and Paris, returning with (to them) rich prizes in the shapes of salacious and vinous anecdotes. This time Edinburgh did not sit back, but sat up shocked and surprised.

However, the great healer set to work, and, by the time at which the history that I am recounting begins, those who cared for Lawrence MacMarr as an artist and a man had begun to see him in something of a true perspective. The controversy was over and, after his own not quite first-class fashion, MacMarr had begun to join posterity.

Apart from anything else, it really had been an extraordinary coincidence that the old woman in the Close had mentioned MacMarr's name to me. For the last twenty-four hours he had been much in my mind, having been absent from it for a long period. Coming up in the train from London the day before I had been reading a book which had been sent to me for review. It was called *Lawrence MacMarr – A Garland of Remembrances*. It was a voluminous collection of MacMarriana by a certain Miss Prudence Muir, who, years before, I had known in Edinburgh. Miss Muir, so she informed us in her preface, had as a young girl in Edinburgh met MacMarr. After his death she had devoted her life to collecting unpublished anecdotes and reminiscences of her hero. These, with the assistance of many pens from all corners of the globe, she had collected together in her 'Garland'. She now published them 'in defence of the fair name of the great Scottish painter and poet'. It must have taken her about forty years to compile. It was an astonishing monument of industry and piety.

Despite the somewhat excessive odour of lavender and forget-me-not that seemed to hang about its pages the book was, to me, quite interesting. And so, despite some rather severe memories I had of Miss Muir when I had been a young man in Edinburgh, I determined to give the book a good review. After all, I could quite honestly praise its interest, its industry and its piety. I had just finished it when a peculiar little incident occurred.

We were leaving Berwick, and had just crossed the line which marks the Border between Scotland and England. I had noticed earlier on an elderly taciturn man of the Edinburgh lawyer type who was sitting opposite me. As we crossed the Border he suddenly spoke:

'We're in Scotland now.'

'I'm very glad to hear it,' I said.

Having broken the ice the elderly man went on:

'I see you're reading a book about Lawrence MacMarr. I once met him.'

'Really, sir? That's very interesting. Are you one of the contributors to this book?'

'I said I *once* met him. Once was quite enough. I never wished to see him again.'

'Indeed, sir?' I said. 'Why?'

'He came to my aunt's house in Drummond Place to dinner. But he was obviously in liquor when he arrived *before* dinner. He was unable to come down from the drawing-room to the dinner-table. He had to be sent home in a cab.'

'That must have been very awkward.'

'It was disgusting.'

No further remarks were made until we got to Edinburgh, where my companion bade me good night. For a moment I had toyed with including this anecdote in my review of the book. But I quickly dismissed it from my mind. I had no very pleasant memories of Miss Muir's treatment of me years ago, but that seemed no justification for a public and ill-mannered gibe such as including this incident in my review would be.

And now on the top of this there had come this adventure in MacGregor's Close. I stepped on my way to Roy's office rather more quickly. It was too good a story to waste. I looked forward to telling it to him.

When I got to the offices of the St Ninian's Society in George Street I was kept waiting in the hall outside Roy's office for ten minutes. This affectation of Roy's (for I felt sure it was an affectation to make himself appear more important in my eyes) never failed to irritate me. He had practised it every time I had called on him. Now, when I really did want to see him, it had the effect of considerably lowering the temporary warmth of feeling for him that I had succeeded in arousing. When at length I was ushered into his room he rose with an air of gaunt abstraction from a table on which maps and plans were scattered in a manner which I could not help feeling had been prepared. He adjusted his large horn-rimmed spectacles and, with the genial smile of the busy man who is good enough to spare a few moments of his time, greeted me.

'Ah, so you've come to see what we've been doing.'

'Yes, Roy. I've had a glance at some of the suppurating wounds on the body of our mother-city on which you have been spreading your antiseptic.'

Roy did not quite like this.

'Oh, ah, I see what you mean. What have you had a look at?'

'I've seen MacGregor's Close. You've done an extraordinarily good job there, Roy. Honestly you have.'

Roy sat back, and put the tips of his fingers together in a Gothic vane.

'Yes, we took a good deal of trouble over that. I think we succeeded. We cleaned it right up, but we managed to preserve everything essential from the old place.'

'Including the essential smell.'

'Oh, you noticed that, did you? It's a nuisance, but we can't do anything about it. The architect thinks it's something to do with the earth underneath.'

'I confess to a slight feeling of relief that even you can't change the quality of the earth.'

Roy smiled his wintry smile, but said nothing; so I went on:

'And there are other things that remain there too. I met an astonishing old woman who sells shoe-laces and matches at the corner of the Close.'

Roy shook his head disapprovingly.

'Yes, we didn't like to clear off all the old people at once. But they'll soon die off.'

'Well, I strongly advise you to get hold of this old woman before she dies off.'

'Why?'

'She claims with some vigour, and with a ring of truth in her voice, that she was the mistress of Lawrence MacMarr.'

I used the stronger, more vivid Scottish phrase. I saw Roy obviously wince.

'What has that to do with me?' he asked.

'You ought to get her to deliver a lecture to the St Ninian's Society.'

Roy pursed his lips in genuine disapproval.

'Oh, I wouldn't dream of doing such a thing.'

I had not, of course, made the suggestion completely seriously. But something in Roy's tone and attitude so irritated me that I gave wings to my fantasy and went on:

'Why ever not? If you could resuscitate Jean Armour you wouldn't hesitate to get her to give a lecture on Burns. A hundred years from now, if the St Ninian's Society is still in existence, members would pay a hundred guineas to hear what this old lady has to say – if they could bring her alive again.'

Roy thought for a moment. Then, with an air of conspiracy he said, in a lowered voice:

'We might arrange with the B.B.C. to get her voice recorded and locked away. But it would be rather awkward with the Director ...'

'I've got an even better idea, Roy. She's very old. Give her five pounds for the use of her body after she's dead. She'd probably drink herself dead at once on the money, so you wouldn't have long to wait for your money's worth. Then you could get her stuffed, and put in the hall here in a glass case with a notice under it "This was the mistress of Lawrence MacMarr." You might include some lines from *Ae Fond Kiss*, or a verse or two of MacMarr's own poem to Jeannie.'

Roy's face was now a sight to behold, but I went on:

'It would, apart from the local interest, be the most poignant reminder to members of your society that "Beauty vanishes, Beauty passes." That is to say, if any of them need reminding of it.'

Roy could stand no more.

'I think that's the most disgusting idea I have ever heard of,' he said.

'I'm sorry, Roy,' I apologized. 'But when will you dear fellow-citizens of mine learn to distinguish between fact and fantasy?'

'I'm glad to hear you did not mean the suggestion seriously,' Roy replied, still looking at me acidly.

'No, I did not,' I said, as I took my leave.

As I wandered down from George Street into Princes Street I found myself, I am afraid, in an unwarrantable state of petulance. By now I ought long ago to have learned to accept certain facets in the Edinburgh mentality as inevitable and not to have bothered about them. But there was something in Roy Crann's extravagantly prosaic Edinburgh attitude that had ruffled me — perhaps it was because he was not an Edinburgh man.

When I was walking along Princes Street towards my hotel in Charlotte Square I passed a big bookshop. One entire window was completely full of copies of Prudence Muir's *Garland of Remembrances*. It was the sight of this window that evoked a long-dead memory in me and prompted me to a foolish and ill-mannered action.

In a flash I was back twenty-odd years in time. I, a shy, eager youth, reputed to be interested in literary matters, had been kindly asked to one of Miss Prudence Muir's literary at-homes in her house in Queen Street. Even at that date Miss Muir was something out of Edinburgh's literary past. She had grown enormously fat, but preserved a fashion of dressing which allowed women to be fat and still keep their dignity. She was also large in build and had a swarthy complexion and a hooked nose. Altogether an alarming person. She ruled her salons with the authority that Queen Victoria used to exercise over her Court. Her literary productions had up till then been slight; but it was always with a shock of surprise that one recollected that this commanding personality had been the authoress of such fragrant fragments.

On the evening which I recalled there were about a dozen people present. Some were nondescript; some were those sub-fuse eccentrics which Edinburgh manages to produce each decade. The conversation, as it always did at these gatherings, eventually came round to Lawrence MacMarr. I was then thrilled to hear for the first time authentic stories about the great man which have since become familiar to me. I longed to contribute something to the discussion. Then there was pause, and the moment came. I remembered seeing in some French paper some mildly interesting reminiscences of the short time when MacMarr was studying in Paris in the Quartier Latin. It was, therefore, with no *arrière-pensée* that I said:

'I believe some very interesting stuff could be collected about the Bohemian side of MacMarr's life.'

Yes, the innocent epithet Bohemian was the word I used, but there was no doubt of the construction placed upon it by the literary salon and its queen. There was an audible silence. Then she spoke:

'I always think that those who mention that side of poor Lawrence's life are a trifle unnecessary.'

As I write these words they do not appear particularly oppressive. At the time, in the manner, and in the circumstances in which they were uttered, they were devastating. I was at the age of eighteen damned, cast into literary outer darkness, for ever dismissed as a 'trifle unnecessary'.

It was only when I had made my escape from Queen Street that I fully realized what Miss Muir had been driving at. Even that did not diminish my discomfort and anger. Why should one side of MacMarr's life, which had gone to his making as a man and an artist, be the subject of an absolute taboo? I agreed that those who dwelt upon it did so from prurient or stupidly iconoclastic motives. Was it not a sign of an equally prurient mind to pretend that it had never existed? Why had I not had the courage to say so? How humiliated, how angry I was!

All this had happened more than twenty years ago. Yet the sight of that well-stocked window in the Princes Street bookshop brought it all before me again with painful distinctness. There was only one difference now. I had the courage of my opinions. Had I not been so exacerbated by the morning's proceedings, however, I do not think I would have behaved as badly as I did.

I turned in to my hotel in Charlotte Square where I was staying. I took a sheet of notepaper and wrote the following letter:

DEAR MISS MUIR, You may not remember it, but years ago you were kind enough to receive me at your monthly literary gatherings. For my part, I have the liveliest recollections of the discussions and arguments we had, particularly about Lawrence MacMarr. I have just been reviewing your book for — and have devoted what skill I have with my pen to praising its industry and its piety. I hope the review will please you.

By a strange coincidence I met, upon my return to Edinburgh today, someone who claims to have known Lawrence MacMarr well, whose memoirs, however, do not appear in the pages of your book. Should you be contemplating a second edition I feel that you might care to include what she has to say: and I would be only too pleased to arrange an introduction.

She is an old lady who sells matches and shoe-laces at the corner of MacGregor's Close. My talk with her was of the briefest. Nevertheless what she said seemed to me to have the ring of truth about it. Her Scots is broad, antique and vigorous. But I feel sure that you, who are so great an amateur of our native Doric, will have no difficulty in understanding her.

She says (and since I am writing in English I will put what she said into English, though she expressed it much more forcibly), she says that she was the mistress of Lawrence MacMarr. Believe me, yours very sincerely,

MORAY MCLAREN

No sooner had I posted the letter in the large post office opposite the hotel than I was seized with remorse. I would have given a sovereign to have recalled it. Almost I contemplated going into the post office and trying to get it back. But I knew that would be no good. What an ill-mannered, foolish, wanton thing to have done. What a needless insult to an inoffensive old lady. If I had outgrown my youthful timidity I did not appear to have outgrown my gaucherie. A little later I did my best to excuse myself. After all was it so wanton? The Fates in making me meet in twenty-four hours the old lawyer in the train, the old lady of the Close and finally Roy Crann had clearly pointed the way. I had but obeyed. It was the best excuse I could offer myself.

Two mornings later as I was dressing I wondered if there would be a reply for me when I came down to breakfast. Once again I tried to palliate my offence. After all, I had not used the old woman's words, I had only said 'she says she was the mistress of Lawrence MacMarr.' In these days that would not pass for a very strong remark.

On my breakfast-table there was only one communication for me. It was a postcard in the thin Italianate hand which I now remembered over the years:

> *Moray McLaren, Esquire,*
> at The — Hotel,
> *Edinburgh.*

I paused for half a minute before I turned it over. When I did so I received the most stunning rebuke I have ever had administered to me. Whether Miss Muir had been stung by jealousy or by my ill manners into what would have been for her a fantastic falsehood, or whether she calmly produced on a postcard a secret over half a century old I do not know. In either event it was a knock-out for me.

On the other side of the postcard above her signature there were written only three words:

> *So was I.*

Naomi Mitchison

MITHRAS, MY SAVIOUR

I WAS posted to Britain last year. It was not what I had wanted but in the Legions you must take what's coming to you. It can't be Rome every time. And there are worse places in the Empire than Britain but not many with the same fogs and rain. There is this difference too in the north: the long, long days in the mid of the year – His time – and then the terrible quick shortening and His face hidden in the river fogs – the sucking river that goes down past Londinium with the tides rushing up and down, the moon-governed river of Britain!

My Centurion said it is nature. There is moon-governed sea in Spain and North Gaul. But nobody told me anything of this when I started my service. And when I was posted to Britain they did not tell me about the fogs coming knee-high, breast-high and, at last, swirling and choking over one's helmet. You hear someone laughing in the fog but you cannot catch him. The tide might creep up through the reeds right onto your feet and you would not know, not till it was on you. Coming quick and creeping cold.

Here, as you might say, on the flat ground, are our quarters, spread out proper as a Roman camp should be and there, all up and down and crowded and stinking, is their town that we call Londinium. The British town. The rivers coming off the low hills at the back go sneaking down through the town and lose themselves in the marshes. But there are ways all through the marshland, not rightly paved, but duckboards or sometimes stepping stones going away down to the wooden jetties that stick out over the mud and the crawling tides. The Gaulish boats come into them with their great leather sails marked for their Gaulish gods whose names I do not like even to think. Ourselves, we cross by the military ferry boats or, if on our private concerns, in the skin coracles that the British make.

Handy little things if one knows the way of them as these Britons do. But I am always thankful when I get out of one safe. And between the camp and the Britons, in the part of Londinium where we go ourselves, the path that is laid out and clean and decent, is our Cave. The rest of the camp know as much about it as is good for them to know. But for us it is the centre.

My Centurion, he is a Lion. If you know what that means, well and good. Me, I am a Soldier. And maybe you know what that means too. Yes, a Soldier of Mithras, the Unconquered. Most of the rest of the congregation are men in my own Legion but there are some of the permanent Staff of the camp and queerly enough some Britons. The old boy that keeps the wine shop for instance, you'll be surprised how high up he is. No, he doesn't use his own wine though he has some good jars. Just smiles a bit if anyone that doesn't know asks him to have one with him. He's put all that behind him.

This isn't to say there aren't other ways of thinking in the Legion. There are some that follow Eppona but those are mostly the chaps that have exchanged out of the Cavalry. I can understand a horseman following Eppona. And you get a few who are in the other Mysteries; in Massilia where we were quartered for a bit I came across some Christians but I didn't think much of them. It seemed to me, as far as I got them to talk about their Mystery, that they had part of it straight the way it is and always will be. So why didn't they see it right and come in with us? But it'll die out, this Christian Mystery, you mark my words.

Well, we had our Hunt. You can't do that the proper way in cities; it has to be more of a procession there. But here in Britain we could go the old way about it. A bit north of Londinium, over the rise there is oak forest and the white British bulls with black points, as noble a beast as one could see from here to Africa. Whatever else I have against Britain it's not those wild cattle of theirs. So we went quietly among the oaks and chose out a bull and roped him by the horns and legs, taking care not to break bone or horn. He was raging mad and there were twenty of us on him holding tight to the rope ends and singing. Everyone else who saw us was scared stiff and ran. That's part of it, of course. So we came down to the Cave.

All that was in plain sight of everybody though most of them were watching from a good way off or were up the trees. You feel proud and glad doing it, using all your strength against the Bull. You are going on His way doing it. As we got near the Cave there was a crowd looking out of windows mostly, but a few came nearer. They'd know right enough. You would hear them saying that these chaps were followers of Mithras and mind you, they were taking it dead serious. I'd been laughed at in my time – who hasn't? – with the old joke about the crow's head, which only shows, yes just shows, they don't know a thing! And I hadn't answered back in case I was to say more than I should. But this with the crowds was halfway to worship. It would be likely that some might come and ask – serious – a bit later on, and they'd be told enough to start them and that way we would get a new brother.

Well then, the Bull was put where he should be and the Fathers went to work on him, changing him, making him into something other than a wild bull of the forest. The rest of us were taking turns at the well. That isn't maybe the kind of cleanliness that matters most, yet it has to be done too. Since in life one thing is a mirror of another.

A man came up to us. He was white-looking and breathing quick. As well as that he was no beauty and he was wearing a uniform we didn't like much. It showed he was one of the slaves that belonged to the Commander's wife. Well, she came from one of these big Roman families, owned half the Mons Caelius if one can believe all one's told. Bad for the Commander she was, and I know what I'm talking about. She'd think things up and if he wasn't keen, well she'd lay off about her family. A moon-governed woman if ever there was one. She'd a whole crowd of slaves all dressed in this uniform more or less and there was an overseer that none of us thought much of. It shows on a man after a while, treating human bodies the way he did, even if they were nothing but slaves. Real nasty he used to be, this overseer, thinking things up to do to those slaves. And the mistress would laugh at it, so we heard.

Well, so this chap that was one of her slaves, he was looking hard at us and we were looking away. You could see how scared he was. Then suddenly he drops on his knees and draws something on the ground. I rub it out quick with my foot for one doesn't want *that* to be seen by anyone, but then I ask him the questions. You know, the questions of the Mystery of Mithras. He answers a bit different to us but I am pretty sure that's only with him being from another country. It is the same everywhere surely, but the words may be a little different between here and, say, Dacia, or Syria.

Well, you can see how I was placed. I was making up my mind what to do and he says, low and harsh and catching his breath: 'Oh quick, they'll get me!' So I knew he must have run away from that woman's household. It was awkward right enough. And then he says: 'By the Light of the Sun – save me!'

Well, there it was; there wasn't much choice, I passed him in. And a minute or two later I saw that overseer of hers come shouldering through. Someone was saying something to him and he came up to me and asked just the exact thing I knew he was going to ask. Well, naturally, I wasn't saying anything. It's an odd thing, right enough, but the more we're truthful to one another – and that's something that's dead serious to me anyway, the whole truth – the easier it comes to lie on someone that's outside. Someone that has no knowledge of our Brotherhood.

He didn't believe me. He gave a nasty look towards the door of the Cave. But he knew better than to try and come in. He blustered a bit all the same. It seemed this man was one of the litter slaves; she made them trot too with a whip at their backs. All up and down those hilly, slippery little streets of Londinium, letting on to herself it was like Rome. Which it isn't. And if one of them slipped they'd lash him to bits. So the chap had bolted.

You know they let women into some of the Mysteries. The Greeks do that and so do the Egyptians. No, I couldn't say about the Christians. But not us. We know. Moon-governed, that's what they are; even the best of them. And the Commander's wife was far from the best.

So then it was dusk and we went in between the Torch Bearers. And the Bull that was by then more than a bull, he died. And we were partakers of the blood. I see you know what I mean. Yes, you know. And this ugly, scarred little chap that was a runaway slave he was with us. They'd taken off that uniform of hers that he was wearing, burned it, I shouldn't wonder. He was wearing the right robes for what he was.

We kept him there inside the Cave for a month, just let him go out a bit at night when there was no one about. We'd see that overseer prowling around. He knew right enough where the runaway was. But he couldn't get at him.

As a matter of fact, the Commander sent for my Centurion. And a man can't lie the same way to his Commanding Officer. As I make out, my Centurion let him know in a respectful kind of manner, but straight all the same, that this man had taken sanctuary and if the sanctuary was broken by force, then all the followers of the way of Mithras would be against him wherever he went, Gaul, Germania, Dalmatia, Macedonia, anywhere you'd find the Legions. You see there'd be bound to be some of us everywhere and we'd get word around. That can be done. It has been done before. So it just wasn't worth the Commander's while to do the thing that wife of his wanted.

And me. That man had asked me to save him and that was just what I'd done. To save someone, even in this kind of small way, that makes a sort of mirror image again. I mean – He is the Saviour. You know that as well as I do. He hunted the bull that is Himself. He is the Way between us and the Light and if you save anyone, well you get a kind of glimpse. Not that I can put it into words. But that kind of thing that wasn't prepared, that I had just to do when it came on me, well maybe it was the biggest thing I'll ever have in my life. Bigger than anything I could ever do in battle. Bigger perhaps than if I was to die for the Eagles of the Legion. I mean, it wasn't much in itself but it got me a bit nearer. Yes, a bit nearer to Him. Mithras my Saviour.

Neil Paterson

SCOTCH SETTLEMENT

It was Harry got the picture. At school. The earth was too
hard to work in winter and so Harry was goin' to school, and
big Andra Jamieson he had the picture, he was allowed books
with pictures in his house, he had hundreds, he said, mebbe
thousands, he had this picture down the leg of his pants and
Harry said, 'Give us it.' Harry said he said, 'Please, Andra.'
'You don't have to beg,' Andra said. 'It's yourn.' And he gave
Harry the picture, and Harry took me down past the clearing to
the hemlocks and showed me.

'Mutts,' I said.

'No,' Harry said. 'Dawgs. These are English setter dawgs
and mighty rare. Real dawgs.'

We looked at the picture. There was two dawgs. One was
settin' on his backside and one was on his four legs. The one
that was settin' was squintin' up at the one that was standin',
an' he was tongue out and rarin' to go. I guess he was grinnin'
straight at me. He was the dawg I liked the best of them.

'They're red dawgs,' Harry said, 'and their picture was took
for sellin'. Anybody wants them dawgs he can have them, it
says, for twenty-five dollars apiece.'

'Is twenty-five dollars a deal of money, Harry?' I asked.

'Twenty-five dollars,' Harry said. 'Ah, yes.'

We looked at the picture for a long time and Harry let me
hold it.

'Ain't none of the kids in the whole of Canada belongs a
pair of two dawgs like this,' Harry said. 'I aim to call mine
Rover. What you goin' to call yours, Dave?'

'I was aimin' to call mine Rover too,' I said.

We had a hide-out Harry built down there in the hemlocks
at the edge of the water. There was no wet settin' on account
of the canoe birch we laid down in strips for floor. We set on

the floor of our own two's secret house and looked for a long, long time at the picture of the red dawgs. They sure was pretty.

'There's Gramma hollerin',' Harry said at last.

'I don't hear her.'

'You never hear,' Harry said. 'Come on.' He folded the picture and put it in his pocket, and we rolled up my trousers so as my gramma would not see the ends was wet and say, You been down by the hemlocks again, and then we went on up for our rations.

'Do you know where I aim to hide this picture?' Harry said.

'No,' I said.

'In my grandaddy's boots.'

I looked into Harry's eyes to see what he meant, and I saw that Harry meant what he said.

'But, Harry,' I said. It was no use. Harry could speak faster'n me, and I never yet talked him into anything or out of any other thing. Harry was eight and smart, and I was but four.

'No other place,' Harry said, his mind was made up. 'Grandaddy's boots.'

I thought of my grandaddy's boots and of my grandaddy. I had a bad stomach, thinkin'. 'I wouldn't, Harry,' I said.

'Safest place,' Harry said. 'My grandaddy has been to the Convention, and his boots is oiled and on the shelf. Come the spring, my grandaddy will put on his boots and go down to the Houses again, but till the spring there will be no comin' and goin' among people and no need for the boots, and no sich safe place in all the house as the insides of them. You take it from me, Dave,' Harry said.

I shook my head. I didn't like it at all. I knew it was two sins. It was a sin to have a picture in the house, and it was a sin to touch my grandaddy's boots. My grandaddy was death on sin. He had eyes sharp as a woodcock for wrong-doin', and when he saw a sin he raised his voice to Heaven and said so, and if it was us had done the sins he took us into the wood-shed and beat us. Once he beat Harry justly till he bled. My grandaddy was a just and terrible man. He was bigger'n anybody's door I ever seen except our own, and he'd a bin bigger'n ourn too if it hadn't been he built the hole to fit hisself. He was thick as two towny men put together, and he had a black beard shaped like a spade that he could a dusted the crumbs off the table with by noddin' his head if he had had a mind to, which he hadn't. He could not write except for J. Mackenzie, his mark, and he could not read, only some capital letters and the names of God and Jesus and numbers up to 793, which is the end of the Bible, Amen, and he had not any yap like the village men but Conventions, when he sat down Harry said the place where he sat became the top of the table and men pointed their talk at him and kept their traps shut when he opened his. He was a true Christian. He knew God's will, and wreaked it on us.

His boots was the best of all the things my grandaddy had, nobody had their like, they was fifteen years old, and he was famed for them. The folks down at the Houses had an idea he wore them boots every day of the year, and they rated him high, Harry said, for this. Folks never guessed that he carried the boots to the outside of the village and put them on behind a tree. Folks did not know that when they came visitin', mebbe once twice a year, my gramma spied them in the valley and beat on the gong and my grandaddy would even come runnin' to get shod before the company arrived. They was black beautiful boots, none of us was ever let touch them, and there was Harry aimin' to hide a picture in them, and pictures was agin God and so was a finger on the boots, and my stomach was jest plain draggin' itself up the track to our house.

My grandaddy was not in the house. You could kinda smell when my grandaddy was in and when he wasn't, not sniff-sniff with your nose, not that kind of a smell, but you could jest smell the nice slack feel of the house.

'Where's my grandaddy?' Harry asked.

'Outside,' my gramma said. 'Now go and git washed, and hurry, and Davy, you scour them hands. Harry, see he does it.'

We came in cleaned and knelt down at our chairs.

'Lord,' Harry said, 'Father chart hum hum bout to receive hum hum blessed portion hum hum hummy umhum day and night. Amen. Gramma, whereabouts outside is my grandaddy?'

'Amen, Davy!' my gramma said.

'Amen,' I said.

'Is he in the wood-shed?' Harry said.

'Now pull your chair up afore you set on to it,' my gramma said to me. 'And never mind the knife. Use that spoon. What was it you was sayin', Harry?'

'I said, where's my grandaddy,' Harry said.

'He's had *his* meat a half-hour,' my gramma said.

'But where is he? Davy wants to speak to him.'

'Me?' I said.

'Your grandaddy is out by the fallen tree,' my gramma said. 'He's amakin' of fish-hooks. Drink up your goat now, Davy.'

'Davy aims to ask him for a dawg,' Harry said.

I laid down my spoon and stared at Harry.

'Well, *I* asked last time,' Harry said. 'Of course, if you're feart to ask.'

'I'm not feart,' I said.

'Stop gabbin', Davy,' my gramma said. 'Jest let off gabbin' this instant and eat up your meat.'

I ate up and drank my goat. My gramma was for ever pickin' on me, but she had only a little voice — she was small-sized — and meant no harm by it. Although she was small-sized, mind, she was clever. She could weave and, not only, she could read and write, and had spectacles to prove it. She did what my grandaddy said like the rest of us, but once when my grandaddy had me by the pants and there was high words flyin' round my ears, my gramma spoke a piece on her own, and that time it was my grandaddy did what *she* said.

'Gramma,' I asked, 'why won't Grandaddy let us git a dawg?'

'On account of its rations,' my gramma said.

'We could git a little tiny dawg.'

'It wouldn't eat but bucket scraps,' my brother Harry said. 'It would catch all the rats. It'll be a little white rattin' dawg, and we'll call it Rover.'

'You'll hev to ask your grandaddy,' my gramma said. She

took the done dish off the table and went to scrape it in the backyard.

'You finished?' Harry asked.

'Near enough,' I said.

'Lord,' Harry said. I bowed my head. 'Lord hum hum thank God. Amen. Amen, Dave!'

'Amen,' I said. 'Harry, I never yet seen a red dawg. Did you, Harry?'

'No,' Harry said. 'But them's red dawgs, sure enough. It says so in the writing. Now go and git down to the tree and ask Grandaddy.'

'Okay,' I said. 'You comin'?'

'No,' Harry said.

I went half across the clearing, then I stopped and looked back. 'What'll I say, Harry?' I asked.

'Jest say you want a dawg. Go on. There's nothing to be scared of.'

When I had gone a little farther Harry shouted, 'If he won't let us git a dawg, try him for some other kind of crittur.'

'What other kind of crittur?' I asked.

'Any kind,' Harry said. It was nothing to him. He was kicking stones round the front door, his hands in his pockets. 'Hurry up,' he said.

My grandaddy had a fire lit down by the tree. He had got horses' nails off old Neil Munro in the spring, they was the best and softest iron, and my grandaddy knew a way to burn them nails and make them into a steel bar, and then when he had filed a hook on the end of the bar he cut it off, heated it red-hot and tossed it in a bucket of water, and then he picked the hook out of the water and laid it on a hot iron till it was bright blue, and to finish off he dropped it in a fishin'-can full of candle grease, and it got black then, and when it got black it was finished. It was the best and strongest hook you ever seen.

When I got down to the tree my grandaddy was jest cuttin' a hook off the bar. He had his back to me and I could not see, but I knew that was what he was doin' on account of his arm went in and out like a saw. I thought I would wait till he finished cuttin', so I waited. I walked up close, and waited till the hook fell off the bar. My grandaddy had tongs, and he took the hook in the tongs and put it in the fire.

'Grandaddy,' I said, 'Harry and me wants a dawg.'

My grandaddy twisted the hook in the flames and laid it in a red nest in the fire. He had a very black face with the beard, but not his eyes, they was blue and dug right into you.

'Jest even a little mutt,' I said.

'What do you want a dawg for?' my grandaddy said.

I could not tell. I knew that we wanted a dawg better nor anything, but I could not jest think what we wanted it for.

'A dawg is no use,' my grandaddy said. 'You can't eat a dawg.'

I could not think of anything to say. I waited a bit, but there was no more talk from him and nothing more comin' from me, and so I went away.

Harry let off kickin' stones and came to meet me. 'Well, let's hear it,' he said. 'What did he say?'

'Said no,' I said. 'Said you can't eat a dawg.'

We walked round to the side of the house without speakin'. We heard my gramma come out the front and start hollerin'.

'Wants you,' Harry said.

I looked at the sun. Was my bedtime.

'Harry, I want to be shook if I'm sleepin',' I said, 'an' see them dawgs again. Will you, Harry?'

'All right,' Harry said. He put up his hands for shoutin'. 'He's comin', Gramma!'

I went round the front to my gramma.

'Davy,' she said, 'was it you hid the scrubber agin?'

I would have said no, but she had a hard face on. 'I think it's settin' up there on the kitchen couples, Gramma,' I said.

It was tub night. When I was in the tub I told her about my grandaddy. I told her my grandaddy was set agin a dawg.

'Gramma,' I said, 'I don't like my grandaddy.'

'Hush,' my gramma said. 'Hush now, that's a terrible thing to say. Everybody likes their grandaddy.'

'No,' I said. 'Gramma, Alec Stewart has a grandaddy is on his side.'

'Is on his side?' my gramma said, and she left off with the towel.

'Is on his side,' I said, noddin'. 'Alec Stewart's grandaddy is. He told me.'

'Your grandaddy sometimes does not always understand young uns,' my gramma said, 'and you are too small a young un to understand grandaddies.' She rubbed the skin near off me. 'Now get shirted up afore I lose patience, and take a great leap into the bed.'

I got into the bed.

'If we had a little white rattin' dawg,' I said, 'it wouldn't eat but rats, and it could have a wee end offa my rations on the Sunday.'

'Git over the bed,' my gramma said, sharp, 'and leave his room for Harry, and stop up all this gabbin' and git to sleep.'

'All right. Good night, Gramma.'

'You never can tell,' my gramma said at the door. 'You might git a dawg some day, Dave. Now git to sleep.'

I lay waitin' for Harry.

I could hear next door. I heard my grandaddy come in and grunt, and I heard my gramma, her feet moved round the room, and then she spoke up to him.

'That dawg,' she said. 'The dawg that Davy wants.'

I didn't ketch what my grandaddy said.

'You can't knock mansize sins outa boys that hasn't yit growed up to them,' my gramma said. 'You own son's sons and you adenyin' them and drivin' them the same wrong road.'

'It's God's road,' my grandaddy said.

'It's a fool's road, James Mackenzie,' my gramma said, 'and it ends in cryin'.'

Harry came in then, and there was no more talkin' save Harry, he had some gab, and my gramma said yis and no, and Harry came to bed. It was dark, and we couldn't see the picture, and Harry didn't want to talk. He said he was too damn bitter.

'If we *did* get a dawg,' he said, 'my grandaddy would only eat it.'

I lay on my back for a long time. I heard my gramma and my grandaddy git into their bed and I jest lay on, thinkin'.

'Harry,' I said. I kicked him. 'Would he eat it skin an' all?'

'Eh?' Harry said, he was half asleep. 'Eat what?'

'The dawg.'

'I don't reckon my grandaddy is truly a dawg-eater,' Harry said. 'Good night.'

'You don't reckon he would truly eat a dawg?'

'Not a whole dawg,' Harry said. 'Now shet up and go to sleep.'

'All right, Harry,' I said. 'Good night.'

2

I don't know if it was the next day or some other day, I think it was some other day, the men came to our house. They came ridin' on hosses, and you could see crowds more where they came from, they was without hosses and small as worms way down in the valley. The hosses dug in their heels by our door and the men hollered for my grandaddy.

My gramma put her hand up atop her eyes and took a good hard look at them.

'Where's Jim Mackenzie?' they said. The hosses danced.

'He might be fixin' the fence,' my gramma said at last. 'Up by the oats.'

'Gee-up!' they said. 'G'an!' And I ran out from the side of my gramma to watch them go. It sure was pretty to see them hosses calomphin' along, their hoofs hit sparks off the track and the men's backsides jogged up an' down.

'I reckon they came peaceable,' my gramma said, 'but it don't hurt to make sure. Davy, run down to the wood-pile and tell your grandaddy.'

I told my grandaddy and he hit the axe blade into a hard-wood log and started for home, and I ran beside him.

'There was guns stuck on the hosses' necks,' I said.

My gramma had my grandaddy's boots open for him at the

door. 'There was five of them, Jim,' my gramma said. 'One was Joe Cullis.'

'Was the hosses sweatin'?' my grandaddy asked.

'No.'

My grandaddy laced his boots and took his gun off the top of the door. I ran to git his cartridge belt.

'Thanks, Davy,' he said.

We stood watchin' him till he hit the wood and we could not see him any more.

'Will my grandaddy be killin' the hosses too?' I asked.

'Your grandaddy's not agoin' to kill anything,' my gramma said, 'the idea.' But she stayed at the door, listenin', and I was not sure. 'You bide by the house now,' she said. She took a last hard listen and went in through the door.

Soon I saw Harry, it was his time to be home from school. I gave the scalp whoop and ran across the clearing to meet him.

'Five hosses,' I said. 'Guns. Guns, Harry, and men ridin' fast.'

'That's nothing,' Harry said.

'They went calomphin' up to the oats and my grandaddy's git after them. One of the hosses was white.'

'Nothin',' Harry said. 'Nothin. Listen, where's grandaddy did you say?'

'He went after the hosses. The hosses was ...'

'And Gramma?'

'She's in. Harry, my grandaddy's booted up an' he's got his gun.'

'Listen, will you,' Harry said. 'This is *important*. I got somethin' mighty special. You know what I got? Go on, ask me.'

'What you got, Harry?' I asked.

'Not so loud,' Harry said. 'We'll jest ease down the hemlock way like we wasn't goin' nowhere in particler. Hisht now, I got somethin' you wouldn't guess. I got a babby.'

'A babby!' I said. 'A real babby?'

'Real enough,' Harry said. 'It's settin' on its hunkers in the hut chawin' away at a root. You feel the weight of it you'd know it was real. I've had it since the mornin'.'

'Where'd you git it, Harry?' I asked.

'Found it.'

'And is it really ourn?'

'It's mine,' Harry said. 'But you kin have a loan of it when I got other business. We kin run now.'

We ran.

'It's declarin' again,' Harry said. 'Hear it?'

I heard it plain.

Harry ran on in front, and when I got to the hut he had the babby up in his arms. 'Hisht now,' he was sayin'. 'It had lost its root,' he said to me. The babby was dressed in a shawl and long pink pants. Harry set it down and it rolled over and howled. Harry set it up straight and held out the root, and it took the root and shet up and shoved it in its trap.

'Well, doggone,' I said. 'It's purely real.'

'You kin feel it,' Harry said, 'if you crave to,' so I felt it. The babby did not turn its head to look, but its eyes came round the side of the root and gave me a glower.

'Hullo, babby,' I said.

It never said nothing.

'Kin it speak, Harry?'

'Ain't exactly gabby,' Harry said.

'Is it new-born, mebbe?'

'No, no, it's gittin' on. Listen, Dave,' Harry said, 'you know what a babby needs best of all. It needs milk. So I aim to go an' tap the goat afore my gramma gits there, an' you bide, see, an' mind the babby. If it drops its root it'll holler, so give it its root back, an' if it still hollers sing to it.'

'Okay, Harry,' I said.

When Harry was gone I sat down beside the babby and looked at it, and it looked back at me.

'What's your name, babby?' I asked.

It never said nothing.

I poked round it with my finger to see was it well fattened up, and it was. I stroked the top of its head and it never moved, only its eyes, they squinted up; it was jest a young babby and did not know it could not see the top of its own head. It looked hard at its root.

'Tomorra, babby,' I said, 'I'll cut you a hunk off the old hog. That's better nor root.'

I thought I heard Harry, or mebbe it would be my grandaddy. I got a real skeer. I went out and poked my head round the side of the hut, and whenever I went away the babby let out a holler. 'Wheesht!' I said. I could not see anything. I went back and said, 'Wheesht now!' and when it saw me it stopped hollerin'. It had took a fancy to me. I went away some more times to see would it holler, and every time I went away sure enough it hollered and everytime I went back it let off. I reckoned it was some birds I heard. I put my arms round the babby to lift. The babby was willin', but it was plumb solid. I got it up, but my legs had no notion to walk with it. I could of carried it fine on the flat, only them bits of canoe birch was not safe to walk on with a babby. 'See,' I said, 'you're big as me now.' I heard a curlew whistle and knew it was Harry, so I put the babby down quick and set it right way up, and Harry came in then. He had a half tin of goat.

'Take the root out of its mouth,' he said, 'and let me feed it.'

I took the root out of the babby's mouth and the babby hollered. It wouldn't look at Harry's tin. It was its root it wanted.

'All right, give it the root to have in its hand,' Harry said. He had that babby all weighed off. I gave it the root in its hand, and it shet right up and drank its milk, with Harry holdin' the tin and its face half inside of it.

I laughed to see it drink. 'Sure has a thirst,' I said.

'One thing about a babby,' Harry said, 'you got to wet its whistle near every hour of the day. My gramma near ketched me, Dave. I was jest finished at the goat when she came round the side of the house. Look now, you git up for your rations, it's near your time, in case she starts searchin' for you. I gotta wash up the babby an' do its chores.'

'And then you'll take it up to the house?' I asked.

'No, no,' Harry said. 'I aim to keep it in the hut. There ain't nobody but you and me got to know about this babby. It's ourn.'

I thought about that. That was good.

'Are we goin' to keep it for ever, Harry?'

'I don't know,' Harry said. 'We'll keep it here for a year or two anyways, till it's got a mind of its own, and then if it wants to hit the trail, won't be no stoppin' it. Now go on, Dave, up to the house.'

I would of liked to bide and watch the baby git its wash, but I had to go for fear my gramma came down by the hemlocks, so I said good night to the babby and told it I would see it in the mornin', and went on up to the house.

The first thing I seen was my grandaddy's boots.

'Your grandaddy's at the water-shelf,' my gramma said, 'so say your prayers good.'

I said my prayers and ate my rations and drank the wee drop milk that was all my gramma had gotten off the goat, then I said more good long prayers, then my grandaddy came in from the water-shelf and my gramma took me out and scrubbed my hands and face.

'Gramma,' I said, 'when I was a babby did I have a towel round my middle?'

'You did,' my gramma said. 'And all babbies has.'

'Why?'

'Why?' my gramma said. 'So as the babby is all plugged up, of course. A babby is like a cat, you see. It has got to be teched about sich things, jest like a cat or any other young crittur.'

'But it's better nor a cat,' I said. 'Nor a dawg neither.'

'Granted,' my gramma said. 'Now say good night to your grandaddy and git bedded.'

I said good night to my grandaddy and got into the bed. I clean forgot about the hosses and the guns, I was too busy thinkin' about the babby, the games me and it would play, and what we was goin' to call it, that specially.

When Harry came in I asked him.

'I ain't jest settled on a name yet,' Harry said, he whispered. 'You thought up somethin'?'

'We could call it Rover,' I said.

'No, no.'

'Rover's a good name, Harry,' I said.

'Rover's a dawg name,' Harry said. 'It's a good name for a

202

dawg, but not for a babby. I had a notion now to call it George.'

'George is a good name too,' I admitted, 'but I like Rover best.'

'I tell you t'ain't fitten,' Harry said. 'And whose babby is this babby anyway?'

'It's your babby, Harry,' I said.

'Well,' Harry said, 'I am goin' to call my babby George after the King, an' that is now its name, an' we will have no more argy-bargy outa you, Dave, that is if you crave to keep friendly with me and my babby.'

'I think George is an extra good name, honest, Harry,' I said.

We heard my grandaddy say his prayers through the door, and then we heard the bed creak, and we knew that him and her had gotten into it.

'Harry,' I said, 'how did you know about them wettin' cloths the babby has on round its middle?'

'I remember my mamma with you,' Harry said. 'I used to help her, and times I did you myself.'

I thought about Harry doin' me. I couldn't remember, but Harry remembered near everything that ever happened from the start of him an' me. Harry remembered my daddy and my mamma. He used to tell me pictures of them in bed, and my daddy was a big man in a white shirt, as strong and thick as my grandaddy, but not so hairy and twice as clean, and my mamma was purely beautiful with a soft way of strokin' you and you could tell her anything, and she did a lot of laughin', but never at you, and her face was like in a picture book. Not like my gramma, who was kind, but her face was strictly useful. I asked my gramma about my mamma, but my gramma never liked to look back, she only said, 'Your mamma was somethin' special, even if she did marry our Alec. Remember always she was somethin' special, puir lassie; she had hands fine as a lady's.'

'What are ladies' hands like, Gramma?' I asked.

'Very clean,' my gramma said.

I used to wash my hands sometimes when I was not told, because I wanted to be somethin' special too. I looked at my hands in the dark and I thought about the babby and the babby's hands. The babby's hands was fat and thick and dirty. 'Did you wash the babby's hands, Harry?' I asked.

'Wheesht,' Harry said. 'Yis, I washed it all. I'm goin' now.'

I must a been half asleep, lyin' there thinkin', because I saw that Harry was over by the windy and he was dressed with all his clothes on. 'I'll be back afore they git up in the mornin',' Harry said, and he climbed right out the windy.

I listened for a long time. I couldn't hear but my grandaddy snorin' and the birds, the noises they made in the wood. I wouldn't be surprised if I heard a wolf too. There was a terrible lot of noise in that old dark wood.

'George,' I said. It was a good name right enough, but it wasn't sich a good name as Rover. I put my head under the blankets and went to sleep.

3

Next day my gramma and my grandaddy thought Harry was at school, but Harry was not at school. Harry was down at the hut with the babby and me. Harry was very sleepy on account of he had been too cold to sleep hardly all night, and so he lay in the hut alöngside the babby's nest and slept, and I had the babby to myself. I and the babby had a fine time. The babby had thrée teeth and a brown spot that wouldn't wash off under its chin. It could stand holdin' on, but it didn't aim to stand on its own. I reckon it was a real lazy kind of babby. It was hard to please with its rations too. It did not like salted ham, and it even did not like a tasty hunk of cheese. It liked water and root, and it wanted to eat a stick of wood, but I did not let it until I had washed the stick good in the lake, and then I told the babby it was jest to sook.

When Harry waked up he sent me to the house for sweet taters, and I got that. Then he sent me to the house for a chunk off my gramma's bolt of cotton, that was for wettin' cloths for the babby, he said to wait till my gramma was out the back, then git the big shears and cut off a hunk this size, he showed me, but I could not work the shears. I got the beginnin' of a hole made, then my hand stuck in the handle of the shears and the blade of the shears stuck in the cloth and I thought I heard my gramma comin', and I picked up the whole bolt and shears an' all and ran; it was bigger'n me that cloth, and it tripped my legs, and I could not see where I was goin', and it got real dirty and scratched with us fallin' and I lost the shears some place and could not find them, but Harry said never mind, my gramma did not see me, nobody did, that was all that signified.

I had to go up to the house for my dinner, and I got some in my pockets for Harry and up my jersey too; my grandaddy was not there, and I did not have to say long prayers, and when I got back Harry had a fire built and the sweet taters was roastin' on the fire. We had ample rations, but the babby was plumb finnicky and would not eat its tater, only a mite when it got cold, and a half slice of bread.

Harry watched the sun. He knew the size of the trees' shadders on the lake, and when they was the right size he said it was time for him to be outa school, and he better had go work a hand on that little old goat afore my gramma, she got there.

'Same as yestiddy, Dave,' he said. 'It's all yourn till I get back.' He meant the babby.

I went and looked to see had he really gone, and then I came back and pulled the babby outa its nest, the babby was hollerin', and set it on my knee.

'Wheesht now, you're my babby now,' I said, 'Rover.'

When Harry came back he was shakin' his head. Wasn't no milk but a little, it was a spoon's fill in the bottom of the tin. 'Go up to the house, Dave,' Harry said, 'and git some pure water for mixin' in.' The babby was smart. When it saw the tin it started declarin'. 'Hurry, Dave,' Harry said, so I went runnin'.

I near run right into my grandaddy.

My grandaddy was standin' in the clearing and a big man along of him. That man was Mister McIver the preacher, and he was the dominie too. He was a true Christian like my grandaddy, he was fierce as a wolf, and his beard was red.

'You! Go git Harry,' my grandaddy said, and his voice was small but bad.

I turned and ran back into the trees. I ran my fastest to the hut.

'Red Kiver, Harry!' I said. 'Red Kiver, the dominie! And my grandaddy wants you.'

'Where?' Harry said. 'Where, where, Dave?'

'In the clearing.' I pointed.

Harry laid the babby in its nest and turned his eyes to Heaven.

'My grandaddy's hoppin' mad,' I said, 'on account of he must of got ketched with his boots not on. You better hurry.'

'Lord sweet God, have mercy on me,' Harry said. 'A poor sinner.'

I took his hand and we went up to the clearing.

'Come here,' my grandaddy said. He pointed Harry with his beard. 'Here.' And Harry went and stood at the end of his beard. 'Now,' my grandaddy said, 'you stand for judgement. Hev you aught to say?'

Harry shook his head, he did not look.

'The boy has sinned doubly. He has been absent two days,' the dominie said, and he limbered his arm. 'I maun thrash him, Jim.'

'Ay,' my grandaddy said, 'you maun thrash him, John. This is fair an' fitten since you are his dominie, but you will thrash him in the school's time, I say, an' not in mine.'

A glare got up between my grandaddy and the dominie, their eyes stuck out like the prongs of forks.

'I came as friend, Jim.'

'You kin go as friend, John,' my grandaddy said, 'if you so please. You spoke as dominie. A man sends his childer to school, the dominie has the use of that childer in school-time. But when the school is out, a man has the use of his own childer and his childer's childer, and on my land an' in my time no man thrashes mine but me. Harry, git to the woodshed. An' you, Davy, go up to the house for your rations.'

I went to the house.

'I never called you yit,' my gramma said. 'What ails you?'

'Nothing,' I said. I sat on my stool at the corner of the fire and wisht for a miracle to deliver Harry from the Christians. After a long time my grandaddy came stompin' in, I couldn't look.

'What was John McIver the preacher after?' my gramma said.

'It was John McIver the dominie,' my grandaddy said. 'He came by with a search party. They is searchin' the upper wood an' he stopped by to query for Harry. Harry has been absent the school two days syne.'

My gramma opened her mouth and took that in. 'And where is Harry?' she asked.

'In the woodshed.'

'Hev you beat him?' my gramma said. Her face was shut up tight, and sour.

'No,' my grandaddy said. 'That is for the dominie. I have ast Harry where he has been and what he has been doin', but he does not aim to tell me. He defies me, an' so I hev shut him in the woodshed, an' he will bide there until he sees the error of his ways. He will git no rations but water. We will now pray.'

After we had et, my gramma gave me a cot's lick at the water-shelf and sent me to my bed. I thought mebbe my grandaddy would go and git Harry, and my grandaddy did go to the woodshed, but he came back single. My gramma spoke for Harry, but my grandaddy hit the table a smack and said, 'Silence! I have said he bides, woman. An' bide he will.'

It was dark.

I put on my clothes and opened the windy enough to git through. There was more noises than any other night, and the ground was a long way down from the windy and I could not see it. I did not want to go, but I knew somebody had to guard the babby from the wild beasts and give it its feed. I put my legs over and hung by my hands. I hung for a long time. After a bit I thought I would climb in again, but I couldn't. I couldn't let go neither. If my grandaddy hadn't been there I'd have hollered for my gramma. I jest hung by my fingers till they bent up. Then I fell. I wasn't hurt except my fingers was sore and my knees was scraped.

It was awful dark.

If somebody got lost on a dark night like that they'd mebbe never git found for days, and if they went down by the hemlocks they might fall into the lake too. The beasts was prowlin' around the wood, you could hear them, and the birds was screamin' with fright.

I went to the woodshed and shouted, 'Harry.'

I gave a whole heap of kicks on the door and shouted, 'Harry, Harry, Harry.'

'Is that you, Dave?' Harry said.

'It's me,' I said. 'Harry, I'm not feart. Harry, mebbe I can't find the hut down by the hemlocks an'll fall into the lake. But I'm not feart, not of the wolves neither.'

'I can't hear you,' Harry said. 'Dave, when you git down there, give the babby its drink and change its wettin' cloth. Can you do that, Dave?'

I didn't know could I or not. I was watchin' a square-shaped beast the size of an ox, it was hidden in back of a bush.

'And then,' Harry said, 'see the babby is warm and tucked low in its nest, and you can top it up with my gramma's cloth too.'

'Harry,' I said, 'and I can't get back in the windy, it's too high. Harry, there's a great big beast out here glowerin' at me.'

'There's what?'

'A great big beast,' I said. 'But I'm not feart.'

'Stop screamin',' Harry said. 'It don't do any good to scream.'

'I'm not screamin',' I said. 'I'm not feart, Harry, even if there's two of them. Harry, will it soon be light?'

'No, it won't be light for a long time,' Harry said. 'Dave, is there truly a beast? Are you awful feart?'

I could hear my heart, and my hair was hot.

'Are you, Dave?'

'Yes,' I said. 'And I'm feart of the wolves too, and mebbe I'll fall in the lake and I can't git back in the windy and could be I got lost in the wood and never was found again.'

'Well, shet up for a minute,' Harry said, 'and let me think.'

I shet up. I never looked near the beast again, but it took a step nearer and breathed on the back of my neck.

'Harry,' I said, 'are you still there, thinkin'?'

'Yes,' Harry said. 'Listen, Dave, there is only one thing for it. You are too little to do for the babby. Go on up to the house and tell my gramma. Tell her about the babby needs its milk. Go on now, run.'

I couldn't run. I couldn't move.

'Go on,' Harry said. 'Dave, hev you gone?'

I heard the beast again and I let out a great loud scream. I guess mebbe I thought I would scare that beast away. I jest stood with my eyes shut and the scream kept skirlin' outa me.

'Dave, is that you, Dave? Where are you?' my grandaddy's voice said, and I opened my eyes and saw his lantern.

'Tell my grandaddy!' Harry said. He was shoutin' and hammerin' on the inside of the shed. 'That's grandaddy. Tell grandaddy!'

I ran like a tiger and took a leap at my grandaddy's legs.

'It's the babby,' I said. 'The babby, Grandaddy!'

He picked me up level with his face and I told him. His face was lamp-lit and queer.

'In the hut by the hemlocks,' I said.

'Show me,' he said.

I took him down by the hemlocks. The beasts was fair feart of my grandaddy and was all runnin' far away. We heard the babby's holler, and my grandaddy put his face to the sound and widened his legs, and I had to run to keep with him.

The babby was crinkled up and red with its holler, but it let off when it saw the lantern. It was okay. I had to laugh, I was that pleased. 'It's mine and Harry's, Grandaddy,' I told him. 'Our babby.'

My grandaddy dug his hand under the babby and lifted it, nest an' all, like in a shovel.

'And that's its milk,' I said. 'In the tin.'

My grandaddy went out the door of the hut and up through

the hemlocks towards the house. I was behind and I could not see. I kept fallin'. I ran fast as a hoss, but there was little trees I could not see, and I was scratched an' bleedin' and times I fell in the marsh, and I could not ketch my grandaddy.

'Grandaddy, what are you goin' to do with it?' I cried.

He never said nothing.

'Wait for me, Grandaddy,' I said.

But he never waited, no nor spoke.

I got feart all of a sudden. I was very, very feart. 'It's mine and Harry's,' I shouted. 'It's ourn!'

In the clearing I fell too, but I could run faster then and I ketched him up. I clawed at his leg, but his leg was movin' and I fell.

'It's ourn,' I said. 'Ourn.'

My grandaddy pushed open the door and went in the house, and I fell on the step and was too tired and sad to git up. I jest lay screamin'. 'Don't eat it, Grandaddy,' I said. 'Tain't fitten. Please, please don't eat it.'

My gramma ran and picked me up and rocked me in her arms like I was a babby myself. 'There ain't nobody goin' to eat it,' she said, 'or harm a hair of its mite head. Your grandaddy's going to give it back to its rightful owners, and that is all.'

'But it's ourn,' I cried. 'It's mine and Harry's!'

'Hush now,' my gramma said, 'it's the Donaldson babby, must be. It's been lost two days, an' all the folks from the Houses searchin' for it, an' its mamma an' daddy near demented.'

My grandaddy took the babby to the Houses, and that same night the men came for Harry. They came on hosses. They was hard-faced men, and they stood in a crowd inside the door.

'It's the law,' they said.

My gramma kissed Harry and buttoned his coat.

'You'll take good care o' him?' she asked.

'He won't come to no harm along of us, ma'am,' they said. 'The mob won't git him.'

And then they set him on a hoss and took him away, and the next day but one they tried him.

4

The store was the court. There was a big space in the middle of the store, and it was all filled up with folks settin' on benches, there must a been twenty there, and my grandaddy and me sat on the front bench. It was Mister Cameron's store, so it was Mister Cameron's court, Tom Cameron, and he sat on a high chair behind the counter, and a writer next to him. The writer was from up the river.

Harry had a chair to hisself.

A skinny man in black cloth got up on his feet. He was hairless and a stranger, and he began the gab.

'The case for the Crown,' he said. 'Duction of young female.' Sometimes he pointed at Harry. He spoke for a long time and folks humphed on their seats and scraped their boots; he spoke quiet and used long words; he was not worth listenin' to. 'The Crown rests,' he said, and sat down.

'Accused,' Tom Cameron said.

Sam Howie, standin' back of Harry, poked him with his finger and Harry stood up.

'Harry Mackenzie, you got anythin' to say?' Tom Cameron said.

'The Lord have mercy on me,' Harry said. 'I am eight years old and a sinner, but I aimed at no harm.'

'You understand,' Tom Cameron said, 'this is your defence. Is that all you got to say?'

'Yes, mister,' Harry said.

'Sir,' the writer said. 'You call the court sir.'

'Yes, mister,' Harry said.

Sam Howie poked him with his finger again and Harry sat down. That was the best thing of all. That was right smart. Every time Sam Howie poked Harry he stood up, and if he was standing he sat down. I grinned to Harry, but he was feart to smile back on account of my grandaddy. My grandaddy was settin' with his arms folded and his beard up. He never moved a half-inch.

'Well, then,' Tom Cameron said, 'this is how it looks to me.

First, this female child has not come to a deal of harm. That's right, Bill, isn't it? Where's Bill Donaldson?'

'I'm here,' Bill Donaldson said, and he stood up. He was the babby's daddy. 'Ain't harmed none far as me and my missus can see. Got to admit that.'

'Well, then,' Tom Cameron said, 'on the other side nobody can't deny there's been too much of this particler kind of lawlessness hereabouts. Take last month only. Willie Fleming's daughter. It was that trapper from your way, it was up the river, what was his name, Arch?'

'Foster,' the writer said.

'That Foster,' Tom Cameron said. 'We all know what he did. He had Willie's Sarah off in the woods for twelve days afore the law caught up on him. Well, then we made him marry her right here in this court, and Sarah's got a man and tied up regler and Willie's well pleased, admitted; still an' all, this abductions and crimes has got to cease.'

'Sex crimes,' the writer said.

'That's right,' Tom Cameron said. 'Sex crimes too. Our women rate high with us in this community and, rightly, a woman's purity is a hangin' matter. It was time we showed the wild elements that this is so, and a man tampers with women-folk gits his just deserts.'

There was a kind of soft growl from most everybody, and Tom Cameron nodded right and left and pointed to Harry. 'Well, then,' he said, 'we got here a boy who is guilty of the kidnap and abduction of this young female Margaret, daughter of Bill Donaldson. He says he aimed at no harm, and according to Bill he did no harm, but he admits to kidnap, and that is a hangin' crime and has caused a deal of worry to Bill Donaldson and his missus.'

'Darn right,' Bill Donaldson said.

'Well, now,' Tom Cameron said, 'we do not aim to be hangin' an eight-year-old boy, and the clerk says they will not take him upriver in the prison, but I hear there is schools for young uns where they can be teched to be reformed, and it is my opinion that we should conseeder the sendin' of Harry

Mackenzie to one of them reform schools. Does happen anyone in the court knows aught of them schools?'

My grandaddy stood up and looked round the court, face to face. Nobody spoke, and then my grandaddy looked at Tom Cameron. 'If you send him to a school, Tom,' my grandaddy said, 'I'll shoot you.'

'Sit down, Jim,' Tom Cameron said, 'and don't interfere with the course of justice.'

'Contempt of court,' the writer said.

'You shet up,' my grandaddy said, 'you scribblin' Pharisee. As for you, Tom, you know me well, an' you hev my meaning.' And he sat down.

'Well, now,' Tom Cameron said, and he clucked in his throat and blinked like a little fat owl. 'We was saying. I take it nobody here knows aught of them schools?'

'I could find out,' the writer said.

'So you could,' Tom said. 'So you could. You will notice, Jim, that I did not say we was goin' to send the boy to a reform school. All I said was, did anybody know aught of them schools so as the court could conseeder them. Well, now, it seems to me that the cause of justice would be served if the Clerk here was to find out all about them reform schools and then the court will have the information it needs and can send Harry Mackenzie to a reform school if it thinks fit the *next time* he appears on a similar charge. Case dismissed. That's all today, folks.'

Sam Howie poked Harry with his finger and Harry stood up. 'You're let aff,' Sam said.

Everybody got up, started movin' and speakin'. 'Store's now open,' Tom Cameron said, shoutin'. 'Anybody aims to buy.'

'Harry,' my grandaddy said, 'come here.'

Harry came.

'Hullo, Harry,' I said.

He never spoke or looked at me. He was white as sickly and his eyes was set low.

'Take Davy home,' my grandaddy said. 'Git straight home, the both of you, and you Harry set on your chair and wait there till I get home. Do you hear me?'

'Yis,' Harry said. He whispered.

'Git movin' then,' my grandaddy said.

Harry took my hand and we went home.

'You feelin' okay, Harry?' I asked.

'Yis,' Harry said. 'But there is an awful thing happened. Dave, you guess what's happened? My grandaddy got his boots on, and you know what is in the inside of them boots. It was the left boot.'

I stared at him. I had clean forgot.

'The picture,' Harry said. 'The picture of the dawgs.'

'Ah God,' I said.

'So I will git two thrashings,' Harry said. 'Thrashed on account of the babby and thrashed on account of the picture.'

'Mebbe I will git thrashed too,' I said.

We went straight but slow.

'If he beats me till the blood comes,' Harry said, 'I am goin' to run away. Happen there is bits of my behind that I cannot see myself, so you will look for me, Dave, and if there is blood shows I will run away.'

'I will run away too, Harry,' I said.

'I am not goin' to stay and be beat to death,' Harry said. 'If he bloods me I will truly run away.'

'Me too,' I said.

I thought about runnin' away. I wondered where we would run to.

'Harry,' I said. 'That babby. It was a girl babby.'

'Yis,' Harry said. 'Kin you walk faster, Dave?'

'Me? Easy,' I said.

'Well,' Harry said, 'we better.'

We walked fast. I thought of the places I knew. We could not run away to the Houses on account of we would only git ketched, and we could not run away to the woods on account of there was only beasts in the wood and there would be nobody to give us our meat.

'My gramma is makin' a pie,' I said.

'What kind?' Harry asked.

'I forgit.'

'Was it a berry pie?'

'I purely forgit,' I said. 'Harry, mebbe my gramma would run away with us too. That would be fine, wouldn't it, Harry?'

'No,' Harry said. 'She is on his side.'

'My grandaddy spoke up for you in the court,' I said. 'He was on our side then, Harry.'

'Yis, of course,' Harry said. 'But that is with strangers. Him an' her is on the same side in the family. You tell my gramma a word of this about runnin' away and I will not take you with me. I mean that, Dave.'

'All right,' I said. But I felt sad. 'I won't tell. I swear it, Harry.'

We got to the house and went in.

'So you're home,' my gramma said. 'And hongry, I'll be bound.'

'No, I ain't hongry,' Harry said.

'Ain't hongry!' my gramma said. 'I never. Well, I know somebody that is.'

'Me neither,' I said.

'I got a pie. Blackberry pie.'

'I ain't hongry, Gramma,' Harry said.

He sat down on his chair at the corner of the fire and I sat on my stool. My gramma stood starin'.

'We're waitin' for my grandaddy,' I said. 'My grandaddy said set and wait for him.'

'Oh,' my gramma said. She wiped her hands on her apron and shut her mouth up tight, and after a minute she turned to the skillet.

We waited a long time.

My gramma put the knives and tools on the table. 'Even though you ain't hongry,' she said, 'you jest had better eat.'

'Listen, there's my grandaddy!' Harry said.

I listened.

'Hear him?' Harry said. Harry was begun to shake, and me too, my knees was jiggin'.

My grandaddy opened the door and my gramma slammed the pie on the table. She stood and stared, jest stared.

'You sold them, then, you really did it!' she said. I looked where she was lookin', and saw that my grandaddy was barefit. 'You walked through the Houses in your bare feet, Jim!'

'They are clean,' my grandaddy said. 'My good name is in God's hands and my pride does not rest in ornaments. Harry, git your gramma the quill and parchment.'

Harry's hands was not trusty. He dropped the quill on the floor and I ran and picked it up.

'He will write it his own self,' my gramma said. She spoke firm. 'Harry will.'

My grandaddy did not argue.

'Sit down, Harry,' my gramma said.

My grandaddy plucked a paper outa his pocket and laid it on the table. Harry began to cry. I never seen Harry cry in all my life before. I looked at the paper. It was the picture of the dawgs.

'Take up the quill an' write,' my grandaddy said. 'Write this: "Sir, I here enclose $26.50 for one red setter dawg and carriage of same stop in good condition and oblige." Hev you writ that?'

Harry shook his head.

'Well, write it,' my grandaddy said.

'And add this,' my gramma said. 'Yours in good faith.' She was smilin' pretty as a young mamma, and she spoke slow and proud. 'Yours in good faith,' she said. 'James Mackenzie.'

Harry wrote like fury; my grandaddy leaned over to see every scratch, and my gramma put her hand on my head.

'We're goin' to git a dawg,' I said. 'Are we, Gramma?'

'Yis,' she said, smilin'. 'Yis, Davy.'

'I reckon we'll call it Rover,' I said. 'Eh, Harry?'

Harry looked up for a minute and nodded, grinnin', and my grandaddy nodded too. 'Rover's a right enough name,' he said. I stood close up with my chin on the table, watchin'. I was mighty content, not only on account of the dawg, but on account of I now knew ours was a good family, not like some. In our family we was all on the same side.

Muriel Spark

THE HOUSE OF THE FAMOUS POET

In the summer of 1944, when it was nothing for trains from the provinces to be five or six hours late, I travelled to London on the night train from Edinburgh, which, at York, was already three hours late. There were ten people in the compartment, only two of whom I remember well, and for good reason.

I have the impression, looking back on it, of a row of people opposite me, dozing untidily with heads askew, and, as it often seems when we look at sleeping strangers, their features had assumed extra emphasis and individuality, sometimes disturbing to watch. It was as if they had rendered up their daytime talent for obliterating the outward traces of themselves in exchange for mental obliteration. In this way they resembled a twelfth-century fresco; there was a look of medieval unselfconsciousness about these people, all except one.

This was a private soldier who was awake to a greater degree than most people are when they are not sleeping. He was smoking cigarettes one after the other with long, calm puffs. I thought he looked excessively evil – an atavistic type. His forehead must have been less than two inches high above dark, thick eyebrows, which met. His jaw was not large, but it was ape-like; so was his small nose and so were his deep, close-set eyes. I thought there must have been some consanguinity in the parents. He was quite a throwback.

As it turned out, he was extremely gentle and kind. When I ran out of cigarettes, he fished about in his haversack and produced a packet for me and one for a girl sitting next to me. We both tried, with a flutter of small change, to pay him. Nothing would please him at all but that we should accept his cigarettes, whereupon he returned to his silent, reflective smoking.

I felt a sort of pity for him then, rather as we feel towards animals we know to be harmless, such as monkeys. But I realized that, like the pity we expend on monkeys merely because they are not human beings, this pity was not needed.

Receiving the cigarettes gave the girl and myself common ground, and we conversed quietly for the rest of the journey. She told me she had a job in London as a domestic helper and nursemaid. She looked as if she had come from a country district – her very blonde hair, red face and large bones gave the impression of power, as if she was used to carrying heavy things, perhaps great scuttles of coal, or two children at a time. But what made me curious about her was her voice, which was cultivated, melodious and restrained.

Towards the end of the journey, when the people were beginning to jerk themselves straight and the rushing to and fro in the corridor had started, this girl, Elise, asked me to come with her to the house where she worked. The master, who was something in a university, was away with his wife and family.

I agreed to this, because at that time I was in the way of thinking that the discovery of an educated servant girl was valuable and something to be gone deeper into. It had the element of experience – perhaps, even of truth – and I believed, in those days, that truth is stranger than fiction. Besides, I wanted to spend that Sunday in London. I was due back next day at my job in a branch of the civil service, which had been evacuated to the country and for a reason that is another story, I didn't want to return too soon. I had some telephoning to do. I wanted to wash and change. I wanted to know more about the girl. So I thanked Elise and accepted her invitation.

I regretted it as soon as we got out of the train at King's Cross, some minutes after ten. Standing up tall on the platform, Elise looked unbearably tired, as if not only the last night's journey but every fragment of her unknown life was suddenly heaping up on top of her. The power I had noticed in the train was no longer there. As she called, in her beautiful voice, for a porter, I saw that on the side of her head that had been away from me in the train, her hair was parted in a dark streak, which, by contrast with the yellow, looked navy blue. I had thought, when I first saw her, that possibly her hair was bleached, but now, seeing it so badly done, seeing this navy blue parting pointing like an arrow to the weighted weariness of her face, I, too, got the sensation of great tiredness. And it was not only the strain of the journey that I felt, but the foreknowledge of boredom that comes upon us unaccountably at the beginning of a quest, and that checks, perhaps mercifully, our curiosity.

And, as it happened, there really wasn't much to learn about Elise. The explanation of her that I had been prompted to seek I got in the taxi between King's Cross and the house at Swiss Cottage. She came of a good family, who thought her a pity, and she them. Having no training for anything else, she had taken a domestic job on leaving home. She was engaged to an Australian soldier billeted also at Swiss Cottage.

Perhaps it was the anticipation of a day's boredom, maybe it was the effect of no sleep or the fact that the V-1 sirens were sounding, but I felt some sourness when I saw the house. The garden was growing all over the place. Elise opened the front door, and we entered a darkish room almost wholly taken up with a long, plain wooden work-table. On this, were a half-empty marmalade jar, a pile of papers, and a dried-up ink bottle. There was a steel-canopied bed, known as a Morrison shelter, in one corner and some photographs on the mantelpiece, one of a schoolboy wearing glasses. Everything was tainted with Elise's weariness and my own distaste. But Elise didn't seem to be aware of the exhaustion so plainly revealed on her face. She did not even bother to take her coat off, and as it was too tight for her I wondered how she could move about so quickly with this restriction added to the weight of her tiredness. But, with her coat still buttoned tight Elise phoned her boy-friend and made breakfast, while I washed in a dim, blue, cracked bathroom upstairs.

When I found that she had opened my hold-all without asking me and had taken out my rations, I was a little pleased. It seemed a friendly action, with some measure of reality about it, and I felt better. But I was still irritated by the house. I felt there was no justification for the positive lack of consequence which was lying about here and there. I asked no questions about the owner who was something in a university, for fear of getting the answer I expected – that he was away visiting his grandchildren, at some family gathering in the home counties. The owners of the house had no reality for me, and I looked upon the place as belonging to, and permeated with, Elise.

I went with her to a nearby public house, where she met her boy-friend and one or two other Australian soldiers. They had with them a thin Cockney girl with bad teeth. Elise was very happy, and insisted in her lovely voice that they should all come along to a party at the house that evening. In a fine aristocratic tone, she demanded that each should bring a bottle of beer.

During the afternoon Elise said she was going to have a bath, and she showed me a room where I could use the telephone and sleep if I wanted. This was a large, light room with several windows, much more orderly than the rest of the house, and lined with books. There was only one unusual thing about it: beside one of the windows was a bed, but this bed was only a fairly thick mattress made up neatly on the floor. It was obviously a bed on the floor with some purpose, and again I was angered to think of the futile crankiness of the elderly professor who had thought of it.

I did my telephoning, and decided to rest. But first I wanted to find something to read. The books puzzled me. None of them seemed to be automatically part of a scholar's library. An inscription in one book was signed by the author, a well-known novelist. I found another inscribed copy, and this had the name of the recipient. On a sudden idea, I went to the desk, where while I had been telephoning I had noticed a pile of unopened letters. For the first time, I looked at the name of the owner of the house.

I ran to the bathroom and shouted through the door to Elise, 'Is this the house of the famous poet?'

'Yes,' she called. 'I *told* you.'

She had told me nothing of the kind. I felt I had no right at all to be there, for it wasn't, now, the house of Elise acting by proxy for some unknown couple. It was the house of a famous modern poet. The thought that at any moment he and his family might walk in and find me there terrified me. I insisted that Elise should open the bathroom door and tell me to my face that there was no possible chance of their returning for many days to come.

Then I began to think about the house itself, which Elise was no longer accountable for. Its new definition, as the house of a poet whose work I knew well, many of whose poems I knew by heart, gave it altogether a new appearance.

To confirm this, I went outside and stood exactly where I had been when I first saw the garden from the door of the taxi. I wanted to get my first impression for a second time.

And this time I saw an absolute purpose in the overgrown garden, which, since then, I have come to believe existed in the eye of the beholder. But, at the time, the room we had first entered, and which had riled me, now began to give back a meaning, and whatever was, was right. The caked-up bottle of ink, which Elise had put on the mantelpiece, I replaced on the table to make sure. I saw a photograph I hadn't noticed before, and I recognized the famous poet.

It was the same with the upstairs room where Elise had put me, and I handled the books again, not so much with the sense that they belonged to the famous poet but with some curiosity about how they had been made. The sort of question that occurred to me was where the paper had come from and from what sort of vegetation was manufactured the black print, and these things have not troubled me since.

The Australians and the Cockney girl came around about seven. I had planned to catch an eight-thirty train to the country, but when I telephoned to confirm the time I found there were no Sunday trains running. Elise, in her friendly and exhausted way, begged me to stay, without attempting to be too serious about it. The sirens were starting up again. I asked Elise once more to repeat that the poet and his family could by no means return that night. But I asked this question more abstractedly than before, as I was thinking of the sirens and of the exact proportions of the noise they made. I wondered, as well, what sinister genius of the Home Office could have invented so ominous a wail, and why. And I was thinking of the word 'siren'. The sound then became comical, for I imagined some maniac sea nymph from centuries past belching into the year 1944. Actually, the sirens frightened me.

Most of all, I wondered about Elise's party. Everyone roamed about the place as if it were nobody's house in particular, with Elise the best-behaved of the lot. The Cockney girl sat on the long table and gave of her best to the skies every time a bomb exploded. I had the feeling that the house had been requisitioned for an evening by the military. It was so hugely and everywhere occupied that it became not the house I had first entered, nor the house of the famous poet, but a third house – the one I had vaguely prefigured when I stood, bored, on the platform at King's Cross station. I saw a great amount of tiredness among these people, and heard, from the loud noise they made, that they were all lacking sleep. When the beer was finished and they were gone, some to their billets, some to pubs, and the Cockney girl to her Underground shelter where she had slept for weeks past, I asked Elise, 'Don't you feel tired?'

'No,' she said with agonizing weariness, 'I never feel tired.'

I fell asleep myself, as soon as I had got into the bed on the floor in the upstairs room, and overslept until Elise woke me at eight. I had wanted to get up early to catch a nine o'clock train, so I hadn't much time to speak to her. I did notice, though, that she had lost some of her tired look.

I was pushing my things into my hold-all while Elise went up the street to catch a taxi when I heard someone coming upstairs. I thought it was Elise come back, and I looked out of the open door. I saw a man in uniform carrying an enormous parcel in both hands. He looked down as he climbed, and had a cigarette in his mouth.

'Do you want Elise?' I called, thinking it was one of her friends.

He looked up, and I recognized the soldier, the throwback, who had given us cigarettes in the train.

'Well, anyone will do,' he said. 'The thing is, I've got to get back to camp and I'm stuck for the fare – eight and six.'

I told him I could manage it, and was finding the money when he said, putting his parcel on the floor, 'I don't want to borrow it. I wouldn't think of borrowing it. I've got something for sale.'

'What's that?' I said.

'A funeral,' said the soldier. 'I've got it here.'

This alarmed me, and I went to the window. No hearse, no coffin stood below. I saw only the avenue of trees.

The soldier smiled. 'It's an abstract funeral,' he explained, opening the parcel.

He took it out and I examined it carefully, greatly comforted. It was very much the sort of thing I had wanted – rather more purple in parts than I would have liked, for I was not in favour of this colour of mourning. Still, I thought I could tone it down a bit.

Delighted with the bargain, I handed over the eight shillings and sixpence. There was a great deal of this abstract funeral. Hastily, I packed some of it into the holdall. Some I stuffed in my pockets, and there was still some left over. Elise had returned with a cab and I hadn't much time. So I ran for it, out of the door and out of the gate of the house of the famous poet, with the rest of my funeral trailing behind me.

You will complain that I am withholding evidence. Indeed, you may wonder if there is any evidence at all. 'An abstract funeral,' you will say, 'is neither here nor there. It is only a notion. You cannot pack a notion into your bag. You cannot see the colour of a notion.'

You will insinuate that what I have just told you is pure fiction.

Hear me to the end.

I caught the train. Imagine my surprise when I found, sitting opposite me, my friend the soldier, of whose existence you are so sceptical.

'As a matter of interest,' I said, 'how would you describe all this funeral you sold me?'

'Describe it?' he said. 'Nobody describes an abstract funeral. You just conceive it.'

'There is much in what you say,' I replied. 'Still, describe it I must, because it is not every day one comes by an abstract funeral.'

'I am glad you appreciate that,' said the soldier.

'And after the war,' I continued, 'when I am no longer a civil servant, I hope, in a few deftly turned phrases, to write of my experiences at the house of the famous poet, which has culminated like this. But of course,' I added, 'I will need to say what it looks like.'

The soldier did not reply.

'If it were an okapi or a sea-cow,' I said, 'I would have to say what it looked like. No one would believe me otherwise.'

'Do you want your money back?' asked the soldier. 'Because if so, you can't have it. I spent it on my ticket.'

'Don't misunderstand me,' I hastened to say. 'The funeral is a delightful abstraction. Only, I wish to put it down in writing.'

I felt a great pity for the soldier on seeing his worried look. The ape-like head seemed the saddest thing in the world.

'I make them by hand,' he said, 'these abstract funerals.'

A siren sounded somewhere, far away.

'Elise bought one of them last month. She hadn't any complaints. I change at the next stop,' he said, getting down his kit from the rack. 'And what's more,' he said, 'your famous poet bought one.'

'Oh, did he?' I said.

'Yes,' he said. 'No complaints. It was just what he wanted – the idea of a funeral.'

The train pulled up. The soldier leaped down and waved. As the train started again, I unpacked my abstract funeral and looked at if for a few moments.

'To hell with the idea,' I said. 'It's a real funeral I want.'

'All in good time,' said a voice from the corridor.

'*You* again,' I said. It was the soldier.

'No,' he said, 'I got off at the last station. I'm only a notion of myself.'

'Look here,' I said, 'would you be offended if I throw all this away?'

'Of course not,' said the soldier. 'You can't offend a notion.'

'I want a real funeral,' I explained. 'One of my own.'

'That's right,' said the soldier.

'And then I'll be able to write about it and go into all the details,' I said.

'Your own funeral?' he said. 'You want to write it up?'

'Yes,' I said.

'But', said he, 'you're only human. Nobody reports on their own funeral. It's got to be abstract.'

'You see my predicament?' I said.

'I see it,' he replied. 'I get off at this stop.'

This notion of a soldier alighted. Once more the train put on speed. Out of the window I chucked all my eight and sixpence worth of abstract funeral. I watched it fluttering over the fields and around the tops of camouflaged factories with the sun glittering richly upon it, until it was out of sight.

In the summer of 1944 a great many people were harshly and suddenly killed. The papers reported, in due course, those whose names were known to the public. One of these, the famous poet, had returned unexpectedly to his home at Swiss Cottage a few moments before it was hit direct by a flying bomb. Fortunately, he had left his wife and children in the country.

When I got to the place where my job was, I had some time to spare before going on duty. I decided to ring Elise and thank her properly, as I had left in such a hurry. But the lines were out of order, and the operator could not find words enough to express her annoyance with me. Behind this overworked, quarrelsome voice from the exchange I heard the high, long hoot which means that the telephone at the other end is not functioning, and the sound made me infinitely depressed and weary; it was more intolerable to me than the sirens, and I replaced the receiver; and, in fact, Elise had already perished under the house of the famous poet.

The blue cracked bathroom, the bed on the floor, the caked ink bottle, the neglected garden, and the neat rows of books – I try to gather them together in my mind whenever I am enraged by the thought that Elise and the poet were killed outright. The angels of the Resurrection will invoke the dead man and the dead woman, but who will care to restore the fallen house of the famous poet if not myself? Who else will tell its story?

When I reflect how Elise and the poet were taken in – how they calmly allowed a well-meaning soldier to sell them the notion of a funeral, I remind myself that one day I will accept, and so will you, an abstract funeral, and make no complaints.

Fred Urquhart

ELEPHANTS, BAIRNS AND OLD MEN

OLD William Petrie of Duncraggie Mains had five daughters, a son and a horse. After his son was killed at Dunkirk the horse became old Petrie's dearest possession. He had a number of horses, for although his farm was nearly seven hundred acres it was completely unmechanized. But he had only one Horse. It was never called the Stallion. Sometimes it was called the Staig, but mostly just the Horse. The other horses, except an occasional mare for breeding, were beneath old Petrie's attention, except when his daughters and sons-in-law tried to get him to turn to tractors. Then he would defend his horses passionately and say that no tractor would ever come to Duncraggie unless it was over his dead body.

Old Petrie's daughters were a disappointment to him. They all nagged. The two oldest were unmarried, and now that each of them was well over forty they were likely to remain so. They ran his house, and they tried to run his farm and him. The other three were married to neighbouring farmers and they came regularly to Duncraggie Mains with their large quiet husbands and large noisy families. And when they got together the five sisters shrieked and rampaged about so much that old Petrie was always driven outside. Usually he took refuge in the Horse's box where he would sit plaiting straw between his rheumatic-twisted fingers.

He was sitting there late in the afternoon of one Hogmonay. The Horse munched oats placidly, and as old Petrie gazed at its gleaming haunches he was thinking of his son. It was eleven years almost since Alec had been killed on the beaches of Dunkirk. Eleven years.... Ay, man, but it was a long time. He had never thought when he got the news that he would live all this time to remember it. But the years had slipped by and now here they were at another Hogmonay...

They were expecting the Family. Jenny and Margaret and their husbands were coming for tea and supper, and they would stay until the small hours of the morning after they had seen the New Year in. But Nellie and her husband, Dick Jeffreys, were bringing their children with them to spend the night. 'The bairnies'll brighten Grandpa up,' Nellie had said. 'He must have his dear ones around him at a time like this.'

Dick Jeffreys had aye been the old man's favourite son-in-law, although he was the most strident about the supremacy of machinery over horse-flesh. But he had been Alec's great friend, and this in the old man's view made up for his other short-comings. Besides, he was a big fine handsome loon, the kind of man Alec had aye shown promise of growing into. They had been at school together, and it was Alec who had first brought Dick to the house. Every Saturday afternoon the two youths had played rugby, and Dick had aye come back for his tea, and then they had gone to the cinema together.

The old man sighed now at the remembrance of these Satur-day afternoons of so long ago. Fifteen ... ay, going on for twenty years ago. Mrs Petrie had been living then, and many a chuckle she and he had had together when Dick had begun to grow up and the lassies had got their eyes on him. He had been that big and quiet, with never a word to say for himself when the lassies had chaffed and daffed with him. Ay, there had been a fell stramash amongst them to see which was to get him, and it was funny when you thought that it was wee Nellie that had finally nabbed him. Wee Nellie, the quiet one that had aye had her head buried in a book ...

The roaring of a high-powered car through the farm-yard disturbed the old man's thoughts. He hoisted himself onto the corn-bin and peered through the dusty cobweb-smeared window. That was Margaret and Bill Johnston, no need to move just yet. 'I can have another quarter of an hour's peace until the whole circus comes, laddie,' he said to the stallion, reseating himself on the corn-bin.

But a few seconds later there was the roaring of another car, then the banging of doors, the high voices of children, and

Nellie's skirls of welcome. The old man sighed and looked at his watch. 'Ay, man, I wonder ...' he said to the Horse, and he moved over and stroked the beast's neck. Maybe it was better to face them and be done with it? 'Tib and Molly ken I'm deaf,' he muttered. 'But they ken I'm no' so deaf as no' to hear our Nellie!'

'So you're there, Father dear!' Nellie screamed when he poked his head hesitantly around the kitchen door. 'I was just saying to the Girls where on earth could you be at this time of day when there's no work being done on the farm. Come away in and get warmed up. You must be freezing.'

'Ay, where have you been?' Tibby, the eldest girl, snapped, sweeping a lock of grey hair away from her eyes as she bent over the table, cutting sandwiches. 'Sittin' out there on your lone in that smelly horse-box I'll be bound! You'll catch your death of cold, and then who's goin' to nurse you?'

'Ach, I'm fine,' old Petrie said, but he suffered himself to be almost smothered by a hug and kiss from Nellie before he said: 'I'll awa' ben to the sittin'-room and ha'e a crack with the lads.'

His oldest grandchild, Sandy Jeffreys, a loon of ten, was sliding up and down the banisters as the old man went through the hall. 'Ay there, Grandaddy!' he yelled. 'Look at me!'

'I'm lookin' at ye, my man,' old Petrie said. 'And I'll do more than look at ye if ye scratch these banisters. I'll warm your hide for ye.'

He scowled as he opened the sitting-room door. He had always disliked Nellie's eldest, perhaps because she had named him after Alec – hoping by this to win the old man's heart and a good share of his fortune – and then decided to call him Sandy. The old man had often pondered upon this. Once in a moment of lucidity he had thought it was because the child was being conceived when Alec was fighting for his life on a foreign beach that he could not bear the sight of him, but he had thrust this quickly from his mind, and now he preferred to think it was because the boy was wild and uncouth.

Dick Jeffreys was standing with his back to the fire, warming his bottom. Bill Johnston was sitting in his father-in-law's favourite easy chair, but neither of them made any show of moving when the old man entered. 'Ay there, Mr Petrie,' Dick boomed, 'I was just saying to Bill that my new Allis-Chalmers is making a grand job of the ploughing. Especially yon stiff field at the burnside. Man, ye should see it spankin' along. It fair knocks all your horses into a cocked hat!'

'No, bairnies, run away and play!' old Petrie said to little Rose and George, who had rushed screaming from the dining-room and clutched him round the legs, 'Grandaddy wants a rest.'

The children, however, took no heed of him, but, followed by Sandy, they ran ahead of their grandfather into the room, where Sandy immediately threw himself into the only other easy chair.

Old Petrie sat on a stiff-backed chair in front of the piano. He leaned his elbow with a bang on the open keys, but nobody paid the slightest attention to the discordant jangle. 'Have you got all your ploughin' done, Mr Petrie?' Bill asked, taking little Rose between his legs and dancing her up and down.

Dick laughed and stepped away from the fire. He pulled Sandy out of the easy chair and sprawled into it, one enormous tweed-covered thigh dangling over one arm. 'Not him!' he laughed. 'Do ye expect a man that works wi' horses to be done afore the likes of you and me?'

'This was my chair,' Sandy whined, punching his father's arm. 'I was here before you.'

'Get away, loon!' Dick thrust him aside and settled himself more comfortably. 'Get away, all you bairns. Away out of here and give us some peace!'

'Ach, leave the bairnies alone,' Bill said, throwing Rose into the air and laughing with delight at her screech of mock terror. 'They want to see all they can see. Isn't that right, m'dear? You've come to see your Uncle William.'

'Have you got ony sweeties?' Sandy said.

'No, Sandy loon, I haven't any sweeties. Your Uncle William is a poor man and canna afford to buy sweeties.'

'I think I'll put wheat in that field beside the mill,' Dick said. 'It hasna had wheat for two three years, and I had a right guid crop off it the last time.'

'Daddy ate all our sweeties comin' in the car,' Sandy said.

'Whisht, loon, whisht,' Bill said, taking out his cigarette-case. 'Ye manna speak when Daddy's talkin'.' He put a cigarette in his mouth and raked in his waistcoat pocket for his lighter. Dick reached out and gripped his knee. 'Here, you greedy devil!' he said. He took a cigarette from Bill's case, but kept a grip on his brother-in-law's knee until he had got a light. Then he leaned back, puffing contentedly, and said: 'I think I'll put in ten acres o' sugar beet this year. It's a lot of work, but the country's needing sugar. And, man, it's a profitable concern.'

'Ay, but it'll nae be you that has the workin' of it,' Bill grinned. 'Ay, lad, but it must be fine to be a gentleman farmer! I wonder how you'd get on if you just had a wee croftie like me?'

'A wee croftie!' Dick grinned boyishly, and he wriggled about in his chair until the springs squeaked. 'Four hundred acres a croftie!' He guffawed and said: 'Man, that's made me feel right thirsty. What about a wee dram out o' your bottle, Mr Petrie?'

'Ay, let's have a wee dram before that drunken brute, Walter Innes, comes and takes it all,' Bill said.

'You're gettin' nothin' to drink until after tea.' Molly, the second Petrie daughter, had bounced in and heard his remark. 'The idea! Wantin' to deprive poor dear Wattie of his fair share!' And she shook her short dyed-brown bob which fell around her round red face like an O-Cedar mop and switched on the radio. 'There, that's better!' she cried, and she rushed out again, not listening to the blares of jazz mingled with disjointed talk and laughter which comprised a popular so-called comedy programme.

Old William Petrie picked his nose meditatively, looking from the group between him and the fire to the Family Gallery on top of the piano. There were photographs of all the children and grandchildren at different stages of their development. A large studio portrait of Alec in his captain's uniform made the old man look quickly to the three wedding groups arranged near it. The photograph of Nellie and Dick recalled something he thought he had forgotten. *Ay, Alec, loon,* he thought, *you were maybe right when you said yon to him. I was the only one that heard you, and I aye have it up my sleeve to tell her in case our Nellie gets outrageous.* ... He closed his eyes, remembering how Alec had been the best man at the wedding. He had walked around Dick before they set off for the church, smoothing imaginary dust off his enormous shoulders, resetting the carnation in his buttonhole. And old Petrie, peering unobserved through the doorway, had seen him flick the silver horse-shoe hung beneath the flower and heard him say: 'Christ, what does Nellie want you to wear this for? She's got you trickit out like a prize stallion, loon, and, faith, she'll ride you to death.' And he had given Dick a friendly smack on the bottom and said: 'For the last time as a single man!' before they had clattered downstairs and into the waiting car.

The old man sighed and opened his eyes. He peered at the photograph. Nellie, with her head held coyly to the side, was trying to the last to carry on being a Shy Little Thing, her hand clutching Dick's arm firmly, her fingers twined through his. But the camera had caught the twist of triumph in her smile and it had caught, too, the uneasiness behind Dick's boyish grin.

'Here, Sandy!' the old man said. 'Go and ask your mammy if the tea's nae near ready.'

'I will not,' Sandy said.

'Go and do what your grandfather tells you,' Bill said. 'Go on now! See who'll be first!'

But none of the children moved. Sandy leaned against the arm of his father's chair, breathing down the back of his neck and whining. Rose and George looked at each other and giggled.

'Go on now like good bairnies!' Bill said. 'Go on, and Uncle William'll give you all a treat when you come back!'

Sandy rushed to the door, and the two smaller children followed. 'Ay, but I dinna ken what I'm to bribe them with,' Bill sighed, bending down and unlacing his boots. 'I must think up something by the time they come back.'

Do you think I should try Yielder oats in yon field at the back o' the wood?' Dick said, slapping his knee. 'Man, it's kind o' sandy, but I think it might give a fair good crop. What do you think, Bill?'

'I dinna ken,' Bill said, putting his boots beside his chair and stretching out his stockinged feet to the fire. 'What I'm worried about is what I'm to give those bairns when they come back.'

'Tea's nearly ready! Tea's nearly ready! Auntie Tibby's seen Uncle Walter's car comin' up the loan!' The children rushed in, howling, and crowded around Bill. 'You were goin' to give us something, Uncle Bill!'

'Elephants and bairns!' Bill muttered. 'Well now, what was Uncle William goin' to give you? Oh, ay!' he grinned and winked at Dick, then he stretched out his feet. 'Now who would like to smell Uncle William's feet? Who wants the first smell? Come on now, bairnies, I'm only going to charge you a penny each. A penny for a delectable smell of Uncle William's delectable feet!'

The children giggled, nudging each other and shuffling about, feeling that the grown-ups were laughing at them. It was little George who made the first move. 'Give me a penny, Daddy,' he said to Dick.

Without taking his feet off his chair, where he sat like an enormous Buddha, Dick squirmed and shuffled until he had brought some money from his hip-pocket. 'Here,' he said. 'Here's a penny for each of you, then get to the devil out of here.'

George dealt out the pennies, but the children all stood giggling, and again it was George who made the first move. He handed Bill the penny. Then he knelt and solemnly sniffed Bill's foot. 'I've smelled it!' he cried. 'I've smelled it!'

The others followed. Bill laughed, poking his feet in their

faces. 'That's a grand smell, isn't it?' he cried, pinching Sandy's bottom. 'Ye couldna make a smell like that, loon!' He counted the pennies they'd given him. 'Threepence! Man, I never knew there was such a fortune in my feet before.'

'I want another penny, Daddy,' Sandy cried.

'Go to the devil!' Dick said. 'Go on, get out of here, the whole lot of you.'

'I want another penny,' Rose cried.

'Man, I never thought my feet would be so popular,' Bill said. 'I must capitalize this. No, no,' he cried, pushing little George away. 'No smells for nothing! Go on now, the whole lot of you, the fun's finished!'

'Tea's ready!' Tibby screamed, poking her head around the door. 'Come and get it!'

All through tea old William Petrie sat as though mesmerized. Tibby shrieked at one end of the table, dispensing food, and Molly ranted at the other end. All around him his grand-children whined and snuffled; his sons-in-law told each other about their crops, and his daughters yelled at the pitch of their voices. The old man scarcely ate; he sank deeper and deeper into a reverie, remembering tea-parties of long ago. Life hadn't seemed so noisy then. His wife had sat at one end of the table, and he had sat at the other. And Alec had been there...

Ay, it was changed days. The young men that Alec had brought in about had aye been quiet and deferential, saying 'What do you think I should do with this field, Mr Petrie?' or 'Do you think I could be doing with another six kye, Mr Petrie?' And his daughters had not been so much in evidence. They had been so busy watching the lads that they hadn't had time to talk. Ay, and wee Nellie there, that was roaring her head off just now, had been the quietest of the lot. Her head had aye been buried in a book. The only times she had looked up had been when Dick came to the house after a rugby match, and then she had watched him with adoring eyes. ... Ay, but she had aye made certain when they piled into two or three cars on a Saturday evening to go to the pictures in the nearest town that she had been crushed against Dick, holding his arm . . .

After tea the children were put to bed much against their will, and their mother and aunts screamed even more than they did. The three young men sat down to play three-handed bridge. Their wives and sisters-in-law congregated around the fire, some with knitting, and Nellie, sitting close to the blaring wireless, held a book firmly against her face. The old man sat on the chair beside the piano, sipping the meagre glass of watered whisky which Tibby had handed him.

'Can ye nae get another programme, Nellie?' he said after a while.

'What's wrong with this, Father dear?' Nellie glanced up from her book, then looked down quickly again in case she missed anything. 'I'm sure we all like this. Don't we, Girls?'

'Ay, this is a fine programme,' Tibby said, craning her neck over the shoulders of the card-players. 'I'm fair enjoyin' it. It's a real fine programme for a Hogmonay night.'

'What about another dram, Tib?' Bill said.

'Ach, have ye nae had enough?' Tibby laughed and went to the sideboard. 'Mind, you lads, this bottle's got to last us till twelve o'clock.'

'Ay, but ye've got plenty more in the cupboard!' Bill winked and threw down his ace. 'There, ma bonnie loons, this is my game again! Now, let's see now!' He began to count his score. 'How much is that you both owe me?'

'Och, leave the payin' up till the end,' Walter Innes cried. 'We've got plenty time for a wheen more games yet. Dinna you think that I'm lettin' you get away with this. I'll have my money back from you and more before the New Year's in!'

'Playin' cards on a Hogmonay!' Margaret cried. 'And nae only a Hogmonay, but a Sabbath into the bargain! My faith, what would my mother have thought if she'd seen ye?'

'Ach, haud your tongue, wife! The better the day the better the deed!' Bill grinned. 'And Mrs Petrie liked her wee gamie as much as anybody else!'

Old William held out his empty glass to Molly, but she cried:

'Oh no, Father, you've had enough. You've had three nips already, and you ken what the doctor-mannie said. No, no, Father dear, you'll get another one to bring in the New Year and no more!'

The old man hunched in his chair, glancing from the card-players to the clock. Ten o'clock ... half past ... Bill was winning, and his howls of glee drowned his brothers-in-law's groans of exasperation. Eleven o'clock. ... Ay, eleven years ago. The old man looked up at his son's photograph and wondered once again what would have been happening here tonight had Alec been alive. Alec would never have held with all this talk of tractors, and he would never have let Tib and Molly interfere with the running of the farm. Alec had aye been a lad after his own heart ... fond of horses, not like his brothers-in-law who kept saying that they 'couldn't abide the brutes. ...'

Half past eleven. ... He looked again at his son's photograph, then he rose. He was making his way unsteadily to the door when Tibby cried sharply:

'Where are you going, Father?'

'Damn it all,' the old man spluttered. 'Can a man nae ging for a wee walk in his ain hoose?'

He went to the lavatory beside the kitchen, then after a few minutes, listening to see that the coast was clear, he unsnecked the back door and slipped out. It was a clear, frosty night, and the waning moon shone on the rime on the cart-tracks. The old man sniffed, his head lifted to the sky. From the near-by cottar houses he could hear sounds of singing and merriment. Ay, they were all awake tonight, ready to drink their drams, if they had them, and see the New Year in.

He hobbled across the yard and opened the door of the stable. As he went into the Horse's box, there was a scuffling of straw and snorting as the stallion lumbered to its feet. 'It's only me, laddie,'' the old man said softly, and the beast gave a low nicker of welcome.

For a long time he stood, rubbing his hand gently up and down the stallion's nose, leaning his thin body against the beast's massive chest for warmth and company. 'Ay, laddie,' he murmured. 'Another year's near gone by, and where are we? How much longer, man, will it be?' He sighed, and the stallion nosed his shoulder in sympathy. 'How long will it be before we're both nae here?' the old man said. And a little later as he heard the ringing of church bells borne on the cold night air from the nearest village, welcoming in the New Year, he muttered: 'Elephants and bairns, Bill said. Ay, and he might well have said "and old men . . ."'

ACKNOWLEDGEMENTS

DUE acknowledgement is made to the following authors, agents and publishers for permission to reprint the stories in this volume: to the author, the Hogarth Press and Messrs Harcourt, Brace Jovanovich, Inc. for 'The Story of Jorkel Hayforks', from *A Calendar of Love* by George Mackay Brown; the authoress and Scottish International for 'Out of Hand' by Elspeth Davie; the author and the Castle Wynd Printers, Edinburgh, for 'The Money' and 'The Potato Planters', from *The Sea-bed and Other Stories* by Ian Hamilton Finlay; the author and the Editor of the *Glasgow Herald* for 'The Devil and the Deep Blue Sea' by J. A. Ford; Mr Charles Turner, Executor of the late Mr Edward Gaitens, and William Maclellan, Publisher, for 'A Wee Nip', from *Dance of the Apprentices* by Edward Gaitens; Messrs Curtis Brown, Messrs Jarrolds and the Executrix of the late Lewis Grassic Gibbon for 'Smeddum', from *Scottish Scene* by Lewis Grassic Gibbon; Mrs Tschiffeley, John Johnston and Messrs Duckworth, for 'Mirahu-ano', from *Hope*, by R. B. Cunninghame-Graham; the author and Messrs Faber & Faber for 'The Old Man' by Neil Gunn; the authoress for 'Choice' by Margaret Hamilton; the authoress for 'Vocation' by Dorothy K. Haynes; the author for 'Christian Justice' by Robert Jenkins; the author and Messrs A. D. Peters & Co. for 'Sealskin Trousers' by Eric Linklater; the author and Serif Books, Edinburgh, for 'A Trifle Unnecessary', from *Dinner with the Dead*, by Moray McLaren; the author and Messrs Cassell for 'A House in Sicily', from *My Enemies Have Sweet Voices*, by Neil McCallum; the authoress and David Higham Associates, for 'Mithras My Saviour' by Naomi Mitchison; the author and Messrs Hodder & Stoughton for 'Scotch Settlement', from *And Delilah*, by Neil Paterson; the authoress and Harold Ober Associates, New York, as well as Messrs Alfred Knopf, New York, and Messrs Macmillan, London, for 'The House of the Famous Poet' by Muriel Spark, first published in the *New Yorker*; and the author and Arco Publishers, for 'Elephants, Bairns and Old Men', from *The Laundry Girl and the Pole*, by Fred Urquhart.

He just wanted a decent book to read ...

Not too much to ask, is it? It was in 1935 when Allen Lane, Managing Director of Bodley Head Publishers, stood on a platform at Exeter railway station looking for something good to read on his journey back to London. His choice was limited to popular magazines and poor-quality paperbacks – the same choice faced every day by the vast majority of readers, few of whom could afford hardbacks. Lane's disappointment and subsequent anger at the range of books generally available led him to found a company – and change the world.

'We believed in the existence in this country of a vast reading public for intelligent books at a low price, and staked everything on it'
Sir Allen Lane, 1902–1970, founder of Penguin Books

The quality paperback had arrived – and not just in bookshops. Lane was adamant that his Penguins should appear in chain stores and tobacconists, and should cost no more than a packet of cigarettes.

Reading habits (and cigarette prices) have changed since 1935, but Penguin still believes in publishing the best books for everybody to enjoy. We still believe that good design costs no more than bad design, and we still believe that quality books published passionately and responsibly make the world a better place.

So wherever you see the little bird – whether it's on a piece of prize-winning literary fiction or a celebrity autobiography, political tour de force or historical masterpiece, a serial-killer thriller, reference book, world classic or a piece of pure escapism – you can bet that it represents the very best that the genre has to offer.

Whatever you like to read – trust Penguin.